Price to Pay

BOOK 2 IN THE
PHILIPPE DUVAL SERIES

J MARY MASTERS

WWW.PMABOOKS.COM

First published 2024 by PMA Books,
A divn of Peter Masters & Associates, ABN 72 172 119 877
Unit 111, 1 Halcyon Way, Bli Bli Qld 4560, Australia

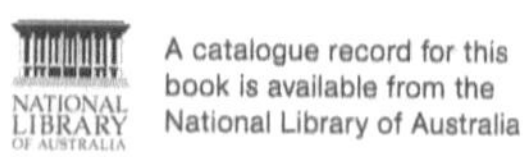

A catalogue record for this
book is available from the
National Library of Australia

ISBN 978-0-6458637-3-4

Cover design: J D Smith Design, UK
www.jdsmith-design.co.uk
Author photograph: Sheree McArthur
www.shereemcarthurphotography.com.au

www.pmabooks.com
Tel + (61) (0) 488 224 929
Email enquiries@pmabooks.com

Dedicated to my dear husband Peter
and to my readers.
Your enjoyment of my books makes
the task of writing worthwhile.

About the author

J Mary Masters (Judith) born in Rockhampton, Queensland, Australia in the 1950s, is the youngest of four children and was raised on a cattle property. For more than twenty years, she was involved in the magazine publishing industry as a senior executive.

Having now given up full time magazine work, Judith is devoting her time to her writing career, with an emphasis on writing for women readers. Her stories feature a mix of town and country settings, drawing heavily on her early country life and also paying homage to her favourite city: Sydney.

She is a member of the Queensland Writers Centre (QWC) and the Australian Society of Authors (ASA). Judith has also completed a fiction writing course with noted literary agency Curtis Brown.

Judith now lives on Queensland's Sunshine Coast with her husband Peter.

Readers are invited to contact Judith through the following channels.

Website	jmarymasters.com
Facebook	www.facebook.com/JudithMMasters
Instagram	@jmarymasters
Blog	jmarymasters.blog
Email	jmarymasters1@gmail.com

Belleville series

BOOK 1 Julia's Story
BOOK 2 To Love, Honour and Betray
BOOK 3 Return to Prior Park
BOOK 4 Heirs and Successors (2023)
BOOK 5 Winds of Change (2025)

Philippe Duval series

BOOK 1 First Born Son (2023)
BOOK 2 Price to Pay (2024)

Back Story

First Born Son, the first book in the Philippe Duval series, was conceived as a companion book to the fourth book in my Belleville family series, *Heirs and Successors,* because it covers a similar timeframe to that book but its focus shifts away from the Belleville family to the life of Dr Philippe Duval.

Book two, *Price to Pay,* takes up where *First Born Son* leaves off.

Philippe Duval was Julia Belleville's first love (see *Julia's Story,* Book 1 in the Belleville series). He was born illegitimately in Sag Harbor, NY, and raised by a single mother who struggled to provide a life for him. It was the war that brought him to Australia as a doctor in the US Army.

For Julia, her meeting with him is life-changing. Yet both their lives evolve in ways no one could foresee.

For readers meeting these characters for the first time, I hope I have provided enough background information in the prologue. I also encourage readers to check out the cast of characters.

I hope you enjoy the book. And if you do, please tell your friends.

Good reading.

J Mary Masters (Judy)

Key characters

Dr Philippe Duval   Surgeon
Julia Duval (formerly Belleville/Fitzroy)   Philippe's wife
Pippa Duval   Julia & Philippe's daughter

AMERICA

Walter William Cox IV   Son of Philippe's half-brother
Barbara Cox   Walter's mother
Virginia Cox   Walter's sister
Clarence White   Butler at Eastbury Hall
Frederick   Chauffeur
Mrs Anderson   Housekeeper
Howard Davis   Lawyer

Arabella Courtenay   Executive Director
                              Ella Duval Foundation

AUSTRALIA

SYDNEY
Dr Joel Tynan   Executive Director
                              Ella Duval Foundation, Sydney

Dr Robert Clarke   Registrar/Surgeon
Patricia Clarke   His wife
Anita Clarke   Their daughter & Pippa's friend
David Clarke   Robert Clarke's brother
Deborah Clarke   His wife
Karen Clarke   Their daughter
Bianca Ferrari   Karen's business partner
Ian Dixon   Barrister
Angela Dixon   His wife
Lucy Dixon   Their daughter & Pippa's friend
Nancy Lester   Pippa's friend
Kenneth Wright   Lawyer
Nicholas Gleeson   Lawyer
BELLEVILLE FAMILY
Richard Belleville   Julia's elder brother
Kate Belleville (formerly Lester)   Richard's second wife
William Belleville   Julia's second brother
Alice Belleville (formerly Fitzroy)   William's wife
Paul Belleville   Richard's son from 1st marriage
Anthony Belleville   Richard's son from 1st marriage
Susan Belleville   Richard & Kate's daughter
Marianne Belleville   William & Alice's daughter
James Fitzroy   Julia's former husband
John Fitzroy   James & Julia's son

PROLOGUE

April 1969

AS PHILIPPE DUVAL, former eminent surgeon, settled into his first class seat on the flight taking him back to America, he began to reflect on how much his life had changed in less than a year.

He now had at his disposal a personal fortune he could not yet quite comprehend. But he doubted in his heart this grand gesture from the father he never knew until the last few weeks of his life would ever make up for the shame of his early life as an illegitimate child.

Nor could it make up for the way his mother had been treated throughout her life. But now there was no way to make amends to her.

In those moments of quiet clarity, he knew too he had behaved in ways he would always regret. He had agreed to separate from his wife, Julia. It seemed the only course of action. His mind went back to the day he had first met her. He had been a young US Army doctor, she the daughter of a wealthy Australian pastoral family. But for war, their paths would never have crossed.

And their daughter Pippa would never have been born. Illegitimate like me, he thought.

He marvelled at the series of unlikely events that had brought the three of them together years later. Was it really fair for Pippa to go on resenting the fact her mother had been forced to give her up for adoption? He couldn't decide. One thing was for sure, their daughter had suffered, as he had done, because of the circumstances of her birth.

And now she'll hate me, he thought. She'll hate me for breaking up my marriage to her mother.

Can I go back, he wondered? Can I go back to Julia and give up Karen? He shook his head slightly from side to side as if arguing the point with himself. Beautiful, capricious, demanding Karen. He had given her up once, before he married Julia. But now? It was a question he couldn't yet answer. Not honestly.

And yet the thought of Julia no longer being in his life left him feeling bereft. She had been his first love, just as he had been hers.

Why has my personal life become so filled with uncertainty, he asked himself? He shook his head slightly as if to dismiss the question from his mind.

But one thing was certain, the moment he touched down in New York and headed to his estate on Long Island, he would assume the mantle so unexpectedly thrust upon him by his late father. As the acknowledged head of the Cox family. As the decision-maker who would guide the family's wealth. As master of Eastbury Hall. As head of the Ella Duval Foundation. He was fashioning a new life. A life he had never imagined for himself. And in that new life, he understood the challenges, marking them off subconsciously.

An embittered sister-in-law Barbara Cox, who had long imagined herself mistress of Eastbury Hall, except her husband the late Walter William Cox III had been sidelined by his father. He had died a disappointed and angry man.

And then he thought of their son, Walter William Cox IV. He

had grown close to his grandfather in his final years. Philippe was grateful for his presence. And for his willingness to act as a bridge between the two households. He hoped Walter would at least calm his sister Virginia who continued to support her mother's belief the inheritance had been stolen from their family.

Philippe let out a long sigh. He hadn't asked for any of it. He hadn't expected any of it. But he knew he would be a hypocrite to deny he didn't enjoy the sudden wealth that had come his way.

For the first time, he understood how wealth could ease his way through life. Was he wrong to enjoy it? Was he wrong to enjoy the chauffeur-driven car that would collect him from the airport? Or the butler Clarence who saw to his every need without query? Was he wrong to indulge the women in his life?

He smiled to himself. If only his mother had been alive to see the great wrong righted. To know his father had regretted not marrying her until his dying day. But she had borne her lot in life with dignity and grace. And now he could do nothing to make amends, except in the one way available to him. His charitable foundation would honour her name. It seemed so inadequate but it was all he could do.

He settled back in the seat and closed his eyes. Take each day as it comes, he told himself. Take each day as it comes, as he drifted into an uneasy sleep, lulled by the throb of the aircraft engines.

CHAPTER 1

America—April 1969

PHILIPPE DUVAL PULLED off his tie and coffee-stained shirt in one quick movement. Nearby, Arabella Courtenay sat on the edge of one of the two chairs in his bedroom, fully aware she was in his private space.

Philippe had insisted she accompany him while he changed his shirt so she could continue her briefing about the function they were due to attend that evening. He had tried and failed to suppress his irritation when a new employee had stumbled handing him a cup of coffee.

Arabella had been one of four candidates put forward by the executive search firm and the only woman on the list. English by birth. Mid-thirties. Cambridge educated. Elegant. Sophisticated but warm and friendly. And highly recommended by previous employers. Philippe had liked her immediately and appointed her as executive director of the Ella Duval Foundation. She had been in the job for just three weeks.

Arabella looked up from her notes as Philippe walked back into the bedroom from his dressing room, a fresh shirt partly buttoned, his tie draped around his neck.

'What pitfalls await me, Arabella?' he asked as he concentrated on dressing.

She laughed. She could list a few but just for a moment she was distracted by her new employer. And then she looked back to her notes.

'Let me put it this way,' she said. 'There'll be a few unscrupulous people wanting funding for marginal projects with high overheads, meaning high salaries for them, and no reasonable hope of producing useful research. And they will go out of their way to meet you and flatter you.'

'Thanks for the warning,' he said and smiled at her. 'Your job will be to rescue me if I look like I need it.'

She returned the smile. He was so different from other men she had worked with. He treated her as an equal. Listened to her opinion. Took her advice.

'I don't think you look like someone who will need rescuing,' she said, 'except from cups of coffee.'

He laughed. He was dressed again now except for his cufflinks.

'Would you mind?'

He held out his right arm. She put her notes down and began the fiddly task of inserting the cufflink into the correct buttonholes.

'Very patriotic,' she said, noticing the fine etching of the American flag.

'They're my favourite. I have others including some ugly Cox cufflinks but I decided I needed a new updated design. The jewellers are working on it for me.'

'I thought you might have something acknowledging your Australian life?'

He nodded his head slightly and smiled.

'I do. From my wife with her family crest,' he said. 'I left them behind in Sydney. My wife and I have separated.'

She had not asked about his private life but she had been given a quiet briefing by the indispensable Clarence, who, she thought, seemed to know everything. She suspected he saw much more than he would ever speak about.

And then she remembered the warnings from her friends.

He's a womanizer, Arabella. He finally married the woman he left in Australia, unmarried and pregnant. But rumour has it the marriage is on the rocks. He had a gorgeous redhead on his arm at the Vogue party in February. His mistress apparently. There's a long list of women happy to take her place. Brilliant surgeon but he's given up his medical career. Inherited a fortune unexpectedly. Oh, he's charming and good-looking too. Whatever you do, don't fall under his spell.

'I understand your wife is coming over next month for the opening of the grounds here.'

She already knew his wife had been offered a board position on the Australian branch of the Foundation.

'She is indeed as is my daughter Pippa who will be involved with the Foundation in Australia.'

Up until that point, he had told only Clarence and Walter of his separation. Neither of them had been surprised but they were both disappointed. Walter, of course, had been the one to ask the other question. What about Karen?

But Philippe had been evasive in his reply. The question remained unanswered.

'Thank you for that,' he said, adjusting his sleeve and reaching for his suit coat. 'I'm sorry if I embarrassed you by bringing you into my bedroom. Perhaps that was unprofessional of me.'

Her office was on the ground floor of Eastbury Hall, the Long Island mansion he had inherited unexpectedly from his father. The Foundation staff, of whom there were now five people, were banned from the upper floors. She looked around her. It was a gloomy room lacking feminine touches.

'Perhaps it's time to call the decorators in.'

It had been a light-hearted observation to ease the tension of the moment.

'It is indeed time to call in the decorators,' he said. 'In fact I need to get at least three of the bedrooms on this floor redone quickly.'

'Three?'

He smiled as she quickly realised why he would want three bedrooms redone.

'Do you know anyone suitable for the job? I'm sure I could rely on your recommendation.'

She nodded, thinking of her close friend Claudia Rossi.

'I do know someone as a matter of fact. Would you like me to call her tomorrow?'

'Please. And I know it's not part of your job description, but can I ask you to oversee it for me. I can see your taste is impeccable,' he said, looking at her elegant, understated dress.

He liked her smile. It lit up her face, especially her deep blue eyes. And he liked how her dark blonde hair framed her face.

'Are you sure Clarence won't be put out if I do this?'

He shrugged.

'Clarence will get over it. He's got enough to do anyway without worrying about this.'

At that moment, she glimpsed the hint of arrogance others had spoken of. He wasn't a man to apologise for wanting things to be done his own way.

'And this room? Masculine and unfussy or some feminine touches?' she asked as they headed to the door.

He smiled again and put his hand lightly on her back to guide her out of the room.

'Not too masculine,' he said. 'I don't expect to be occupying it alone indefinitely.'

He noticed then a slight blush colour her cheeks. He hadn't needed to be told she would have heard all the gossip about his private life. Looked at objectively, it makes me sound like a philanderer, he thought. He worried then what he had said had been inappropriate.

They walked down the main staircase together where Walter William Cox IV was waiting patiently. The first thing Walter noticed was the slight blush of colour on Arabella's cheeks and then he saw a quick almost surreptitious movement as Philippe pulled his arm away from her back.

What's she doing in the private quarters? Is he doing what I think he's doing? His wife isn't here with him because his marriage is in trouble. And there's been no mention of Karen. Has he found a new target for his attentions?

For Walter these were fleeting but troubling thoughts as he held the front door open for them and then, without explanation, guided Arabella towards his car.

'I'll drive you,' he whispered to her. 'You looked a bit uncomfortable with Philippe just now.'

He opened the car door for her and she got in without comment. Philippe smiled to himself as Frederick, his chauffeur, closed the car door behind him. He understood exactly what Walter was thinking. But to him it had all been just mild flirtatious chatter with an attractive woman. Nothing more.

As Walter warmed the Camaro's powerful engine, he smiled across at his passenger.

'Did I misinterpret what I saw, Arabella?' he asked. 'Was Philippe exercising his famous charm on you?'

She laughed quietly, amused by Walter's earnestness.

'He is charming, isn't he?'

'So I'm told,' he said, 'and his bed has a vacancy at the present time.'

He said it in the hope of shocking her to see how she would react. To find out if she had designs on Philippe. But she was equal to his challenge.

'I know he's separated from his wife,' she said, laughing out loud, 'but what happened to the redhead? I didn't realise he was taking applications to fill that vacancy.'

Walter shook his head and laughed too.

'Not sure, he's simply not talking about his private life. Not to me anyway.'

While they were talking about Philippe, she decided to risk another question, a question that had aroused her curiosity.

'I take it you've met his wife,' she asked, interested now to know more. 'And his mistress too when she came to New York a few months back?'

She was intrigued. What type of women had Philippe chosen?

'I have met them both,' he said, taking his time to reply. 'His wife Julia is delightful. Blonde, elegant, very friendly, not unlike yourself.'

'And the mistress?'

'She's delightful too in a different sort of way. Beautiful long auburn hair that shines red in the light, eyes that sparkle with mischief, alabaster skin, very shapely. And besotted with him. He's bought her diamonds and furs. Funded her fashion business. And he's the envy of every man who's ever set eyes on her because she's available to him whenever he wants her.'

She thought about this new information for a few moments.

'So why does he seem so lonely now?'

'I'm guessing it's because he's separated from his wife. And he's not sure where it will all end up.'

'Meaning?'

'Will they reconcile which means he'll have to give up Karen. Or will they divorce which means Karen is going to expect the one thing he's denied her so far – a wedding ring.'

He let the clutch out and simultaneously accelerated hard. She felt the sudden thrust of power as the big car leapt forward.

'If you want my advice, Arabella, don't get in the middle of it.'

He almost had to shout to make himself heard over the roar of the engine.

'Did you think I was planning to?'

He risked a sideways glance at her.

'Not planning exactly,' he said, 'but he's got a lot to offer that might tempt a woman.'

'You mean the expensive gifts or the cachet of being his mistress? Or perhaps his next wife?'

He wished she hadn't said that. Was it just light-hearted banter? But it told him she had been thinking about Philippe. Thinking about him in quite the wrong context.

'Perhaps I've said enough, Arabella,' he said. 'I just didn't want you to be uncomfortable around him.'

'I'm not uncomfortable around him, Walter,' she said with a smile. 'I find him polite and charming. He's actually asked me to oversee the decorating of some of the upstairs bedrooms as a favour. That's what we were talking about when you saw us. I've promised to call my friend Claudia to get the job done quickly.'

'Well, the rooms certainly need updating, but isn't that somewhat outside your job description.'

He didn't say but he thought immediately it should be Clarence looking after it. Clarence had run the household for more than twenty years. Nothing happened at Eastbury Hall unless Clarence approved it.

'Of course it is but I'll do it for him as a favour,' she said. 'What I had asked him was whether he wanted his bedroom to be *masculine and unfussy* or with *some feminine touches*.'

'And his reply?'

'He said *not too masculine. I don't expect to be occupying it alone indefinitely.*'

Walter laughed to himself then. He began to wonder if Philippe would be foolish enough to complicate his life by romancing another woman. Or was the redecoration of the rooms a good sign that he expected to reconcile with Julia. He hoped it was the latter. For all their sakes.

'Well, I think I survived unscathed, Arabella,' Philippe said as he stood back and let Frederick open the door of the car for her. 'And I've convinced Walter you are safe with me and my chauffeur.'

'I'm sorry he did rather hijack me,' she said with a smile that contained just a hint of apology.

'That's fine,' he said. 'He meant well. He was just looking out for your interests.'

What am I meant to say to that, she wondered? She was keen to change the subject.

'Are you getting your head around how the Foundation should work now?' she asked, wondering if he found the detail rather tedious.

They had, over the weeks she had been in the job, discussed the criteria for grant applications and how the board should assess applications for research funding. She had raised another issue too, making sure the Foundation had a high profile to encourage philanthropic donors.

'I am, Arabella,' he said. 'I've even begun schmoozing the widows as you suggested to get them to leave us a legacy.'

'I knew you would be excellent at it,' she said unsurprised. 'You must have seen the ripple of gossip that went around the room when you walked in. You haven't been about much since you took over here, have you?'

'No, I've not had much opportunity really,' he said. 'And what were the gossips saying about me, if I may ask?'

But she shook her head. She couldn't repeat what she had overheard but she was sure he would know.

'Let me guess,' he said. 'It would either be *his wife's not with him, they say he's heading for the divorce court* or *what happened to the redhead?*'

She was grateful for the darkness in the car. Her face flushed hot and red. She had asked that very question of Walter earlier in the evening.

He glanced at her. He could sense a sudden tension between them. Years of medical practice had honed his perceptiveness. He was good at detecting changes in mood or changes in emotional states.

'I shouldn't have said that, should I?' he said. 'But I find it helps to talk to someone.'

'To talk to someone about?'

She was unsure what he meant. Or at least she was pretending to be unsure what he meant.

'About what's going on in my life,' he said. 'I'm sure Clarence or Walter would have given you some insight into my complicated personal life.'

She nodded. What could she say?

'I didn't ask,' she said finally. 'Clarence volunteered a few sketchy details.'

'And Walter?'

'Filled in some of the gaps,' she said.

He relaxed back into the luxuriously padded seat.

'So they shredded my reputation very successfully, I take it?'

'Well, let me just say, it wasn't what I expected to hear.'

'I know what you expected to hear,' he said. 'That I'd had a career as a top surgeon, inherited a massive fortune from the father I'd never known. That I'm happily married to Julia with whom I have a daughter I hadn't met until she was in her early teens.'

She gestured as if to say *that about sums it up.*

'If only life was that simple,' he said. 'As I said before, my wife and I have separated. I have no idea whether we'll get back together again. My daughter doesn't like me much anymore because I was unfaithful to her mother. And the redhead? The redhead is my weakness.'

He looked across at her. Had he been too frank with her? But he felt relaxed with her. He hadn't realised how lonely he'd become. He was missing Julia. He was missing Karen.

'But tell me, what's going on in your life apart from your work?'

He knew very little about her except that she had one failed marriage behind her and had reverted to her maiden name. Her husband had been American and she had stayed on after their separation.

'Nothing of interest,' she said. 'Absolutely nothing of interest really.'

'You mean compared with my complicated personal life?'

'Compared with almost anyone else's life really.'

'Is that deliberate?'

He wondered if she had been badly hurt by the failure of her marriage.

'Possibly,' she said, 'but the fact remains women have to be twice as good at their jobs to compete. I decided to focus on my career.'

He understood that. Hadn't he done that in his days as a surgeon? Medicine had been everything to him. He missed the daily demands of it. He missed his colleagues. He was about to say *but it makes for lonely nights* and then he stopped.

The car came to a standstill and Frederick jumped out to open the door to hand her out of the car. Philippe glanced at his watch. It wasn't especially late.

'Come in and have a nightcap before you go home,' he said.

She looked at him and hesitated. Was this a good idea?

He knew why she was hesitating.

'It's nice to have someone to talk to,' he persisted.

She relented and together they walked up to the front door to be greeted by Clarence who had been looking out for Philippe's return.

'Arabella is going to have a nightcap with me,' he said leading the way to the first floor.

'In your study?'

'Yes, Clarence, in my study. Can you come up and make us some drinks?'

Arabella looked at him enquiringly.

'Is your study a no go area?'

He laughed.

'It is, according to Clarence, unless it's lawyers,' he said, 'And it's the room where I found out about the inheritance from my father.'

'That must have been quite an occasion for you.'

'It was.'

As they entered the room together, she walked across to the sideboard and picked up a framed photo.

'Your wife and daughter?'

'Yes, that's Julia and Pippa.'

'They could be sisters,' she said. 'They look very much alike.'

She put the photograph back on the polished surface and sat down on the sofa. He stood by the fire, stirring it back to life.

'Clarence does a great martini. I hope you like martinis.'

With an almost unnatural silence, Clarence appeared suddenly.

'Martinis, Dr Duval?'

'Thanks, Clarence.'

Within minutes, he had handed them their drinks and backed out of the room but not before Philippe had time to register Clarence's look of disapproval.

'He's not very happy with me,' Philippe said with a half smile.

'Because you've invited me in for a drink.'

He nodded.

'Because I've invited you in for a drink.'

He continued to stand near the fire at some distance from her. He always found the old house chilly regardless of the season.

'It's just pleasant to have some company,' he said.

'I do understand that,' she said. 'It took me some time to get used to living alone again when my marriage broke up.'

He looked at her and wondered why a smart, attractive woman like her would be alone.

'I'm surprised you didn't go back to England. I assume you have family there?'

'I do have family there. Well, a younger sister Elise whose main aim in life is to get her photograph in Tatler magazine. And a mother who still believes I should be hankering for a good marriage instead of a career. She had several suitors lined up for my inspection when I returned to England briefly after my marriage failed.'

'And did you inspect any of them?' he asked, amused by her description of her mother's matchmaking.

She shook her head slowly.

'I told my mother one marriage was enough,' she said, with a hint of sadness. 'He was very controlling towards the end.'

He could see her dreams had been shattered by what marriage had turned out to be for her.

'And then you concentrated on your career.'

'I did,' she said, 'but I always knew it would be difficult to get beyond a certain level because of my sex, so I was delighted when you gave me the opportunity.'

He could see she was genuinely grateful.

'To be honest,' he said, 'given a choice, I had no desire to be surrounded by men in grey suits.'

'But you would have been mostly surrounded by men in your profession, surely?'

'That's true but more women are coming into the profession and I tried to help their careers. And I tried to shield them from the awful bullying of my male colleagues where I could.'

He was enjoying getting to know her, getting to understand her motivations, hoping it would be the start of a genuine friendship.

'By the way I have an invitation to the Met Gala on Monday. I don't suppose you'd like to come with me?'

'But don't worry if you already have plans,' he added quickly.

She sipped her drink trying to think of a good reason to decline the invitation but she could think of nothing. Instead, she found herself accepting.

'I've got nothing planned,' she said. 'That sounds delightful.'

And then he came to sit alongside her. Not close. Not touching her. Keeping space between them.

'I'm pleased you can come with me,' he said. 'I'm told it's quite an event. I'll get Frederick to pick you up.'

'There's no need for that,' she said. 'I can drive myself and meet you there.'

But he shook his head.

'Certainly not. That's what I keep a chauffeur for.'

He sipped his drink and looked at her closely. She possessed a natural friendliness that appealed to him. Am I putting her in a difficult position, he wondered? He hoped not.

For just a moment, their eyes met until she glanced away. She put her drink down on the coffee table.

'I think it's time I went.'

He didn't try to dissuade her. He recognised the danger of the intimacy that was developing between them. They walked down the stairs to the front door together where Clarence was waiting to lock up behind her.

'Can you organise Frederick to pick Arabella up Monday evening around six,' Philippe said. 'She's coming to the Met Gala with me.'

He saw Clarence's look of surprise. He waited until Arabella was out of earshot.

'Before you say something you shouldn't, Clarence, just let me say there's nothing more than friendship between us.'

Clarence nodded, acknowledging the reprimand but he smiled quietly to himself. He had seen where friendship could lead a man. And Philippe Duval was, at this point, particularly vulnerable, he thought. Very vulnerable indeed.

CHAPTER 2

Australia

AS THE PLANE TAXIED towards the terminal, the flight atten-
dant handed Philippe his briefcase and his jacket. He smiled his
thanks. There were distinct advantages in flying in the first class
cabin but even the comforts of first class failed to alleviate the tedium
of the long haul travel between New York and Sydney.

'We look forward to seeing you again soon, Dr Duval.'

He nodded. It would be soon. Too soon. He needed to be back at
Eastbury Hall well before the opening of the gardens to the public.
He had left just as the decorators were ready to gut the master bedroom he normally occupied. He had marvelled at the speed with
which the other two bedrooms had been redecorated. It had all been
down to Arabella.

He smiled to himself as he thought about her. Good at her job but
fun to be with too. Happy to be his partner at the functions he wanted
to attend. He was relieved the gossip columnists had not linked them
romantically. But it was only a matter of time, she had warned him.

And now, as he arrived back in Sydney, he began to feel a vague sense of guilt at the pleasure he had taken in Arabella's company and yet he had done nothing more than put his arm around her waist on one or two occasions. But even doing that had seemed slightly improper. Except that she had not objected. Had she moved just a little closer to him on those occasions? Or had he just imagined it?

He shook his head, trying to rid himself of thoughts of Arabella as he directed the limousine driver to his house at Point Piper. The purchase of it had been settled in his absence. His new housekeeper had prepared the house for his return but he felt the emptiness of it as soon as he entered.

Was this home, he wondered? Could it ever really be home with just him in it? Or was it that Sydney was no longer his home? Slowly he was adjusting to the fact that the centre of his life was now Long Island and New York. America had begun to feel like home again. He gazed out over the harbour but for the first time it failed to lift his spirits. Not because the scene had changed but because he had changed. And now his life felt more uncertain than ever. But that was wrong, he thought. It's not my life that feels uncertain. It's my relationships that feel uncertain.

Can I reconcile with Julia, he wondered, and expect her to spend the greater part of her life in America? Early in their marriage he had rejected the idea he could go back to medical practice in New York. And now? His circumstances were very different. But he still did not believe she would settle happily in America so far away from her family. And would she want to anyway? Perhaps she was ready to divorce him. Perhaps she had moved on from him.

And then his thoughts moved to Karen. With her fashion business she had more reason to be in New York, but not permanently. He knew she couldn't walk out on Bianca, on what they had built together. And he couldn't deprive her parents of their only surviving child.

For the time being he could see no solution. He walked back inside and picked up the phone to dial Pippa's number.

An hour later Pippa knocked on the door and greeted her father with unexpected warmth. He was relieved there was no hint of the animosity she had felt towards him months earlier when she had first learnt of his affair with Karen.

'You look tired,' she said, concerned at how weary he looked. 'It's a long flight. You should get an early night.'

He smiled, delighted to see her.

'I will,' he said. 'I promise. But tell me what's been going on in my absence.'

She wondered then if he had called her before calling anyone else. She had half expected to see Karen with him.

'I love this view,' she said, heading straight to the terrace. 'It's magical.'

'But a little chilly this afternoon.'

He handed her a glass of wine.

'Your hospital career is finally over, I guess,' he said. 'How are the plans taking shape for the office?'

He had left all that decision-making to her.

'The agents found me a sub-let in a building down towards Circular Quay,' she said. 'It will be ready mid next month.'

'And staff?'

'I've lined up some interviews for the executive director role starting tomorrow,' she said. 'I hope that's OK?'

He nodded.

'I hope you've vetted them.'

He was in no mood to waste time on interviews with unsuitable candidates. If Arabella had been with him, he would have asked her to do the interviews. She had quickly learned to relieve him of the tedium of the administrative work he had no interest in doing.

'I have,' she assured him. 'There are only three candidates worth considering. Once that person is appointed, I can deal with hiring the other staff with the director.'

He admired her new found confidence.

'That's good,' he said.

They lapsed into silence for a few moments. Pippa turned away from the terrace to face him.

'I thought I might find Karen here with you.'

She was watching his reaction carefully. Did he know Karen was disappointed in how few times he had contacted her in nearly two months?

Her good friend Anita, Karen's cousin, had confided in her, wondering if it meant her father had moved on from Karen.

He shook his head.

'I haven't told her I'm back yet,' he said.

'Are you planning to?'

'Of course. Just not today.'

'And are you planning to see my mother?'

'Yes, if she wants to see me.'

But in his answer Pippa detected the unspoken question about her mother.

'What you're really asking is, has she moved on from you?'

He shrugged.

'Well, she would have been seeing quite a bit of her first husband lately. John's twenty-first birthday. Marianne's wedding. I wondered if she had changed her mind. She told me she wasn't planning to go back to him. But events might have moved on while I've been away. Or is that something I shouldn't ask you?'

She sipped her wine. It was time they all acted like adults, she decided.

'I have no idea what my mother is planning for her future. To me, it seems as if her life is adrift. You and your work at the hospital formed the whole framework for her life. And now that's been stripped away she's having to reinvent her life. I don't know how far she's got with that yet.'

He nodded.

'I understand,' he said. What else could he say?

But she wondered if he really did understand. Marriage had been her mother's whole life, her whole identity. Take that away and what was she left with, she wanted to say. But she had no desire to act as a go-between in their relationship.

'When we went up north for John's birthday, the four of us had lunch together. John and his father James. My mother and me. It was the first time ever.'

She paused to gauge his reaction.

'That's a surprise,' he said. 'How was it? Civilised?'

'It was. I hope this doesn't sound disloyal to you but we felt like a family.'

He shook his head. He was pleased his daughter had a good relationship with her half-brother. But with his father? He was less certain. And for her to even consider thinking of the four of them as a family annoyed him. But he tried not to show it. He was responsible for breaking up their small family of three. How could he criticise her for turning towards John and his father?

'Until recently, I never realised how much John suffered because of his father's attitude to their breakup,' she said. 'It was all because of me. He's certainly apologetic about it now.'

'And trying to make it up to your mother,' he said, 'and succeeding it seems.'

'That was a rather unnecessary remark,' she said with just a hint of rebuke in her voice. She had almost said *it's nice to see them getting along so well now* but thought better of it. She knew, looking into the future, she would walk a tightrope between her parents until everything was settled between them.

'And Marianne's wedding? How did that go? I imagine her father was incandescent at the news she had to get married.'

She smiled, recalling what she had been told.

'He was. But she looked beautiful. All white satin and lace. She hardly looked pregnant at all.'

'And the bridesmaid?'

'Blue satin. Flowers in my hair. Absolutely ghastly, but Marianne loved it.'

They laughed together. He knew his daughter well enough to know she had no taste for the long-established rituals of a wedding ceremony. She hadn't always been like that, he thought, but she had certainly become very cynical about marriage. Had he been responsible for that, he wondered?

'When is her baby due?'

'September, I believe.'

'And her husband? One of the stockmen I think you told me. No doubt he saw considerable advantage for himself in seducing the boss's daughter.'

But she was inclined to defend Alex.

'Alex is very charming actually. His story should resonate with you. His mother was a governess who died shortly after his birth. He was working on Glenmoral where Uncle Richard met him. That's where Paul's plane went down. Uncle Richard subsequently offered him a job at Prior Park.'

'But still, a guy with few prospects.'

'You're right. Marrying Marianne has changed his life. But she's completely in love with him.'

'Does he feel the same way about her, do you think?'

She paused.

'Of course, he does.'

It was probably a little white lie, she thought, but Alex had seemed genuinely excited about the marriage and the prospect of fatherhood.

'You're being left behind, my dear daughter,' he said. 'Not even a permanent boyfriend. Or am I just out of the loop?'

She threw back her head and laughed heartily.

'Anita and I are determined spinsters,' she said. 'Careers first and last.'

'You'll get on well with Arabella then,' he said.

'So your new executive director is a committed career woman too, is she? She sounds formidable from what you've told me so far.'

But then she saw the hint of a smile on her father's face.

'No, she's not formidable. I wouldn't describe her as formidable.'

He was about to say *she's lovely* and then he stopped himself, choosing his words more carefully.

'She's very well credentialled. Very career focused. Understands what it takes for a woman to succeed in a man's world. She's got most of the office systems in place already. She's acting as my mentor, not the other way around.'

'It's great that you've found someone so competent,' she said, 'but I take it she's not a woman in her late fifties wearing sensible shoes and no make up?'

He shook his head slowly and laughed quietly. There was nothing about her that fitted that description.

'No, she isn't. She's thirty-something. English by birth. Very stylish. Has been married but isn't now. She's delightful company.'

She looked closely at her father. She thought she knew what the smile now meant each time he mentioned her name but she hesitated. Did she have the right to ask him?

'Sounds like it's something more than a professional relationship then?'

He looked up suddenly, shocked at what his daughter was suggesting. He answered her with a determined shake of his head.

'Of course I'm not sleeping with her if that's what you're suggesting, Pippa,' he snapped. 'She works for me. That would be totally unprofessional. We've become friends, that's all.'

She shrugged her shoulders. Only part of her believed him. Perhaps he hasn't slept with her yet, she thought, but that didn't mean he didn't want to. Or that he wouldn't sleep with her in the future. How much trouble can one man create for himself? Was that why Karen hadn't heard from him so much and why Karen wasn't the first call he made on his return?

She sighed. Perhaps I'm reading too much into it. Perhaps I'm way off the mark. She got up then and headed towards the kitchen.

'Has your housekeeper stocked your kitchen?' she asked. 'I think it's time we had some dinner.'

He followed and watched her work her way through the cupboards and the refrigerator.

'Pasta?'

'Pasta sounds fine,' he said.

He was simply enjoying having his daughter with him for the evening.

'You could move in here if you like,' he said. 'The house needs people, not to be standing empty when I'm not here.'

'I was going to suggest it,' she said, 'but I thought it might intrude on your privacy.'

'It won't,' he reassured her. 'It would be nice to have you here when I'm in Sydney.'

'Which sounds as if you'll only be spending some of your time in Sydney in the future?'

'I think that's how everything is panning out. Having to manage the family's investments and the Foundation, I think America has almost reclaimed me. There are decisions only I can make. I find it's better to be on the spot than to do it all remotely.'

She realised then he had also lost the anchors of his life in Sydney. His job at the hospital and most likely his marriage. And Karen? She suddenly felt a surge of sympathy for Karen.

'Which makes divorce inevitable, I suppose,' she said.

'Perhaps. Perhaps not.'

She sensed his uncertainty.

'But you don't honestly believe my mother would want to live the rest of her life on the other side of the world, do you?'

'No, I just can't picture it if I'm honest.'

'And Karen?'

He smiled that his daughter was suddenly concerned for his mistress.

'She has a life, a family and a business here in Sydney. It wouldn't be fair to ask her to give up everything to fit her life around mine.'

'So the solution is?'

'To do nothing at the moment,' he said. 'To make no firm decisions.'

'In the hope that these problems will resolve themselves?'

'Perhaps.'

But she knew his unwillingness to decide would only create more not less uncertainty for her mother. But she could do nothing to influence the situation.

And then she recalled her half-brother's words. *This mess just has to play out.*

She pulled the largest saucepan from the cupboard and began to fill it with water. She was grateful for the distraction of cooking. In the background she could hear the familiar sound of her father's favourite jazz record. The music wafted through the house.

Why can't he live here for at least half the year, she wondered? Why did it have to be all or nothing? Is there something I'm missing, she wondered? Could it be he's moved on from both my mother and Karen and he's using everything as an excuse or a reason to move on?

She knew there was one person she could ask. Walter. Perhaps he could shed some light on his life over there. She quickly calculated the time difference. She would call him late that evening.

Eastbury Hall was a hive of activity in advance of the big day when the gardens would officially open to the public. The builders were putting the finishing touches to the ground floor suite of offices for the Foundation, including a boardroom that commanded a view of the gardens. Outside, work was underway at a similar frenzied pace to create the facilities to turn the gardens into a public park. Clarence was calm despite the activity around him. He had a clear plan of how the work should proceed.

Arabella, using all her diplomatic skills, had managed to convince him her small role in overseeing the redecoration of three of the upstairs bedrooms was simply a way to relieve his workload and free him for more important work. Her smile and subtle flattery had won him over.

But all the same, he was curious to know why Pippa Duval was calling Walter. He wondered what was going on back in Sydney that had prompted her call.

'Not bad news I hope, young Walter?' he asked.

Walter smiled to himself. He knew Clarence was desperate to know why Pippa had called him but he wasn't sure himself after he had hung up from the call.

'No, Clarence, not bad news.'

He paused. Should he say more? He had observed the increasingly close relationship between Philippe and Arabella but he didn't know whether it was meaningful. Would Clarence know? But how exactly to ask him was a dilemma.

'She was checking up on her father actually,' he said. 'I think that's what it was all about.'

'On his life here, I suppose?'

Walter nodded.

'She told me he's become convinced he'll be spending most of his time over here now. That Sydney will no longer be his home.'

'Meaning?'

'She didn't say as much but she inferred that he thought it unlikely her mother would want to spend her life in America away from her family. She even mentioned Karen. He has the same concerns there apparently.'

'Which led her to think there might be another reason altogether, am I right?'

'Something like that, Clarence,' he said, 'but I said I didn't think so. But he's certainly been going about to more functions. He seems to be enjoying the social side of things more than I expected.'

'And you and I know it's all because of Arabella Courtenay.'

Walter looked at Clarence. He knew from experience that Clarence missed nothing.

'Philippe seems to get on very well with her,' Walter observed. 'And this morning I notice she's overseeing the redecoration of his bedroom. It was almost as if it's going to be her bedroom too the way she was expressing her opinions.'

Clarence allowed himself the luxury of a raised eyebrow and a slight smile.

'Oh, I think she's set her cap at him, if I may use a very old fashioned term. But she's very clever. And patient. She hasn't made one false move as far as I can see.'

'And Philippe? Is he interested in her? Interested enough to ditch his wife and his mistress for her?'

Clarence laughed quietly to himself.

'Why do you think I would know the answer to that question when I don't think he quite knows it himself yet.'

Walter was thinking back over his conversations with Arabella.

'Maybe it was just that he was lonely being here by himself. That's how Arabella herself described him to me some time back.'

Clarence shrugged.

'A lonely man, in my experience, is a vulnerable man. Perhaps seeing his wife again or his mistress will give him a different perspective.'

But there was one more question Walter wanted to ask. Should he ask it? Would Clarence be shocked at the question? But he decided to risk it anyway.

'Is he sleeping with her?'

Clarence paused for some time before answering. Should he really be speaking about Philippe's private life in this way?

'Not as far as I know, Walter,' he said.

And then he turned and walked away.

CHAPTER 3

Australia—May1969

PHILIPPE AND HIS DAUGHTER sat discussing the three candidates they had interviewed that morning.

'What do you think, Pippa? Who impressed you the most?'

He had his own opinion but he wanted to hear her opinion first.

'Well, not the patronising lawyer,' she said, immediately ruling out the humourless fifty-year-old who addressed all his answers directly to her father.

He laughed.

'I agree. I couldn't work with him either.'

'So that means it's between the young guy with the finance background and the doctor wanting to use his medical background in another capacity,' she said, knowing her father would opt for the doctor who had worked in exotic places in terrible conditions.

She could see her father admired his dedication. And his aim to see funding go to under-researched areas of medicine and public health.

'I think that's an easy choice, actually,' he said. 'Dr Joel Tynan gets my vote.'

She smiled and nodded her approval.

'He gets mine too. But what are we going to do about experience in the philanthropy sector? He doesn't bring that to the table. And I know you decided against linking up with another foundation.'

But he already had the answer to that.

'The lawyers have found me a consultant who will do the job. For a big fee. He will help us set up all the systems and the grant documentation and so on and then leave us to get on with it.'

'And the local board?'

There seemed to be so much still to discuss.

'Names are under consideration. Hopefully Robert Clarke will agree to join the board.'

'And my role?'

She was still unclear exactly what her role would be.

'I thought you were too young and inexperienced to take on the executive director role,' he explained. 'I expect you'll work alongside Dr Tynan and the other staff. I guess you'll be their direct link to me. I think Joel Tynan will see that as an advantage.'

He looked at his watch.

'Are you meant to be somewhere?' she asked.

He smiled and nodded.

'On second thoughts, don't answer that,' she said.

'I'll see you later then,' he said.

He handed her a set of house keys including a key to the garage.

'Come and go as you please,' he said.

'Thanks.'

She sat for a few moments thinking about the interviews. It was the first time she had seen her father in his new role as Foundation chairman, rather than celebrated surgeon. She admired the ease with which he had slipped into it.

She began to gather her belongings together and then stopped as the door opened. They had used one of the meeting rooms at the law firm her father retained.

Nicholas Gleeson had been waiting, hoping that Philippe would leave first. He put his head around the door.

'I hope I'm not interrupting.'

She shook her head.

'No, we're finished but you've just missed my father. Nicholas, isn't it?'

She remembered him from the Clarke's pre-Christmas drinks party. He held out his hand to her.

'It's nice to see you again, Pippa. I heard you were doing some interviews this morning for the local branch of the Foundation your father is setting up. How did that go?'

'It went well. We have decided on a candidate,' she said. 'I think my father will call the executive search firm this afternoon to let them know but he was in a rush to leave. Running late for his next appointment.'

Nicholas Gleeson smiled that knowing smile that told Pippa he knew exactly where her father was headed. Would he say anything, she wondered?

'I see you're holding a set of keys. Moving house perhaps?'

She smiled. He didn't miss much.

'My father has asked me to move in with him. You probably know he bought a new house at Point Piper. It has a beautiful harbour view.'

'Yes, I know. And your mother has remained in their old house. Or is she moving in with your father too?'

'I think you know the situation there, Nicholas. Don't you do some legal work for my mother? I'm sure she'll tell you what she wants you to know.'

He had annoyed Pippa with his slightly patronising smile.

'Well, I think your mother is in limbo at the moment if you want my opinion, wondering when the divorce papers are going to arrive.'

'I don't think my father has any plans to initiate divorce at the moment,' she said, her voice betraying her irritation at his questions.

And then she looked at him, wondering if he was trying to persuade her mother to initiate divorce proceedings.

'Will you be acting for my mother if she divorces my father?' she asked.

Her mother had never discussed the matter with her beyond acknowledging they had separated to give each other time to consider the future.

He nodded.

'I will, Pippa. Your mother appointed me as her lawyer some time ago.'

'I didn't know that,' she said.

'No, well perhaps she didn't want your father to know either so perhaps it's best if you don't mention it to him.'

'You can be absolutely sure I won't mention it to him,' she replied. 'I'm trying to stay out of the line of fire.'

'Has it come to that?' he asked, trying not to sound hopeful.

'Just a figure of speech, Nicholas,' she replied with a half smile. 'I'd say it's a classic standoff at the moment to which I just happen to have a front row seat unfortunately.'

He smiled at her description of her role.

'Well, I hope they sort it out for your sake, Pippa. It must be difficult at times for you.'

She nodded.

'It is indeed,' she said. 'It is indeed.'

He held the door open for her and then escorted her to the lift.

'Give my regards to your mother,' he said as the lift doors closed.

'I will,' she said.

And then she noticed the fleeting look of pleasure on his face at the mention of her mother's name. With that one unguarded moment, Pippa knew he was harbouring hopes of becoming more than just her mother's lawyer. She prayed his ambitions would come to nothing.

Philippe hesitated before heading into the restaurant where he had arranged to meet Karen. This had been his longest separation from her and he was uncertain how she would greet him, uncertain even how he still felt about her.

But as soon as he saw her, all his doubts vanished. He wondered how he had ever been foolish enough to think he could keep her at arm's length. Or that he would even want to keep her at arm's length.

And her doubts vanished too as he embraced her and then kissed her, oblivious to the stares of disapproval from the other patrons.

'It's wonderful to see you,' she whispered to him, 'but there'll be more gossip about us now.'

She had spotted one or two people in the restaurant who would delight in recounting the titillating scene that had just played out in front of them.

He shrugged. What did it matter now? He was separated from Julia.

Over lunch, she quizzed him endlessly about what he had been doing.

'I took your advice about the gloomy house,' he said. 'Three of the bedrooms have been redecorated. Or at least two are finished. Mine is being done while I'm over here.'

'I hope it's not all very masculine,' she said. 'I should have been there to oversee it.'

He smiled at her, recalling the discussions he'd had with Arabella on that very topic.

'I'm sure you'll like it,' he reassured her. 'The decorator had strict instructions not to make it too masculine.'

For a fleeting moment, he wondered how well she would get on with Arabella. But he knew the answer without even thinking about it. She wouldn't. She would see Arabella as a potential rival, regardless of what he said.

'And your US contracts?' he asked. 'Are they going according to plan?'

She bubbled over with excitement at the business prospects opening up for them.

'Thanks to you, Philippe,' she said. 'Very much thanks to you. I will need to go across for the first delivery, probably in June.'

He refilled their champagne glasses to toast her success. And then she asked him the question that was always uppermost in her mind.

'Is your separation permanent? Are you and Julia going to divorce?'

But he sidestepped the question.

'We haven't had a chance to discuss it since I got back,' he said.

'So you've not seen her?'

She couldn't resist the question.

'No, I haven't seen my wife,' he said. 'Pippa came over last night. We had some catching up to do. And I've asked her to move in with me.'

Would it be her home one day, she wondered? She had admired the house when he had shown her over it.

'Does that mean Pippa's not quite so angry with you now?'

He laughed.

'Deep down, I think she still is. But she's agreed to work with me. She's quite tough on me really.'

She considered this for a few moments.

'Because you feel your wife should take some of the blame for the state of your marriage?'

He looked at her then. She was asking him questions she would once have never dared to ask him.

'If I'm honest, the blame is almost exclusively mine. I neglected her, almost from the moment I realised you were going to be back in my life again.'

She laughed then.

'So it's my fault,' she said, her eyes twinkling with mischief.

'It is,' he said with a smile. 'Of course it is. You remember. You came to my office before I left for New York last winter. I knew as soon as I got back to Sydney, I would want to see you again. I wouldn't be able to stop myself.'

She leant across the table then and kissed him. He knew he wanted her just as much as he had before.

'I think it's time we left,' he said, as he threw some cash on the table for the meal. 'Let's go to my place so we can enjoy the harbour view as the sun goes down.'

She was surprised. What if his daughter came home?

'Is that a good idea? What will Pippa think?'

He kissed her again as he held the car door open for her.

'She'll get used to having you around,' he said.

He knew then he had been right to describe her as *his weakness*.

Later, as she lay in his arms, he kissed her lightly on the cheek.

'When were you going to tell me?' he asked.

'Tell you what?' she said but a secret smile hovered on her lips.

'That you're pregnant, my darling,' he said, as he ran his hand over her stomach. 'Did you think I wouldn't notice?'

He had seen the telltale signs almost immediately.

'I hope you're not angry with me,' she said turning to look at him. 'If you don't want to take responsibility for it, that's fine. I can do this by myself.'

He shook his head and kissed her gently.

'No, I'm not angry,' he said, 'and of course I'll take responsibility as the father. When is the baby due?'

'Around early October,' she said.

He did a quick calculation.

'Our New York baby.'

She nodded.

'Does your family know?'

She shook her head.

'No, only Bianca. And Uncle Robert knows. He guessed.'

'I'm pleased I know now. I'm due to see him tomorrow. That might have been awkward.'

She looked at him, relieved that he was taking the news so well.

'I'm sorry I didn't tell you I wanted to have a baby. I was running out of time. And then I wanted to be sure I didn't miscarry again.'

But he could not be angry with her. She had suffered for loving him in the past. He began to contemplate the implications for his life. And hers. And for him, now, there was no option. He would have to divorce Julia.

'I'll get my lawyers to begin divorce proceedings,' he said, 'but it will take quite a while to finalise. It will be some time before I can marry you.'

'I realise that,' she said. 'Unfortunately, the baby won't wait.'

He smiled to himself. How was it, he wondered, that both the children he fathered would end up being born illegitimately. First Pippa. Now Karen's baby.

'And there'll be a lot of gossip, I'm afraid.'

'To be honest, I don't care about that at all,' she said, 'but you should tell your wife before she finds out via other means.'

That, he thought, would be the most difficult thing he would have to do. His affair with Karen was one thing but for everyone to know Karen was now carrying his child would be humiliating for Julia and there was nothing he could do to lessen that humiliation. She's going to hate me forever, he thought sadly.

And his future? He knew he had no option but to offer marriage to her. No option at all. And his concerns about where his life would be lived? All those concerns now seemed irrelevant. The future would just have to take care of itself.

As he lay with her in his arms, he tried to decide if he was sorry Karen had trapped him in this way. He had not expected it. Would he have agreed to her getting pregnant if she had asked him? Probably not, given his age, he thought. But it was done now. Her pregnancy was well established. Within a few weeks, everyone would know.

He eased himself out of the bed and dressed. She was sleeping peacefully so he did not disturb her. He pulled the door of his bedroom shut just as he heard Pippa's voice calling him.

She took one look at him as he descended the stairs from the upper floor. She knew immediately what he had been doing, who he had been with.

'Karen's with you, isn't she?'

He nodded.

'She is, Pippa. She's asleep actually.'

She was about to make a light-hearted remark and then thought better of it. She had no experience of what to say to a father caught with his mistress in his bed in the late afternoon.

'No doubt she was delighted to see you.'

He could hear the bitterness returning to Pippa's voice.

'And I was delighted to see her, Pippa, don't forget that.'

'Obviously,' she said.

He didn't miss the slight sneer in her voice.

'There's something I have to tell you,' he said. 'Let's sit down.'

But she had already guessed. Anita had hinted at it when she had seen her earlier.

'She's pregnant, isn't she?'

He nodded.

'How did you know?'

But he answered his own question.

'Anita, I suppose. Karen told me Robert knows.'

'And that divorce you were in two minds about?'

'I'll instruct my lawyers to begin divorce proceedings immediately but I will need to tell your mother first.'

She pursed her lips, imagining the awkward conversation that lay ahead of him.

'She's going to feel humiliated. You know that, don't you?'

'Yes, I know that. Becoming a father again at my age wasn't part of my plan.'

'But you have to take responsibility for it,' she said. 'Unless she's been sleeping with someone else. Maybe you should ask her, just to be sure.'

It was the angriest he had ever been with his daughter. It was an unnecessary slur.

'I'll pretend I never heard you say that, Pippa,' he snapped. 'Karen is going to be my wife. And the baby will be your half-sister or half-brother. You need to remember that.'

She knew she had overstepped the mark.

'I'm sorry. I didn't mean to say such a hurtful thing. When is the baby due?'

'Early October or thereabouts.'

Just as he had done, she did the calculations quickly.

'A New York baby then? Appropriate somehow, isn't it?'

He smiled.

'It is indeed.'

And then she thought about their conversation of the previous day.

'It looks as though the decisions about your life have been taken out of your hands,' she said. 'Weren't you just going to *do nothing* and *make no firm decisions.*'

He laughed and nodded, remembering his words. He gestured helplessly as if to say, *that was yesterday, this is today.*

They both looked around as they heard Karen's footsteps on the stairs.

She looked at Pippa, not quite knowing what reaction to expect. She was relieved that Philippe stood and held out his hand towards her.

'I've told Pippa our news,' he said.

Karen looked at her cautiously. And then Pippa smiled at her and got up and hugged her.

'A bouncing red headed boy, Karen. What do you think?

She laughed.

'Early days, but I think it's a boy. As to how he will look, I think he'll be the spitting image of his father.'

'He'll like that,' Pippa said. 'I didn't favour his looks at all.'

As the sun set over the harbour, the three of them sat together chatting as if it was something they had done many times before. Pippa noticed how affectionate Karen was towards her father. And her father? She could see he was still absorbing the news that had upended his life.

There was one thing she knew for sure. She knew her mother would hate him for what he had done to her. Or maybe not hate him. Maybe that was too strong a word, she thought. But she would feel rejected. Embarrassed. And humiliated by him.

She hoped her mother would move on to find happiness again. She thought about her conversation with Nicholas Gleeson and smiled to herself. He's going to be all over this as soon as he hears this news. And personally? I think he's going to be delighted, Pippa thought. Absolutely delighted.

Chapter 4

May 1969

'BUSY DAY AHEAD of you?' Pippa asked as she sipped her coffee.

Philippe nodded. 'Obviously I will have to see my lawyer. And I'm seeing Robert Clarke for lunch.'

He had already delegated the task of contacting the executive recruiters to advise the candidate they had chosen to Pippa.

'I thought the most important thing might be for you to see my mother and tell her about Karen,' she said, as if he needed reminding.

'Don't worry, I'll do that today.'

'And Karen?'

'I'll see her later. And, yes, I have a lot to talk about with her.'

'Is she going to move in here with you?'

'We haven't discussed that yet. She may prefer to stay in her own apartment for the time being. I don't know.'

'Well, twenty-four hours have brought big changes in your life.'

He smiled.

'Indeed. I hadn't thought about the possibility Karen would want to try for a baby.'

'How do you feel about it?' she asked.

'I'm OK,' he said.

And then he smiled.

'After all she didn't manage to get pregnant all by herself.'

Pippa doubted it would still be the closely guarded secret Karen thought it was. If Anita knew, then her mother Patricia would know. And Patricia Clarke's reputation as a gossip was well established. Poor Karen, she thought. All eyes are going to be focused on her figure, looking for the first obvious signs.

And then the ringing of the telephone shattered the morning silence.

Pippa answered it and heard her mother's voice on the other end of the line. She listened intently and then she hung up. She looked across at her father.

'She knows.'

'How?'

He was stunned. He had only found out from Karen the previous evening. How was it that Julia had found out so quickly?

'She had lunch with Patricia Clarke yesterday.'

He closed his eyes briefly.

'I'm sorry she found out that way. I should have been the one to tell her. I'll go and see her.'

But Pippa shook her head.

'Perhaps give her a day or two to calm down. I won't repeat what she said except the final message was that she's already told her lawyer to begin divorce proceedings.'

'Her lawyer being Nicholas Gleeson, I assume?'

Pippa nodded.

'I never meant for it to happen this way, Pippa,' he said. 'I loved your mother. If Karen hadn't come along, I'd still be happily married to her.'

'But Karen did come along. And Karen has always been there in the background, hasn't she?'

He shrugged his shoulders. What could he say now that would make any difference? It no longer mattered that he had avoided Karen for years.

'Yes, I guess that's true.'

'Somehow, for my sake, you need to make it up to my mother.'

'I will. I promise. I will try.'

He got up and walked onto the terrace to enjoy the morning light over the harbour. He thought of Julia. There was a part of him that would always love her. Karen's pregnancy had forced his hand. Without that he knew he would have delayed their divorce. But now the decision was irrevocable. He understood her anger with him. But did she understand the last thing he wanted was to hurt her in this way. He had hoped the dissolution of their marriage, if that's what eventuated, would have been amicable. But he understood how deeply he had hurt her. And now he was left wondering what he could do to make amends.

He stood staring at the harbour for some time until the shrill sound of the telephone brought him back to the realities of the day.

Before Kenneth Wright had even had a chance to review his appointments for the day, Nicholas Gleeson tapped on his colleague's office door.

He was surprised at the early interruption.

'Can I help you with something, Nicholas?' he asked, hardly looking up. He was, in fact, distracted by the growing number of urgent matters demanding his attention and hadn't welcomed the intrusion.

'The starting gun's just been fired, Kenneth.'

His colleague looked up, perplexed.

'Sorry, what did you say?'

'I had a call early this morning from my client,' he said obliquely. 'She wants to begin divorce proceedings immediately.'

And then he realised what Nicholas was telling him.

'I take it you mean Mrs Julia Duval.'

He nodded.

'I do,' he said. 'And I'm working on a proposal for her settlement too.'

'Grounds, Nicholas?'

But he already knew, of course.

'We'll be citing his adultery.'

'And you have evidence of this that will satisfy the court?'

'Oh, yes, we have evidence, Kenneth,' he said, with a smile of satisfaction on his face. 'Evidence your client won't contest I don't think.'

'And what evidence would that be, Nicholas.'

Kenneth Wright was not in the habit of conceding any point in such negotiations.

'Karen Clarke is pregnant, Kenneth. I imagine you'll find this out very soon.'

There was silence in the room as both men took in the implications of the news.

'So you're assuming Philippe Duval is the father. Has he accepted paternity? I'm conceding nothing here until I've spoken to my client. She may have other men friends for all we know.'

Nicholas laughed out loud then.

'Admirable tactics, Kenneth, but you and I both know she's besotted with her wealthy lover. And he with her.'

He turned to go.

'And you, Nicholas?' he asked. 'He may decide to enquire into exactly how close you are with your client?'

'Don't go there, Kenneth. That line of enquiry would yield nothing. You've been listening to too much idle gossip.'

Despite the busy day that lay ahead of him, Kenneth Wright sat back in his chair and began to contemplate the fallout from what he imagined was about to become a very acrimonious divorce negotiation. He felt sorry for Julia Duval. She had deserved better treatment than she had received at the hands of her wealthy husband.

But it was a familiar story. There was nothing unique about it in his experience, except perhaps the extent of Philippe Duval's wealth. But his job now was to represent his client and reject any outlandish settlement proposed by his colleague.

He picked up the telephone and dialled Philippe's number. This can't wait, he thought. He looked at the carefully typed list of appointments his secretary left on his desk each evening before she left for the day. This would have to take priority above everything else. After a brief conversation, he hung up the phone and carefully crossed out his next appointment and wrote down Philippe's name, before calling his secretary in to rearrange his day.

It was left to Pippa to drive the short distance to her mother's house. The front door was open despite the chilly breeze. She called out as she entered. The house seemed silent, almost unlived in. All her father's personal possessions had been packed and transported to his new house.

It was then she realised how little impact her mother had made on the house. It looked forlorn. The bookcase mostly empty. His jazz records all gone. On the wall, the dusty outline of where his awards and citations had once hung. Only a picture of their wedding remained. And a picture of her own graduation.

She moved along the hallway. The bedroom he had occupied in the past few months showed no sign of his recent occupancy.

She was startled then by her mother's voice.

'It's a sad place now, isn't it? The removalists came last week to take the rest of his stuff. He didn't want our wedding photo though.'

'Nor my graduation photo, it seems.'

Julia shook her head.

'No, he already has that. There was a spare copy in one of our albums. He asked for it specifically along with a selection from your teen years.'

She put her arm around her mother then.

'It wasn't meant to end like this,' Pippa said, fighting back the tears she had managed to hold in check so far. 'How did it end like this? He seemed happy with you. We seemed happy as a family.'

They walked through to the back porch together. It was mostly protected from the chilly wind that had sprung up.

'Karen Clarke is what happened,' Julia said, bitterness and anger fighting to get the upper hand. 'I guess she trapped him. Am I right?'

Pippa nodded.

'Pretty much, I think. Let me put it this way, I don't think he was planning on fatherhood again. But he is now.'

'How far along is she? Patricia didn't know for sure but she thought probably as much as four months.'

'That's about right I think,' Pippa said.

'You've seen her then?'

'Yesterday afternoon.'

Julia noticed her daughter didn't elaborate on the circumstances of their meeting.

'I assume that's when your father found out?'

She nodded. Please don't ask me anything more, she prayed silently.

'You could have moved back here with me, Pippa, instead of moving in with your father. You'd have been spared the embarrassment of having to be polite to his mistress.'

Pippa shrugged her shoulders. She had known everything about this encounter was going to be awkward.

'I accepted the offer to move in with him before all this happened. He indicated he wasn't going to spend as much time in Sydney as before.'

'And now?'

'I don't know what his plans are. You know he's appointed an executive director for the Foundation in America.'

She wondered if Arabella Courtenay would be disappointed too at the news of her father's impending marriage.

'No, I didn't,' Julia said, barely interested in it now. 'I've heard nothing of what he's been doing since he left to go to America. He felt we needed time to ourselves to consider our relationship and whether we might get back together again.'

'Did you ever really think that was likely?'

How could she say to her daughter the way he had made love to her just before he left had raised her hopes? That was impossible.

'I thought our relationship was getting back to what it had been,' she said, without being specific. 'I thought perhaps he was getting over his infatuation with Karen Clarke.'

Having seen him with Karen, Pippa knew it had been wishful thinking on her mother's part. Perhaps even on his part.

'Well, if he was getting over her, he isn't now.'

Julia laughed.

'Serves him right,' she said. 'I'm finished with him.'

'But please tell me you don't hate him,' Pippa said. 'I know this is humiliating for you but he didn't plan it this way.'

Julia turned and looked at her daughter.

'You're quite an advocate for him, aren't you?' she said, almost accusing her of choosing sides. 'How do you think I feel? Patricia Clarke felt sorry for me. That's why she called me to meet for lunch to tell me.'

She heard the bitterness in her mother's voice. The disappointment too.

'That must have been hard for you to hear.'

'It was hard. It was embarrassing. Patricia was remarkably sympathetic but I know she'll spread the gossip. I think once she told me, she would feel free to talk about it to the rest of her friends.'

'I think Dr Clarke would be furious if he found out. In fact, he's likely to find out today because my father is having lunch with him.'

Julia got up and walked into the kitchen to make herself a cup of tea until Pippa took over the task from her. Tea had always been her mother's preferred drink, particularly in moments of crisis.

'What now for you, Mother?' she asked. 'What do you plan to do?'

'I've already called my lawyer to start divorce proceedings. I've called the real estate agent to sell this house. After that, I don't know.'

Pippa listened to all this without comment. They sat together at the kitchen table in silence for a few minutes. Julia sipped her tea, all the time wondering how her life had disintegrated so spectacularly.

'I thought you might have headed back up north,' Pippa said.

'I may do that but I haven't decided. I'll call Alice later to tell her what's happening.'

Pippa was relieved her mother seemed calmer now. More settled. More accepting of what was going to happen.

'My father would like to come and see you,' she said. 'He really wanted to tell you the news in person, not have someone else tell you.'

Julia shrugged as if she no longer cared.

'If he wants to, he can. But tell him not to expect a warm welcome.'

Pippa looked closely at her mother. Physically, she looked the same. But she had never heard her mother sound so embittered.

'Don't let this ruin your life,' she pleaded. 'Please don't become a bitter and twisted person because of this. I know you've endured a lot in your life. But just be thankful we all found one another and had almost a decade together as a family. That means something. It means a lot to me.'

Julia smiled at her daughter. She realised, without Philippe, she would never have met her daughter, never have known her. That counted for a lot.

'We did have a good time together as a family,' she said, smiling. 'I'll always remember that.'

'And now it's time to get out of this gloomy place and go and drink champagne and crack open some oysters,' Pippa said, relieved to see her mother smile briefly. 'And I'll tell you about Dr Joel Tynan, the new executive director of the Foundation in Australia.'

Across town, Robert Clarke had made an overly long study of the lunch menu at his favourite Rose Bay restaurant. He had greeted Philippe warmly enough but he was cautious. Had Philippe seen Karen since his return? Did he know about Karen's condition?

'How's everything going at the hospital, Robert?' Philippe asked, his interest genuine.

'Pretty well,' Robert replied. 'Usual scheduling problems for operations. Staff shortages as the winter flu season kicks in. And your expertise was hard to replace.'

'Well, I guess, given what you know about Karen's condition, you'll be pleased to be spared the scandal that is now about to break over my head,' Philippe said.

Robert was relieved the subject was out in the open.

'I was wondering if you knew about Karen's pregnancy,' he said, finally tossing the menu down on the table.

'I do, Robert. I must say it came as something of a surprise. Has Karen consulted you? Is her pregnancy going along as expected?'

He shrugged his shoulders.

'She didn't consult me about it. As a matter of fact, I guessed. She stayed over with us one night a couple of months ago. I know morning sickness when I see it.'

'Is she getting good care? I haven't had a chance to ask her yet.'

'I gave her the name of an obstetrician and organised an appointment for her. As far as I know, it's a normal pregnancy.'

Philippe set his menu aside too and looked around for a waiter.

'I have to say I didn't appreciate your wife telling my wife about Karen. It would have been better coming from me.'

He saw the look of shock on his former colleague's face.

'I didn't know that Philippe. I'm sorry. She's always felt sympathetic towards your wife.'

But he was annoyed with his wife. She shouldn't have meddled in that way. He could see how it had irritated Philippe.

'Sympathetic or not, she should not have done it, Robert,'

Philippe replied with just a hint of anger remaining in his voice. 'I have to deal with the fallout now.'

'What can I do but apologise again, Philippe. I agree. She shouldn't have said anything. But you know how my wife gossips. Everyone will know now.'

'Including your brother, I assume?'

Robert nodded.

'He knows. He rang me this morning wondering why Karen hadn't told him herself.'

Philippe let out a long sigh of frustration.

'Does it occur to anyone she wanted me to be the first to know? Or at least among the first to know.'

Robert understood his frustration. Having people gossiping about Karen before he found out himself would have been annoying.

'So what happens now, Philippe?'

Both men were ignoring the waiter standing beside their table until he coughed slightly. For a few minutes, they turned their attention to ordering their meals and drinks.

'What do you think happens now, Robert? I spent the morning with my lawyer. I'm being sued for divorce on the grounds of adultery by my wife. Unfortunately, Karen's name can't be kept out of it.'

Robert Clarke was silent, thinking of the implications for Julia and remembering back to the night of Philippe's farewell dinner. Somehow their divorce still didn't seem right to him despite his loyalty to his niece.

'That's going to take some time, I imagine,' Robert said, having only a vague idea of the long legal process involved in divorce.

'It will, Robert. Possibly a year or more. Which means Karen's child is going to be born illegitimate.'

'But she would have known that was a risk. You would have known it was a risk.'

Philippe laughed then. The sound was more cynical than he intended.

'This pregnancy wasn't a joint decision, Robert. It was Karen's decision.'

'You mean she trapped you? Isn't that the word men normally use about women who do that?'

Philippe began to wonder why his conversations with Robert Clarke always seemed to descend into an unwelcome dissection of his private life.

'I'd never use that word, Robert. That's not the way I speak about Karen. You should know that.'

But he wondered why Robert had pushed him into denying he felt trapped. Did he feel he'd been trapped by her? He didn't know for sure. But he was beginning to see she had closed off options in his life with her pregnancy. But he couldn't blame her. Didn't blame her.

'And after the divorce is final?'

'I'd expect Karen to become my wife,' Philippe said, without any ambiguity.

'Her father will be pleased to hear that.'

'What are you suggesting? Did he think I wouldn't be prepared to do the right thing?'

Robert shrugged.

'I think he always felt there was a chance you wouldn't. That when you tired of her, you'd walk away from her. Go back to your wife. Or move on and relocate to America permanently.'

Philippe paused. It was as if, in a very few words, Robert Clarke had laid out all the possibilities for his life that had existed up until twenty-four hours ago.

'Obviously, Karen's pregnancy changes many things,' he said, 'but not the fact that I will be spending more time in America, which brings me to the reason for this lunch. I need good people on the local board. Are you still up for the challenge, Robert?'

'Of course. I'd be delighted,' he said, 'and I have a couple of suggestions from academia and research who would add a certain amount of kudos to your new enterprise.'

'Good. I'm pleased. Let's drink to its success.'

Robert sensed Philippe was finished talking about his private life. He wondered if Karen was going to live with him while his divorce was being finalised. Wasn't that happening now in these more permissive times?

It was as if the topic of Philippe's private life was off limits for the rest of the lunch. They chatted as old friends about the medical matters that had previously consumed so much of Philippe's life.

For Robert Clarke, it was safe ground. For Philippe, it was a reminder of how much he missed the day-to-day challenge of medicine. Inheriting great wealth had been a blessing mostly but it had robbed him prematurely of the career he had loved. And then he understood, there was always a price to pay. Always a price.

CHAPTER 5

May 1969

THERE IS ALWAYS a price to pay.

These words echoed through Philippe's mind as, days later, he parked in front of the house he had once shared with Julia. The house looked as it had always looked. Red brick solid. Reassuring. Dependable. He had always liked the pleasing symmetry of its elegant Federation design.

He remembered how thrilled Pippa had been when he had bought it shortly after settling in Sydney permanently. He tried to remember exactly when. More than ten years ago surely. And they had been happy. Mostly. And he had been fulfilled in his career.

But he knew all that had changed. Changed because of his inheritance. Changed because he had pursued Karen again. And now? His life was different. Vastly different from what it had been.

As he looked into the future, he was gripped by a profound sadness knowing Julia would no longer be part of his life. He could not escape the fact he had hurt her deeply.

He walked to the front door, which stood open. It was the first time he had ever knocked on the front door. He could see her walking towards the front of the house, her silhouette cutting through the darkness of the hallway.

She did not smile at him. She did not greet him.

'I wanted to see you,' he said quietly. 'I wanted to apologise.'

His voice was calm, sympathetic, sincere.

'For what? I think apologies are a bit late to be honest. After all, your mistress is pregnant. In a few months' time, she'll have your baby. I hope you'll all be very happy together.'

He heard the unmistakeable bitterness in her voice.

She turned and walked away from him towards the kitchen. He followed her noticing as he walked through the house how bare it all looked now.

'I'm selling the house by the way,' she said, with a dismissive wave of her arm. 'I don't want to live here anymore.'

He nodded. He had expected that.

'You're free to do whatever you want with it. The lawyers are working out a financial settlement for you. We should meet with them next week to discuss it.'

She shrugged as if it meant nothing to her. Money to placate me, she wanted to say. To help me forget how much you've humiliated me. But she knew even acknowledging it was a further humiliation. As if she could be bought off. As if his sins against their marriage could be absolved for a price. But she hesitated. She did not want their divorce to descend into name calling. Not for her sake, but for her daughter's sake.

'Nicholas has already told me that. He's taking care of it for me.'

But he hadn't come to talk to her about their divorce. It all seemed so tawdry and distasteful. He put his hand on her arm. She looked at him in alarm as if his touch would burn her flesh.

'I'm sorry our marriage has ended this way,' he said. 'Very sorry. It's not something I planned or expected. There was always a part of me that felt we would get back together and resume our life together.'

She laughed at him. It was a sound that conveyed only contempt.

'What, when you had tired of your dalliance with Karen? Or she had booted you because you wouldn't offer her marriage.'

'That's not what I meant,' he said.

'Well, what did you mean then?'

He closed his eyes briefly, trying to conjure up the right words to tell her how he felt. He tried again.

'What I mean is there is a part of me that will always wonder if I've made the worst mistake of my life in ruining our marriage.'

There, he had said it. He waited for her to say something.

After a long pause, she finally spoke.

'It's very easy for you to say that now, knowing that you have to do the right thing by Karen.'

'But it's the truth,' he said. He wanted her to know how he felt. 'I never meant to hurt you. And yet that's exactly what I have done. I'm sorry for it. Very sorry. I never meant for this to happen.'

He was close enough to see tears gathering in her eyes. He reached out and touched her cheek gently with his fingers.

'Please don't hate me,' he begged. 'We've shared too much to hate one another.'

She shook her head. What was she supposed to do? Go on loving him as he moved on to Karen and their child?

And then, for just a few moments, he held her in his arms again.

'You will always be precious to me,' he whispered. 'We should have grown old together. It's my fault we won't be. Please forgive me.'

He turned then and walked away, leaving the house quickly without a backward glance. If he had looked back, he would have seen the tears streaming down her face.

But he could not bear to look back. He could not bear to look back and be reminded of what he had lost. Because, for the first time, he began to understand what he had lost. And how he must now live with the choices he had made. And the consequences of those choices.

Julia sat for a long time looking out on the back garden but seeing nothing. Not the first winter leaves falling. Not the chrysanthemums in full bloom. Not the last of the summer flowers now faded to brown and in need of pruning.

Her mind, instead, replayed Philippe's short visit over and over, as if it was on a continuous cinema loop. Had he really admitted he had made a mistake in destroying their marriage? She was unsure now. But what did it matter anyway? Karen had made sure she would be his next wife. In a week or two her pregnancy would be obvious and everyone would know. And everyone is going to look at me with pity, she thought.

And then she heard another knock on the door. But this time it was followed by a familiar voice. A welcome voice. She hugged her elder brother as if he was her saviour.

'I decided to surprise you,' Richard said as he headed to the kitchen to begin the familiar task of making a cup of tea.

He handed her a fresh handkerchief.

'If crying helps, by all means cry,' he said.

'You've just missed Philippe, actually,' she said, dabbing at her eyes.

'So what did he have to say for himself? That he was sorry he hurt you?'

He could imagine all the things he probably said.

She nodded.

'That and he was sorry he ruined our marriage.'

'A bit bloody late for that,' Richard said, as he took the boiling kettle off the stove to make the tea.

'So what brings you to Sydney? I didn't know you were coming down?'

He finished pouring the water into the teapot and set the kettle back on the stove before he put his arm around her again.

'You brought me to Sydney,' he said gently. 'We were all worried about you. And Kate and Susan were on their way to Bowral anyway. It's school holidays.'

'But not you? You're not going to Bowral?'

He shook his head.

'Actually, the less I'm there the better,' he said. 'Her son Tim doesn't like me very much actually.'

'Because you took his mother away, I suppose. In the same way John has never liked Philippe.'

'Pretty much,' he said. 'He was quite forceful in telling me what he thought of me on the night of Paul and Nancy's engagement dinner.'

'I didn't know that. How did Kate react to that? I assume she was part of the conversation.'

'Oh, she heard it. She's been a bit unsettled since then to be honest. She decided she wants to stay with Tim and Nancy until the wedding now. I think she feels she's neglected them because she's been living so far away with me.'

'And Susan?'

'She wants to enrol her in the local school down there for the next term.'

'How do you feel about that?'

He sighed deeply. How do I really feel about it, he wondered? What's the truth?

'Not ecstatic. To some people it might look like a separation.'

Julia looked at her brother carefully, trying to gauge his reaction.

'Is it? A separation I mean.'

'No, of course not,' he said quickly.

But he was more uncertain than he let on. He knew she enjoyed returning to Berrima Park and being there with her children. He hadn't wanted to deprive her of this last opportunity before Nancy's wedding for them to be together as a family again. But still he felt a sense of irritation at being excluded.

'Tell me, how did you know about the latest sordid chapter in my life?' she finally asked. 'I haven't spoken to anyone.'

'You'll be surprised at this but David Clarke called me. He

thought I would want to know which was very decent of him really. He reminded me of a conversation we'd had last year. That one of us would end up consoling a disappointed woman. As it turns out, it's me.'

She managed to raise half a smile. But the news that Karen's father had called her brother surprised her.

'He doesn't like Philippe very much. That's going to be a tense relationship.'

'Serves him right,' Richard said.

She laughed. She knew David Clarke had the ability to irritate Philippe.

'What does he think of his daughter being pregnant? There's no way she'll be married to Philippe before the baby is born. Pippa told me she's four months along already.'

Richard shrugged.

'I think he's willing to trade that off for the arrival of a grandson he thought he would never have. But he told me there's no way the child is having Philippe's name until they are married. For some reason he doesn't trust Philippe to do the right thing.'

'I think he will. He was brought up as an illegitimate child. He won't want that for his child. He didn't want it for Pippa.'

'And speaking of Pippa, I don't see any sign of her here.'

'She's moved in with her father.'

He wondered if that meant she had chosen sides. He would be disappointed in her if that was the case. But he didn't quite know how to ask that question.

'She agreed to move in with him before all this happened. She's unhappy about what her father has done but she's going to be working closely with him in future.'

He didn't envy being Pippa caught in the middle of her parents' marriage breakdown. He remembered how difficult it had been for his children when his marriage to Catherine had broken down.

'Does it help to talk?' Richard asked.

'It does,' she said, sipping the hot tea. She was pleased to have her brother's company. 'I actually found out about Karen's pregnancy from Patricia Clarke, not from Philippe.'

He remembered Patricia Clarke. The fact she had thought it appropriate to tell his sister about Karen's condition did not surprise him. He was sure it was gossip that fuelled Patricia Clarke's life.

'That must have been a tough conversation. I imagine she thought she was doing you a favour.'

'Doing herself a favour more like it. Once she'd told me, I think she felt free to tell the rest of her friends. In confidence of course.'

She paused and looked at her brother.

'By the way, have you told John what's happened?'

He nodded.

'I have. I avoided having to call in and see him with his father. I saw him in town yesterday morning, quite by chance.'

'Which means James will know too of course.'

'He will. Is that a problem for you?'

She shook her head.

'No, not really. Everyone's been expecting it since I separated from Philippe.'

'But you're worried James might now have expectations?'

He didn't quite know how else to frame the question. He could see she was thinking about what to say, perhaps even how much to confide in him.

'Not expectations exactly,' she said, 'but I think the impending divorce will raise his hopes.'

'And you?'

'It would be easy to go back,' she said, 'but I'm not sure that's what I want. I'm not going to make any decisions at the moment.'

'If I may say so, he seems very much a changed man since you came back into his life. He seems happier, much more relaxed.'

They sat together in silence for some time, each contemplating the challenges ahead in their own lives. She was grateful for Richard's presence. It had calmed her and brought a sense of reality back to her life.

'Why don't you go and change, fix your face and then we can go out and eat an early dinner,' he said finally. 'I'll call John Bertram and see if he's around to join us. He's always good company. We can drown our sorrows.'

'Well, that's an invitation I can't refuse,' she said, laughing for the first time in days as she headed to her bedroom.

He picked up the telephone and called John's number, the arrangements quickly falling into place.

Richard then walked the short distance to the front of the house to close the front door against the growing chill of the late afternoon. He noticed the front gate open and a man, similar in age to himself, juggling a briefcase and a large bunch of red roses in his efforts to close the gate behind him. Her lawyer for sure, Richard thought, simply by the way he was dressed. But red roses? What did that signify?

'Can I help you?' Richard said as Nicholas Gleeson approached the front door. 'Julia's just getting changed.'

Nicholas Gleeson had no idea who had addressed him.

'I've come to drop off some documents for Julia to look at. My name's Nicholas Gleeson,' he said, extending his hand towards Richard. 'And you are?'

'Richard Belleville, her brother, providing moral support. Come in.'

He ushered Nicholas into the living room. He put his briefcase down on the coffee table with the flowers alongside it.

'Red roses. A nice touch. Unusual though. I've never had red roses from my lawyer,' Richard said with a smile.

There was something about Nicholas Gleeson's smile that made Richard feel slightly uncomfortable. And something about the unconvincing way he explained away the roses that made him feel suspicious.

'I thought your sister might need cheering up,' he said. 'Flowers will do it every time in my experience.'

'Well, she certainly needs cheering up. But it was always likely to end in tears,' Richard said.

'Why do you say that?' Nicholas was intrigued.

'Philippe's history with Karen isn't recent,' Richard said. 'They were lovers before he married my sister. Karen's always had a very strong hold over him.'

'You know her then?'

'Oh, yes, I know her. I met her at Robert Clarke's house one evening just before he married Julia. And I know her father David. We sit on a board together.'

Nicholas was beginning to piece it all together now.

'Am I to assume you found out about Karen's condition via David Clarke rather than your sister?'

'That's right,' Richard said. 'I was pleased he called me.'

'I should tell you up front David Clarke is also a client of mine.'

'Well, it's all very cosy, isn't it?' Richard said. 'I hope that's not going to compromise your representation of my sister in her divorce. He's humiliated her. She deserves a decent settlement from him.'

'Oh, she'll get a decent settlement alright.'

Richard laughed. In those few words he heard a determination that exceeded a lawyer's brief.

'And you're going to enjoy the prospect of relieving him of some of his fortune, if I'm not mistaken.'

They both turned as Julia walked into the living room. She had heard Nicholas's voice from her bedroom. Nicholas stood and moved towards her but he saw the warning look in her eye. He kissed her lightly on the cheek and presented the flowers to her.

'Lovely roses, thank you,' she said.

He held out some documents for her.

'Take a look at these documents when you have a chance and then we can go over them in the next day or two.'

'Thanks, Nicholas,' she said. 'I will.'

'If you don't want to run the risk of seeing your husband in our offices, it might be better if I came to see you here. Or you could come to my house, whichever you prefer.'

She smiled. Going to his house presented some risk. Was she prepared for that?

'I'll call you,' she said, as she ushered him out the door.

When he was gone, Richard turned to look at her.

'Well, that's a potentially dangerous situation. A lawyer who clearly wants to romance his client.'

He noticed the slight flush of colour on his sister's face.

'Be careful, Julia,' he said. 'Philippe might decide to be difficult if he thought there was something going on between you and your lawyer.'

'There isn't,' she said, with a smile. At least not now, she might have added.

Richard was vaguely satisfied with his sister's answer. He hoped the admiration was all on one side.

'Let's go and eat. I'm starving. John Bertram is going to meet us at the restaurant.'

'Which restaurant did he suggest?'

'The Coachman. He says it's very good. I've written down the address.'

'I know where it is,' she said.

'Not a good choice?' he asked, noticing her grimace at the name.

'Oh, it's a lovely restaurant,' she said. 'A lovely restaurant where you can wine and dine your wife when you're trying to convince her she's the only woman in your life. It was where Philippe gave me a beautiful sapphire and diamond necklace. Only it was probably the same day he gave Karen a stunning platinum and diamond pendant with her initial picked out in perfectly matched diamonds.'

She paused, thinking back to the dinner.

'The jeweller assured me mine was the more expensive,' she added.

Richard laughed at how audacious his sister had become.

'You asked the jeweller?'

'I did,' she said. 'I had to get the clasp fixed.'

For just a fleeting moment she remembered when she had last worn it. And how Philippe had unclipped it from her neck. And what had followed. Would she ever wear it again?

She handed her car keys to her brother.

'Will you drive? I'll tell you how to get there.'

'Sure,' he said as he held the passenger door open for her and then slid behind the wheel, quickly pushing the seat back to accommodate his height.

He hoped her more positive frame of mind was a sign that she was over her tears. Over her disappointment at her failed marriage. And, most of all, over Philippe.

CHAPTER 6

May 1969

PHILIPPE SAT ALONE on the terrace, staring out at the harbour. He had done quite a lot of that in recent days. Am I unhappy at the turn of events? Unhappy with Karen? He didn't know. He couldn't answer those questions. He couldn't separate the issues in his mind.

In the past, he had simply been her lover. Being with her when he could. No real commitment, at least on his side. A clandestine relationship he had enjoyed. Until it was no longer clandestine. A sexual relationship that had been pure pleasure. Had she ever said no to him? And obligation? None beyond kindness and indulgence. Expensive presents had been the currency of their relationship.

He conceded he might have hinted at marriage but he had never promised her marriage. But he had told her he loved her. But he had loved her in the context of a relationship with no commitment beyond being her lover. And now? He had promised her marriage. Because he had to. At some vague time in the future.

He knew there was one thing about her he hadn't understood. Just how much she had wanted a child. His child. But she had known instinctively he would never have agreed to her becoming pregnant if she had asked him. He had written the contraceptive prescription for her himself but had never asked if she was taking it.

'A penny for your thoughts?'

He remembered Pippa had used those words once before. Then he had been musing on the personal obstacles he would face if he had wanted to return to New York to practice as a surgeon. In less than a year, his life had changed beyond recognition. He turned and smiled at her, relieved to have his daughter to talk to.

'I was thinking about how I've complicated my life.'

'You mean how Karen's complicated your life.'

He inclined his head.

'If you like.'

He was not prepared to argue such a trivial point.

'Have you spoken with her about what comes next? Do you want her to move in here with you?'

'I've offered her that option but she's declined because I'll be absent so much in the next few months. I think she simply wants us to go on as we are until we can be married.'

'When the baby is born, what happens then?'

'She's going to have a couple of months off and then go back to work, she told me.'

'And who is going to look after the baby?'

'A nanny, I suppose. Anyway, she's coming across to New York in June for their first department store deliveries. We can talk more then.'

Pippa sat alongside him in silence for some time, wondering just how his life would evolve over the next few years.

'If you marry her, she'll expect you to spend as much time in Sydney as possible,' Pippa warned. 'You should think about that.'

He laughed quietly.

'Do you think I don't know that. But I have to offer her marriage.'

'Do you?'

'Yes, Pippa, I do. She's having my child.'

'Because of the child. Not because you love her.'

He paused. A moment too long.

'Of course I love her,' he said.

'So if you are in love with her, really in love with her, I mean, why didn't you push to divorce my mother months ago and marry her?'

He did not answer her. Because he did not want to answer her. Because he could not answer her.

'Do you want me to answer that for you?' she asked.

He shook his head.

'I know the answer to that, Pippa. Let's leave it.'

He got up then and headed towards the kitchen and she followed him.

'Are you ready to head back to New York tomorrow?'

He nodded.

'I am. And you? Bags packed, are they?'

'They are. I'm looking forward to it,' she said, sorry that the plan for her mother to attend the opening of the gardens hadn't survived the fallout of recent days.

'Is Joel Tynan coming?

Pippa smiled.

'He is. He was surprised. Thrilled to be included actually and pleased to be added to the payroll in advance of the office opening. Did you let Clarence know by the way?'

'I did.'

'And the reason for the change?'

'I think that can wait until I can speak to him and Walter in person but I think he'll guess.'

'And Arabella?'

He shrugged. She was watching his response carefully.

'What about Arabella?'

'Did you tell her about our new local appointment?'

'I did. She was thrilled. Said she looked forward to meeting him. And to meeting you too.'

***

Across the Pacific, the news Julia would not be coming had caused a flurry of speculation. And disappointment. Both Clarence and Walter knew then the death knell had been sounded on Philippe's marriage.

And Arabella? Privately, she had felt a frisson of excitement at hearing the news he was returning without his wife but she was careful to make no comment at all. In quiet moments she knew just how much she was looking forward to seeing Philippe again. Too much, she told herself repeatedly. Much too much.

In Sydney, Karen sat in her father's office, her feet up on the second of his visitors' chairs. She looked at her watch. Philippe's plane would already be heading across the Pacific, halfway to its first stop in Honolulu.

'You look a bit tired,' he said, genuinely concerned for her. 'You're working too hard. Is everything alright?'

She smiled.

'I'm fine,' she said. 'It's been a draining few days.'

'How did he take the news?'

'As well as might have been expected.'

'And he's started divorce proceedings?'

'Julia has,' Karen corrected him. 'The petition will cite adultery of course. My name's all over it. But it's going to take a long time.'

'And, in the meantime, you're going to have his baby. You didn't tell him, did you, that you had this in mind all along?'

She shook her head, her long auburn hair swishing from side to side.

'He wouldn't have agreed. He always said he was too old to be a father.'

'I'm inclined to agree with him.'

'And marriage?'

'He's asked me to marry him when his divorce is final.'

'I'm pleased to hear that,' David Clarke said. He had never been sure Philippe would offer his daughter marriage.

And then he looked across at his daughter.

'That's what you want, isn't it? To marry him.'

'Of course,' she said.

He heard the uncertainty in her voice.

'Of course, it's what I want. But there's something missing. If he had started divorce proceedings and then offered to marry me before he found out I was pregnant, I would have been delighted. But now I sense he's offered marriage out of a sense of responsibility, not because he loves me. It wasn't spontaneous. It wasn't the way I wanted it to be.'

He got up from his chair and walked around his desk. He bent down and put his arm around his daughter. She should be delighted, he thought. She should be smiling and happy and thinking about her future as Philippe's wife. Not disappointed and miserable.

'Of course, he loves you,' her father said. 'He just wasn't expecting to hear about your baby. Remember, it's his child. You have a very real hold over him now.'

He watched helplessly as tears coursed down her face.

'If it helps to cry, then cry,' he said, 'but it will all be fine in the end. Think of the day confetti lands in your hair. The day the champagne corks pop. The day he slides that wedding ring on your finger.'

She smiled and brightened at the picture her father was painting. She hugged him fiercely. He had the knack of saying the right thing at the right time. She loved him for it.

The very next day David Clarke sat opposite Nicholas Gleeson, having insisted he be the lawyer's first appointment of the day.

'What can I do for you today, David?' he asked. 'I thought we'd settled most of your matters for the time being.'

'Not this one we haven't. My daughter Karen and the divorce you're handling on which her future depends. What stage is it up to?'

Nicholas Gleeson pushed his chair back from his desk and stood up.

'David, you know I can't talk about that with you. You're not a party to that matter. My client is Julia Duval.'

'Who is probably very keen to get rid of her two-timing husband as quickly as possible,' David Clarke interjected.

Nicholas shook his head, his face suddenly serious.

'Except that the two-timing husband of hers was two-timing her with your daughter. Have you forgotten that? Anyway, he's jetted back to New York. He won't be back here for months. We've only had the briefest of meetings if you must know. We're not even close to a financial settlement.'

'Playing hardball, is he?'

'I didn't say that, David. These processes take time. And then we have to prepare a case for the court. Dates and times and places if you get my meaning. It's going to take eighteen months at least.'

'Once it gets to the point of going before a judge, is there any way to speed it up?'

Nicholas shook his head.

'Not unless the judge is friendly and in a good mood. And not bogged down with too many cases.'

He considered this information for a moment. He stood up and turned to go.

'A friendly judge? A new Mercedes-Benz might make a man more friendly and accommodating.'

Nicholas Gleeson laughed out loud at the audacity of what his client was suggesting but he issued the expected warning.

'I'll pretend I never heard that, David. Bribing a judge is not something I've ever attempted. And it's not something I'm about to try now.'

The older man shrugged his shoulders. He didn't say that if he came to know the name of the judge he might find an excuse to approach him. Keep the lawyer's hands clean, he thought. But he would do anything to speed up the divorce for his daughter's sake.

Privately he felt if it all took too long Philippe Duval might find a reason to avoid marrying his daughter. He firmly believed Philippe had expected to go on enjoying his relationship with her without consequences. And without commitment. He's treated my daughter like a high paid call girl, he thought. Well, now he must pay the price for that. He must learn there are consequences. Unavoidable consequences. There is always a price to pay. And he was determined Philippe Duval would pay it.

America

Walter walked quickly to open Pippa's door even before Frederick had brought the car to a stop at Eastbury Hall. He hugged her in an affectionate brotherly way.

'How was the flight?' he asked before lowering his voice. 'We need to talk. You need to tell me what's going on. Come down early.'

She nodded her head as she looked around her at the changes to the gardens.

'It was a long and boring journey,' she said. 'The gardens look very different. It all looks terrific.'

And then she heard her father's voice.

'Walter, it's good to see you. This is Dr Joel Tynan. He's going to be heading up the Australian branch of the Foundation.'

The two men shook hands. He noticed the newcomer looking at the massive house in front of him with a mixture of awe and uncertainty.

'It's a bit of a monstrosity, I'm afraid,' Walter said, as if he needed to apologise for his family's vulgarity in having built such a place.

Joel Tynan might privately have agreed with Walter's description of the massive house that towered above him but he was hardly going to say so publicly.

'From the gilded age, I assume,' he said diplomatically. 'The age of big fortunes being amassed and spent on such displays of wealth. But I understand it's being put to good use now.'

'It is, Joel,' he said, following his gaze. 'My father was going to have it torn down and turned into a housing estate. But he didn't inherit it as he expected to. And my mother wanted to redecorate it and lord it over her society friends by having the biggest house.'

'Yes, Pippa told me the story of how Philippe came to inherit everything.'

Walter turned and pointed across the garden to a smaller but still impressive mansion.

'That's my family's home now. My father died last year. My mother, sister and I continue to live in the smaller house which was surveyed off from the main estate.'

Smaller perhaps, Joel thought, but not small. Definitely not small. Everywhere he looked Joel Tynan saw privilege. And wealth. Two months earlier he had been working in a central African village try-ing to deliver medical care in the most primitive of conditions to people who struggled to get enough food to eat every day. And now he had suddenly landed a job that brought him into the midst of unimaginable wealth. He had never seen wealth at close quarters. Not wealth of this magnitude.

Pippa had told him her father had set aside half the sale price of the industrial company he had inherited for the purpose of setting up the Foundation. But she had assured him he remained an extremely wealthy man by anyone's measure.

'And what's your role, Walter, if I may ask?'

'Apart from sitting on the Foundation's board, I do anything Philippe needs doing, particularly when he's away. And here's Clarence. Unusually late to the proceedings.'

Clarence, who had been conspicuous by his absence when they

arrived, came hurrying down the front steps.

'Dr Duval, I'm sorry. I was just caught up with a telephone call. It's good to have you back home.'

Philippe smiled and greeted him. Was this really home for him now? Sometimes it felt like it, he thought.

'It's good to see you Clarence,' he said. 'You remember my daughter Pippa and this is Dr Joel Tynan who's going to head the Foundation in Australia.'

'Welcome to Eastbury Hall, Dr Tynan,' Clarence said, adopting his customary formality before turning to greet Pippa with a friendly welcoming smile that held just a hint of the sadness he felt at the absence of Pippa's mother.

'Clarence started here as the butler under my grandfather,' Walter said quietly to Joel, 'but he runs everything now to do with the house. And he mixes a great martini.'

For Joel Tynan, there was a sense of unreality as he walked through the massive doors for the first time. He could see part of the ground floor had been altered to include office space but it had been done carefully to keep the integrity of the interior intact.

As they approached the stairs that led to the upper floor, he caught a glimpse of the Foundation staff busily at work.

'And Arabella Courtenay?' he asked Walter quietly. 'I thought she might be here to greet us. Is she about?'

'She won't be far away. Probably putting on her lipstick.'

And then they heard the clatter of high heels across the marble floor of the entrance.

'Watch this,' Walter whispered. 'She'll go straight to Philippe. She won't even notice anyone else.'

Joel watched as Arabella smiled brightly at Philippe and laid her hand on his arm.

'It's great to see you back, Philippe,' she said. 'I hope you had a good trip. We have a lot to catch up on.'

He smiled at her and then turned to introduce her.

'This is my daughter, Pippa,' he said, 'and Dr Joel Tynan who I told you about.'

Her smile lights up her face and her eyes positively sparkle, Pippa thought. And she's devastatingly pretty too. She noticed Joel Tynan was momentarily lost for words. It was clear, if he had formed a mental picture of Arabella Courtenay at all, it wasn't the vision of loveliness being introduced to him.

And then Pippa looked back at her father. He was smiling at Arabella. It was as if there was some private unspoken communication between them.

'We'll talk later,' Pippa heard him say quietly to her as they headed upstairs to be shown to their bedrooms, all now redecorated under Arabella's watchful eye. Pippa had been given the bedroom next to her father's. Joel was shown to the third of the redecorated bedrooms.

'We'll have drinks before dinner downstairs at six,' Clarence said as he showed Joel to his room. And then the door closed behind him.

It's like a palace, he thought, complete with household staff and beautiful gardens. Would it all be Pippa's one day? Or would Walter and his sister share it too? Whatever the outcome, how was it, he wondered, that these three young people would never need to work for a living while others struggled in abject poverty. The utter unfairness of life sometimes threatened to overwhelm him. He looked around the room. Everything looked new. There was the unmistakable smell of fresh paint. And carpet so thick his feet sank into it. He remembered the threadbare carpet in his family home and his mother shifting furniture to hide the worst of it.

He checked the time. Time enough for a shower and a change of clothes as he began to contemplate the challenges that lay ahead of him.

Pippa too was noticing the redecoration but she was in a hurry. She showered and changed quickly so she could get downstairs ahead of her father with the express aim of seeing Walter alone.

As she reached the bottom of the stairs, Walter, who had been looking out for her, put his arm around her and guided her out into the garden.

'I know what your first question is going to be, Walter,' she said, as they walked through the immaculate gardens. 'You want to know what's happened between my mother and my father.'

'We were shocked to find out she wasn't coming over with your father. What's happened, Pippa? Or are we being left to figure it out ourselves?'

They were sitting side by side now on one of the newly erected garden seats, the paint only just dry.

'I'll tell you, Walter, but you mustn't repeat anything,' she said quietly. 'My mother is filing for divorce on the grounds of his adultery.'

There I've said it out loud, she thought. She watched as Walter dropped his head into his hands. It was obvious he too was disappointed by the news.

'We figured as much,' he said. 'I'm so sorry. It just seems tragic. They seemed so right together. Happy together. Except …'

But he couldn't finish the sentence.

'Except for Karen.'

And then she turned towards him as he sat up again.

'I assume you met her when she was here.'

He nodded.

'I met her the first night they were in New York. I had dinner with her and Bianca. With your father of course. I knew as soon as I met her, she was involved with your father.'

Pippa let out a long sigh of disappointment.

'I found out over Christmas at my cousin's engagement dinner. My half-brother John overheard one of my uncles arguing with my father, accusing him of cheating on my mother. It was just so terrible.'

'I take it he wasn't prepared to give up Karen and go back to your mother?'

Another sigh broke the silence between them.

'I don't know but from very recent conversations I think he might have been having second thoughts. But it's too late for that now.'

'Too late? Because your mother wouldn't forgive him and take him back?'

She laughed mirthlessly and shook her head.

'It's all too late for that, Walter,' she said, as if he hadn't heard or understood the first time she had said it. 'Karen's pregnant. She conceived when she was with him in New York in late January or early February. My father has offered to marry her when his divorce is final, which is going to take some time.'

He was shocked by the revelation. It was something he hadn't thought about.

'Something tells me a baby wasn't in his plans,' he said finally, understanding how Karen's pregnancy changed everything.

Pippa shook her head slowly from side to side.

'No, it wasn't,' she said. 'I think he was stunned by the news.'

'When's the baby due?'

'October some time,' she said, 'and before you ask it will be illegitimate. Just like me. Just like he was. There's a certain irony there, don't you think?'

He put his arm around her then to comfort her. He understood the depths of her disappointment more than most.

'And you've had to observe all this as a bystander, trying not to take sides but probably more disappointed in your father than you want to acknowledge.'

He noticed a tear slide down her cheek. She began to search her pockets for a handkerchief until he came to the rescue, offering his own handkerchief.

'Devastated is the word, Walter. But I just have to learn to accept it.'

'And your mother? How is she coping?'

'How do you think she's coping, Walter? She's shattered by it all.

My father's life and work were the framework for her whole life and now it's been dismantled. She's having to build a new life for herself.'

She knew she had not been quite truthful about her mother but whichever way she looked at it, she considered her father's transgressions had been worse. And that James Fitzroy had taken advantage of her mother at her lowest ebb.

Like Pippa, Walter was devastated by the news. Not because he didn't like Karen but because he admired Julia. He admired them as a family. It had all seemed so perfect. Philippe, Julia, Pippa. They were happy together. They enjoyed each other's company. How did it all go so wrong, he wondered? How did Philippe allow himself to be bewitched by another woman?

He shook his head, knowing he would never understand it. He doubted Pippa would ever understand it either. Not fully.

She got up then.

'Let's head back and have a drink,' she said.

He smiled. He certainly needed one.

'Just a warning. Arabella's staying to have dinner with us.'

She rolled her eyes.

'Does she know about his impending divorce, do you think?'

He shrugged his shoulders.

'Not unless your father has told her but she may have guessed because he's come back without your mother. I've become cautious about talking about your father's personal life with her.'

'Because …?'

'Because Clarence and I both think she has designs on him, so we made a pact not to talk about your father with her. Which leaves him free to tell her what he wants to tell her. Or not tell her as the case may be.'

She stopped and looked at Walter.

'Please tell me my father hasn't become interested in another woman. That would be ridiculous.'

'I think it's mostly one-sided,' he said, unconvincingly, but he wondered if Pippa had thought about the fact her father had spent weeks by himself. And he faced the prospect of weeks, even months, by himself at Eastbury Hall. Did she know how many times her father and Arabella had been out socially under the guise of networking in the Foundation's interests? And how often she ended her day in his study, just the two of them, having drinks together.

'I hope you're right, Walter,' Pippa said. 'His life doesn't need to become any more complicated than it is now.'

As Walter opened the massive oak doors to the house, she was dismayed to see her father and Arabella standing close together deep in conversation, seemingly oblivious to everything going on around them. In that moment, she noticed a familiarity between them that alarmed her. And then her father looked up and moved slightly apart from Arabella, as if he had suddenly become aware of Pippa's scrutiny.

'Arabella's just been filling me in on everything that's been going on in my absence,' he said, 'but there's time enough for that. Let's all go and have a drink and celebrate our progress to date.'

Joel Tynan, walking quietly down the stairs, had seen the intimate exchange and he too was left to ponder what lines his new employer might have crossed. And then he caught Pippa's eye and he knew she too had thought the same thing.

Philippe Duval, he pondered, had everything going for him. An outstanding career as a surgeon. Sophisticated and charming. Now in his fifties, a little grey in his hair only adding to his distinguished good looks. And then suddenly he becomes a very wealthy man. At least he plans to do some good with his wealth, he thought. That's more than many others would.

But Joel had made it his business to find out more about Philippe's private life of which he had known very little. It hadn't been difficult once he tapped into his network of medical professionals. There was always someone who knew someone who knew the latest gossip. And the latest gossip disturbed him. He remembered what he'd been told. *Brilliant surgeon, one of the best, but he's been two-timing his lovely wife with a stunning redhead and now he's been caught out. The girlfriend is pregnant to him and his wife is divorcing him, accusing him of adultery. The question remains though will the girlfriend end up as his next wife or will he just move on.* It seemed opinion was evenly split both ways.

There are weaknesses in every man, he thought. Even the best of men. And then Philippe turned to greet him, making every effort to put him at ease. He smiled and followed Philippe into the dining room where Clarence had already commenced the task of making martinis.

CHAPTER 7

America—May 1969

THE GARDENS AT Eastbury Hall looked to have defied the record temperatures of the days leading up to the Memorial Day weekend. Or perhaps it was because the sprinklers supplied from the estate's own small lake had been working overtime.

No one could remember weather quite so hot and humid before the official start of summer.

But everything was ready for the big day, thanks very much to Clarence. And for the invitation-only event that was to precede the official opening of the gardens.

It was late afternoon and guests would start arriving within the hour but there was no sense of urgency. Not from Clarence and not from Philippe. They stood together before the solid granite memorial that dedicated the gardens to the US military personnel who had fought and died while serving the United States Armed Forces.

'Very appropriate, if I may say so, Dr Duval,' Clarence said, quickly wiping over the bronze plaque to remove a film of dust no one could see.

'I might have been one of them, Clarence,' he said. 'Not that I was on the front line but there were many doctors and nurses killed and injured. Brutal times.'

A separate plaque honoured the doctors, nurses and medical staff who had fallen. Tomorrow he would lay wreaths to honour them all as the gardens opened to the public. But tonight would be different. It was the first time he would host an event at Eastbury Hall. As the sun began to set, the garden came to life, the fairy lights strung from tree to tree creating a magical display.

As the two men headed back towards the house, Clarence laid a hand on Philippe's arm.

'Have you thought about who is going to be greeting the guests with you this evening?' he asked quietly.

'The family group, Clarence. Me and my daughter and Walter and his mother and sister. I've managed to get Barbara Cox to unbend a little towards me. And, of course, her daughter Virginia follows her mother's lead. They'll be in their element, spreading gossip about me.'

Clarence laughed quietly. Perhaps you should not give them quite so much ammunition, he wanted to say, but he was relieved all the same.

'Good choice,' he muttered.

Clarence was about to walk on but he noticed Philippe hesitate.

'Is there something more you need to tell me?'

Clarence knew what was coming. He didn't really need confirmation that Philippe's marriage was over. The absence of his wife from the long-planned opening of the gardens had told him everything he really needed to know.

'There is something more, Clarence. Walter already knows but I'd appreciate it if this goes no further.'

Clarence remained silent, waiting for Philippe to continue.

'My wife is suing me for divorce. It won't surprise you it's over my relationship with Karen. But there's something more you need to know because Karen will be over here next month. In a couple of weeks' time in fact. She may come out here with me.'

Again, Clarence said nothing. He wondered what else there was to tell him.

'Karen is pregnant with my child. When my divorce is finalised, I've offered to marry her. But she will have the baby before I can marry her, of course.'

There was a moment of strained silence that followed Philippe's revelation. Like Walter, Clarence had not thought of the possibility. Had the baby been planned, he wondered? Certainly not by the two of them, he concluded. By her, probably. The classic trap for men. And Philippe had walked right into it.

'I'm sorry to hear about your divorce,' Clarence said finally. 'I really liked your wife.'

He made no comment about Karen or her pregnancy. Was it something he expects me to congratulate him about, he wondered? Somehow, he didn't think so.

And then Clarence caught a hint of sadness in Philippe's face. In his voice too.

'So did I, Clarence. So did I.'

For a fleeting moment, Clarence thought Philippe was about to say more but they walked the rest of the distance back to the house in silence. The big doors already stood wide open ready to receive the invited guests.

The ground floor rooms on the eastern side of the building were brightly lit and decorated with massive vases of flowers. Trays of canapes were ready for the waiters who stood to attention awaiting the arrival of the first guests. Regimented rows of gleaming glassware stood empty, waiting for the uncorking of the wine and champagne. And then Philippe heard the pop of a champagne cork and the first of the glasses being filled.

Across the entry hall, he noticed Arabella busily checking the final details with the catering staff before heading towards the small orchestra that would play light classical music throughout the evening.

'Everything's perfect,' he whispered to her as he came alongside her. 'And you look sensational.'

She was delighted with his compliment and for just the briefest of moments he put his arm around her waist, his cufflink catching the delicate chiffon of her dress for just a second. She turned and smiled at him.

'I wanted everything to be perfect for you,' she said quietly.

'Thank you.'

He would have said something more except he noticed his daughter watching him intently.

'Time for me to go and do my duty,' he said with a slight grimace.

As he turned, he greeted Joel.

'Don't be overawed by it all, Joel. This stuff serves a purpose. If we're going to do some serious good in the future and set the Foundation up for the long term, we're going to need serious money. We need to court the rich.'

Joel smiled. He had never considered his role in life might be to help relieve the rich of some of their wealth to help fund medical research. But if that's what was needed, he would do his bit.

And then Arabella came alongside him and slipped her arm through his. He felt the softness of her body. It's almost provocative, he thought. Not that he minded.

'Everything looks spectacular, Arabella,' he said, knowing a compliment was expected. 'I'm sure the evening will be a great success.'

'It's the first time Philippe has entertained here on this scale. I wanted everything to be perfect for him. But of course Clarence should get a lot of the credit too.'

Very diplomatic of her, he thought.

And he wanted to say *don't get too hopeful where Philippe is concerned* but he needed to make a friend of her, not an enemy. At close quarters, he was able to see how much effort she had put into her own appearance, the subtle colour of her dress setting off her peaches and cream complexion, her blonde hair swept up with a diamond clasp. And then he noticed the diamonds at her throat.

'A lovely necklace,' he said. 'A gift from an admirer?'

She smiled, her eyes lighting up with pleasure. He noticed too the slight flush of colour on her cheeks.

'Yes, a gift, Joel,' she said, without nominating the giver.

The jewellery stores must welcome Philippe with open arms, he thought. Rich. And generous to the women in his life.

'We must spend some time together next week before you head back so I can show you how we work here,' she said, wanting to lead the conversation on to safer ground.

'Of course,' he said. 'I would really appreciate that. This is all new to me. We don't take possession of the office in Sydney for another two weeks. And once everything is set up, we have to decide how to invite applications for funding.'

'There won't be a shortage of those I wouldn't think,' she said. 'Did you know Philippe has already been invited to sit on some research boards?'

'No, he didn't tell me. Is he going to take them up?'

'I think he will. I've advised him to do so.'

'Which will mean he will spend more time in America, I imagine?'

She nodded.

'I think he'll very soon come to regard America as his home again.'

'I wonder if that will be tough on his private life,' Joel replied.

How much does she really know about Philippe, he wondered?

'He told me his wife is divorcing him,' she said. 'That should make it easier for him.'

He was wary. He knew the real reason for Philippe's impending divorce but only because of the gossip he had heard. It had not been discussed with him. He was still an outsider.

'Did he say why his wife is divorcing him?'

She looked at him, trying to decide whether he was actually seeking information he did not know or trying to find out how much she knew. She could not decide.

'He didn't go into details,' she said.

I can hardly say he told me *the redhead had got him into trouble.* She remembered the conversation with a smile. She would have asked him more questions except she could tell he wasn't in the mood.

'Enough about our employer, tell me about yourself,' she said as they watched the first of the guests arrive. 'I take it you haven't moved in these circles before?'

He laughed and shook his head.

'No, my father worked as a supervisor on the production line at the local car plant and my mother stayed at home. They couldn't afford to send me to university. Fortunately, I won a scholarship. And worked in the holidays.'

He hoped by explaining his family background she would understand he wasn't part of this world. Or her world.

She listened carefully.

'And then you practised as a doctor?' she asked, prompting him to say more.

'Yes, initially at a Sydney hospital and then overseas. Two months ago, I was trying to save lives in an African village with almost no resources.'

'What brought you back to Sydney? That sounds like very worthy work. But tough work I imagine.'

'I needed a change,' he said. 'I thought if I didn't leave then I would never leave. And my mother was getting older. I'm an only child. And my father passed away while I was in Africa.'

That was the simplest explanation he thought. Not quite the full explanation but close enough to the truth.

'That's very sad, Joel. I'm so sorry to hear that.'

She too had lost a father unexpectedly so she knew how it felt.

'Is your mother pleased with your new career?'

He smiled. His mother had been delighted.

'Very pleased,' he said. 'Philippe is quite well known in Sydney. She thinks it's a great coup that I landed the job.'

'And it is, Joel,' she said. 'Philippe wasn't brought up to wealth either. I guess you know his story. Perhaps he recognised a kindred spirit.'

He hadn't thought of that but he knew Philippe appreciated having a medical professional he could talk to. But he knew that wasn't the case with Arabella. He wondered about her life story but he didn't get a chance to ask. He wondered too why Philippe had chosen her. He looked at her again and understood that Arabella brought qualities to her role he lacked.

As she moved away from him, he watched her effortlessly move from guest to guest, greeting some with a kiss on the cheek, flattering the men and being friendly with the women. She endured with good grace the men who put their arms around her waist or patted her arm, half of whom probably made improper suggestions to her as she flirted and flitted around the room. She's a natural. She'll charm the money out of them, especially the men. He doubted he was the first man to fall in love with her at first sight. But he was realistic. He didn't stand a chance. With her looks and charm, she could have her pick of the wealthiest of men.

But during the evening, he noticed what others had probably missed. The number of times Arabella looked around quickly to see where Philippe was. And the number of times he looked back at her at that precise moment and smiled across the room. And each time her face registered a look of pure pleasure.

Joel knew then that Walter had been right on the first day they arrived. Arabella had eyes only for Philippe. And Philippe? A harmless flirtation. Or something more? Would he, in the midst of an expensive divorce from his wife and with his mistress pregnant, be bold enough to romance another woman? Perhaps that's what rich men could get away with, he thought. Or thought they could? He smiled to himself. There had to be some benefits, didn't there?

And then a voice cut through his reverie. A hand was thrust in his direction. He looked from the carefully manicured hand to the immaculately made up face. Her dark shoulder length hair was held in place by a diamond clip. Her dark brown eyes were looking at him appraisingly. She smiled but he noticed the smile did not extend to her eyes. Which was a pity, he thought, because she is a very attractive girl, except for the scowl.

'Virginia Cox,' she said, 'and you are?'

But she knew very well who he was.

'Joel Tynan,' he said. 'It's a pleasure to meet you, Virginia. You must be Walter's sister.'

She looked at him for some time, trying to decide what she thought of him, wanting to dislike him because he had been chosen by Philippe Duval. But she found herself liking his slightly unkempt appearance and his unflinching gaze. As she removed her hand from his, she noticed his long, elegant fingers. He might easily have passed for a musician, she thought. But in those hazel eyes, she noticed distaste—or was it contempt—for everything he saw around him, as if it was all too frivolous for his liking. And barely concealed contempt for her.

'They tell me you've spent some years plying your trade in central Africa,' she said, eyeing him carefully.

He smiled. He doubted she would be able to find central Africa on a map. Did she have any idea how other people lived, he wondered?

'That's right but I decided I should come home, otherwise I would spend my entire life there. My mother needs some looking after now my father has died.'

She did not respond in the accepted way. No insincere condolences at the loss of his father. No polite enquiry about his mother.

'No wife, Joel?'

He shook his head slightly. Should he tell the truth? It would emerge sooner or later.

'I was married, Virginia, but not now.'

She reached up and touched a small scar on the side of his cheek.

'Did she throw something at you and walk out?'

She remembered how many times her father had thrown things in anger. Not at her and not at her mother, at the wall mostly. And at Walter. Her brother still had a small scar on the side of his head from their last, most violent argument.

Joel nodded and smiled at her. How had she guessed?

'Good guess. My ex-wife Colette was quite volatile in the way French women can be.'

'What were you arguing about? Maybe you deserved it?'

He remembered the scene vividly. Should he tell her? What did it matter now?

'I had accused her of being unfaithful to me with a visiting Italian doctor.'

'And was she?'

He shrugged. There were times it still hurt to admit it.

'Yes, she was having an affair with him. She left me for him.' He fingered the scar on his face. 'That was her parting gift. And our divorce, which has just been finalised.'

Was that a hint of sadness in his eyes, she wondered? Or just relief it was over? She was curious.

'Are you happy it's over?' she asked.

He hadn't expected that question. He thought about his answer for a few seconds. Time for more honesty, he thought.

'My marriage was a ridiculous mistake from start to finish,' he said finally. 'And you, Virginia? You're too young to have fallen into the marriage trap yet.'

'So that's how you see it? A trap?'

'Well, it was a trap for me. Perhaps not for you.'

She shrugged and pulled a face.

'I have a boyfriend,' she said. 'I think he wants to marry me.'

It was as if marriage was the next obvious step for her. The only step. Yet there was no enthusiasm in her voice at the prospect.

'Is he here tonight? You should introduce him.'

He hadn't noticed her with an escort.

'No, he's not here tonight. He's away for the weekend with some friends. Boating or fishing or something.'

'And your mother? I noticed her arrive. I've yet to meet her. She hasn't been around in the few days since I arrived.'

Virginia laughed then.

'You don't know, do you? We're hardly on good terms with your employer. He inherited what should have been my father's. My mother isn't likely to forget how our family has been cheated. Nor am I.'

He already knew the story but decided to play along with her.

'Really? You don't look poor to me.'

She ignored his jibe if that's what it was. She couldn't decide. Instead, she pointed across the room to a group of people talking animatedly.

'That's my mother over there,' she said. 'I'll introduce you if you like.'

Joel followed the direction she was pointing and noticed a woman in her early fifties, not a hint of grey in her dark hair and wearing probably the most expensive gown in the room. The emeralds she was wearing would feed an African village for a decade, he thought. And even at a distance, he suspected the plastic surgeon had already been at work, trying to recapture the youth that was slowly but surely ebbing away from her.

As if she had sensed the scrutiny, she turned and looked across at her daughter, her face immediately transmitting a hint of displeasure which Virginia ignored. She took Joel by the arm and guided him through the crowd to where her mother stood.

'Mother, this is Dr Joel Tynan. He's heading up the Foundation in Sydney,' she said, forcing her mother to extend her hand towards Joel.

'Dr Tynan, pleased to meet you. My son told me about your appointment.'

Joel took the cool hand in his for the few moments politeness dictated.

'Mrs Cox, the pleasure is all mine,' he said, remembering his manners, except there was nothing about the encounter that involved pleasure. Had the woman ever smiled with genuine delight, he wondered. Should I compliment her on the cosmetic surgeon's excellent job? Probably not, he thought.

'I assume you're here to meet Arabella Courtenay and her staff?'

He nodded. This was safe ground for him.

'Yes, we'll be working together. I need to understand how she runs the office here so we can run the same way in Sydney.'

Barbara Cox smiled then, not with genuine pleasure but malicious delight.

'Well, she's certainly made an impact here. More on some than others. I'm sure she was delighted at the news Philippe Duval's wife has finally had enough of him and is suing for divorce.'

It was dangerous ground. He was cautious. He didn't want to be dragged into the family battle he'd already been warned about.

'I'm not really privy to what goes on in Dr Duval's private life, Mrs Cox,' he said. 'It's not something I've discussed with him.'

'It's not very private at times, Dr Tynan. A few months ago, he was flaunting his mistress over here when his wife didn't come with him. Now he's out every other night with Arabella Courtenay under the guise of networking for the Foundation. People really are starting to gossip about him.'

She turned then and gestured in his direction.

'She's never very far from his side, I'm told.'

As if on cue, Arabella walked quietly to Philippe's side and slipped her arm through his. She whispered something to him, he smiled and nodded.

'I think it's reasonable. They work closely together, Mrs Cox,' he said, trying to deflect her attention. 'People may be reading a lot into a friendly, professional relationship that isn't there.'

Barbara Cox looked at him then with contempt and walked away. He thought Virginia was about to do the same but she surprised him.

'Mother despises him. You must know that,' she said.

'I take it she enjoys spreading gossip about Philippe?'

'Or helps it along its way.'

He laughed, surprised by Virginia's honesty.

'And he's given her plenty to gossip about I understand.'

'Not quite what you told my mother,' she reminded him.

'No, it wasn't but I didn't want to be caught out discussing his private life. I'm sure he's capable of telling people what he wants them to know.'

'Such as his mistress having his baby.'

He knew she had said it to shock him but he only shrugged. He assumed her brother had told her. He seemed to be the one member of the Cox family on good terms with Philippe.

'I'm sorry to disappoint you but it's common knowledge in certain medical circles in Sydney.'

She looked at him. This time there was no scowl, just a conspiratorial smile.

'But you weren't part of those circles, were you? You made it your business to find out about him, didn't you?'

He laughed. She was cleverer than she looked. He nodded.

'I did,' he said. 'I wanted to know more about him. I knew of his outstanding medical career.'

'But the rest was a surprise, I imagine?'

'It was if I'm honest. But it's got nothing to do with me. I'm told most men envy him.'

'Because of the redhead?'

He laughed again.

'Yes, she is a stunning looking woman I'm told.'

'I wonder how Pippa feels about it all and about having a half-brother or a half-sister who will be almost a generation younger than her?'

'I don't know. I haven't asked her and I'm certainly not going to ask her.'

He looked around and noticed Pippa close by. Had Walter been by her side the entire night?

'She seems to get on very well with your brother,' he said, hoping to change the direction of the conversation.

'She does, doesn't she? But, of course, he was her way into the family initially. You should get her to tell you the story some time.'

'I will,' he said. 'Thanks for the tip.'

He took fresh glasses of champagne from the tray as the waiter passed and handed one to her.

'If you're not working all weekend, I could show you around Long Island,' she said. For the first time he noticed a genuine smile in her eyes.

'That would be great, Virginia,' he said. 'I've never been to this part of the world before, but haven't you got better things to do with your friends?'

She shook her head.

'No. It would be fun. I'll give you the grand tour tomorrow. Be ready at ten.'

'I'd like that,' he said, 'very much.'

He watched as she walked away greeting people she knew as she moved through the crowd.

'I see you've made a conquest, Joel,' Pippa said with a smile as she came to stand beside him. 'She's always been a catty bitch to me. I'm pleased to see there's another side to her.'

'Well, she's offered to give me the grand tour of Long Island tomorrow.'

Pippa laughed, remembering what Virginia had done to her mother when Walter had taken her out for the afternoon.

'Well, just be careful she doesn't throw a drink all over you like she did to my mother in a public bar.'

Pippa proceeded to tell him the story.

'Not a nice thing to do. Thanks for the warning. I'll be on my guard.'

But he was intrigued by the girl. She represented everything he had come to despise. Privilege. Entitlement. Superiority. Yet he felt drawn to her. Unexpectedly.

He drained his glass of champagne and looked around for another. And he began to see how easy it was to get used to a privileged lifestyle. Very easy indeed.

CHAPTER 8

'DR TYNAN WAS ON the telephone just now,' Clarence said as he approached Pippa and her father who were sitting together in the garden enjoying the last light of the day. Philippe half turned towards Clarence at the sound of his voice.

'No problem is there, Clarence?'

'No. He was calling to let us know he wouldn't be in for dinner. The guided tour of Long Island with Miss Cox has extended into an early dinner with Miss Cox apparently.'

Philippe made no comment. Was there any reason to be concerned about Virginia taking an interest in Joel Tynan? He couldn't think of any immediately, yet he looked to Pippa for confirmation.

'You know him better than I do. Any reason to be concerned?'

He didn't know much about Joel's private life. He had presented well as a candidate for the job but discussion of his private life had been kept to a minimum. Philippe had wanted to know about his medical training and where he had practised.

'If you're asking if he can be trusted around young women, of course, he can,' she said indignantly, surprised her father might be suggesting otherwise.

'I didn't mean that,' Philippe said, 'not exactly. I was thinking though she's a young woman who could, capriciously, cause trouble if she wanted to.'

He knew from experience if Joel said or did something inappropriate there was a good chance Virginia would overreact. In seeking Joel's company, he worried she might have an ulterior motive. Discredit one of his employees and the Foundation is discredited by association.

At that very moment, Walter came strolling across the grass to join them. He had been enjoying the peace of the gardens at the end of the first day of public access. The main gates had been shut for half an hour and the gardeners were busy cleaning up. But in the quiet of the late afternoon, he had overheard the conversation. He too was concerned. He knew his sister well. And he knew she could make mischief if the mood took her.

'Clarence, did he say where they were going to eat? Which restaurant?'

'No, but knowing your sister, it will be Gosman's at Montauk. People have been raving about it since its refurbishment.'

'Of course,' Walter said.

And then he held out his hand to Pippa.

'Fancy dinner at Gosman's, Pippa?'

'So we can act as a chaperone for your sister?'

But he shook his head.

'No, so we can make sure she's not up to anything. She may simply be enjoying Joel's company and we're jumping at shadows.'

Pippa looked at him. He did not appear concerned but she knew him well enough now to know he did not want to take any chances. His sister had already demonstrated her spitefulness.

'You don't trust your own sister, do you?'

He laughed.

'Not entirely. She can be vindictive if things don't go her way. And I'm not sure she is fully reconciled to the way things turned out.'

'Well, if you put it that way, how can I refuse such a charming invitation. I need fifteen minutes to change.'

He looked at his watch in the fading light.

'I'll time you,' he said with a laugh as he turned to walk back to his house as Pippa walked in the opposite direction.

Philippe had been listening to the exchange with interest. And some alarm. But he was relieved he and Walter were in accord. Virginia could make all sorts of accusations against Joel if she decided to turn nasty. And she would be believed because Joel was an outsider. And she was Virginia Cox. An unwelcome kiss could turn into something else entirely.

'Was I overreacting, Clarence?' Philippe asked.

Clarence took a moment to consider his answer.

'I wish I could say you were overreacting, Dr Duval, but I'm not sure. I think young Walter's concern tells you all you need to know.'

'I hope we're wrong, Clarence. I thought perhaps she had warmed towards us a bit.'

Clarence shook his head.

'I wouldn't count on it. My spies tell me she and her mother are enjoying spreading the latest gossip about your private life and trashing your reputation further.'

Philippe stood up then. Some of the gardeners were close by, too close to be having this conversation.

'Let's walk, Clarence,' he said.

When he was sure they would not be overheard, he spoke again.

'By that I take it you mean about my divorce and about Karen being pregnant?'

Clarence nodded. Did he need to say more?

'Forget the divorce. They would have worked that out because Julia isn't with me. But there are only three people here who know about Karen's condition apart from me. Pippa. Walter. And you. How did they find out?'

Clarence was not surprised to hear he had not told Arabella.

'Perhaps Walter told them?'

'I don't think so. Pippa told Walter in confidence.'

'If you're thinking I said anything to them, you're wrong. I never discuss your private life with anyone,' Clarence replied. Except young Walter, he might have added.

Philippe smiled to himself.

'Clarence, you would be the last person I would ever think of as a gossip. I know you wouldn't break a confidence. I wonder if some-one overhead me on the telephone to Karen. I have asked a couple of times how her pregnancy is going.'

'It's possible, I suppose,' Clarence said.

It was in fact an explanation he thought was entirely feasible. He remembered seeing the Eastbury Hall housekeeper Mrs Anderson deep in conversation with Barbara Cox on more than one occasion. Was it worth mentioning? He decided against it but if he caught her out, that would be quite a different matter altogether.

Clarence said nothing more as they walked on in silence. But it troubled Philippe. If they were spreading gossip about him regarding Karen's pregnancy, he was worried Arabella would hear it eventually. He had simply told her the redhead had got him into trouble. He hadn't specified the trouble. Should he tell her?

And if he decided to tell her, how would he broach the subject? And how would she take the news? His instinct told him whichever way she found out she would be disappointed by the news.

As they reached the house, he headed upstairs to his study and picked up the telephone. He hesitated. Was calling her late on a Saturday afternoon a good idea? Probably not, but he decided to do it anyway.

Gosman's Dock Restaurant borrowed heavily from the sea for its decorative touches. Rusty anchors, ship models, fish floats and other maritime paraphernalia all artfully arranged throughout the space which smelled of the sea. The restaurant was larger than Pippa expected. She guessed it would accommodate several hundred diners. Beyond the window, she could see an expanse of water, unusually calm, and now tinged pink from the dying rays of the late afternoon sun.

After several minutes careful study, she looked across at her companion.

'It's a wonderful place, Walter,' she said. 'What do you recommend? A lot of the food is quite new to me.'

He smiled across the table at her. She had completely transformed her appearance in the allotted fifteen minutes. She was dressed simply but stylishly in a sleeveless minidress that showed off her lightly tanned skin, with her blonde hair falling prettily around her shoulders, her blue eyes exuding warmth and friendliness, her face lightly made up. When they entered the restaurant together, he noticed the admiring glances she attracted from other diners. But she seemed not to notice.

'Well, the soft-shell crabs are great. And the lobster. Or if you like soup, the Manhattan chowder would be my suggestion. It has a tomato base rather than a creamy base.'

She laughed then.

'You sound like the ultimate gourmand, Walter,' she said teasingly. 'I'll have the lobster. I've had that before in Sydney.'

She tossed the menu on the table, content for him to handle the ordering.

'Any sign of your sister?'

He was about to say no and then he noticed his sister walk in with a group of friends. Joel was beside her, his arm around her loosely. He was grateful for the large anchor that shielded their section of tables from the entrance to the restaurant.

'Just walked in. Joel is beside her. I must say she looks relaxed and happy with him.'

She didn't turn around for fear the movement would draw attention to them.

'Does she have a boyfriend, Walter?'

It was the first time she had enquired about his sister. Her first meeting with Virginia had not gone particularly well.

'I know she's been seeing Patrick Boyd for a few months but he's away for the long weekend apparently.'

'What's he like? Do you like him?'

He shrugged.

'He's OK. His family is in the oil business.'

'Does your mother approve of him?'

'Yes, she does. Right pedigree.'

She was tempted to say it sounded as if his mother was choosing a bloodline for breeding but she thought better of it. But Walter could see the mischief in her eyes and he laughed.

'Don't say it, Pippa. I know what you're thinking.'

He looked beyond her then to the table where his sister was sitting alongside Joel who had his arm around the back of her chair and was laughing with her.

Pippa took the risk of turning around to follow Walter's gaze.

'The boyfriend might not be too happy if he saw that,' she said, as she turned back to face Walter.

He laughed dismissively.

'No, he wouldn't. And he does have a bit of a temper. I think Joel would end up with a black eye and a bloody nose.'

She noticed though Walter was totally unconcerned about his sister.

'You don't think there's anything to be alarmed about, am I right?'

He shook his head.

'Nothing at all. I think she's enjoying herself so I think we can enjoy our dinner together and not worry about them.'

She sighed with relief. Perhaps her father had overreacted. She was sorry then they had left him to dine alone. And then she heard the familiar pop of a champagne cork.

'Champagne? What are we celebrating?'

'Our first dinner together. I hope there'll be many more.'

She looked at him quizzically.

'It sounds like we're on a date?'

'I'd like it to be,' he admitted but his tone was cautious. 'I'd very much like it to be a date.' He waited, anxious for her to say something. Had he declared himself too soon?

'Your mother would be incandescent with rage to hear you say that.'

'Well, my mother doesn't control my life,' he said as he reached across the table and took her hand in his.

He held her hand for a few seconds and then she pulled it away. His declaration had been unexpected.

'I don't know what to say,' she said. 'I've been so preoccupied with the mess my parents have made of their lives I haven't really thought about my own.'

'So no boyfriend tucked away in Sydney, pining for your return?'

She shook her head. It had been the same question her father had asked.

'No, nothing serious. Up until recently my medical career was so demanding I really had no time for a social life. When I did go out, it was in a group or with my best friend Anita Clarke, Karen's cousin.'

'That must be a bit awkward now?'

He wondered how much she had learnt about her father's affair from her best friend. She looked at him, trying to decide what she should say, how much she should tell him.

'Not awkward,' she said, shaking her head. 'Not in the way you might think given my father worked with Anita's father at the hospital. Anita and her family have always been very sympathetic to me and my mother. Except it was Anita's mother who broke the news to my mother about Karen's pregnancy. That was the day my mother was forced to face up to the fact she should divorce my father. She called her lawyer immediately.'

He didn't quite know what to say. He felt sorry for her that she had been caught in the middle of it all. But his curiosity got the better of him. There was one question he really wanted to ask.

'Was your father angry with Karen? It must have been a difficult conversation for her to break the news to him.'

Pippa's full-throated laughter stunned him.

'Walter, my guess is she didn't tell him. She waited for him to notice.'

'Waited for him to notice? I suppose she would be beginning to show,' he said, not understanding her amusement.

'Walter, he was bound to notice when she was lying in his bed. I got home late one afternoon to find my father just leaving his bedroom. He was quite open in telling me Karen was with him.'

'I see,' he said, wondering how the situation could have been any more embarrassing for her. 'I didn't know you'd moved in with your father recently. You had moved out of your parents' home as I recall.'

She grimaced.

'I agreed to move into his new house, which is fantastic by the way with a great view of the harbour, before I heard about Karen's situation. My mother is selling the original house they shared which he signed over to her otherwise I could move back with her.'

He was beginning to get a much clearer picture now of how everything had evolved. But still the disappointment remained for him. He had liked Julia. He had admired her and enjoyed her company. He couldn't help but feel she had been badly let down. But the revelations kept coming. For Pippa, it was a relief to talk to someone she could trust.

'I found out recently Karen was pregnant to him before he married my mother.'

Walter was stunned into silence. He hadn't known about Karen's earlier pregnancy and he was sure Clarence didn't know either.

'Shocking, isn't it? She left Sydney for London a month or so before my parents married. She had a miscarriage.'

He wondered then how long the relationship had been going on. Probably years, he thought but how could he ask such a question.

'Did she get tired of waiting for him to leave your mother do you think?'

Pippa shrugged, unsure.

'I think she decided she wanted to have a baby. His baby in particular. And she knew the window was closing for her because of her age.'

And then he noticed the colour drain from her face.

'You look as if a ghost just walked over your grave,' he said, trying to lighten the mood.

She tried to smile.

'Not a ghost, just something I said to Karen. I went to visit her when I first found out about their affair. I told her to keep on taking her little pills. I also asked her if she had flushed them down the toilet and decided to set a trap for him again. Do you think I gave her the idea?'

He was astonished by her admission but he shook his head.

'If what you tell me is correct, I think the idea must have always been there in the back of her mind.'

'But not in my father's, I can assure you.'

They sat back then as their meals were placed in front of them. When the waiter had gone, she felt she had to say something more.

'Now you know much more about the whole sordid story, Walter,' she said. 'I know you admired my father. I imagine your admiration might have been tarnished somewhat by these events.'

He couldn't deny it. Like her, he had been disappointed. Bitterly disappointed.

'But you've reconciled with your father, Pippa. You seem to get on well with him. Do I have the right to judge his private life? Not really.'

She thought about it for a moment before she replied.

'Yes, I get on well with him now but I don't know that I will ever completely forgive him. By marrying my mother, he fulfilled every hope and dream I ever had about us becoming a family. I was no longer the discarded child without a family. But now? He's torn it all down. But at least we had some good years together as a family.'

He was pleased she was taking a pragmatic approach. But what else could she do, he thought.

'And your mother? What will she do?'

'I don't know to be honest but her first husband James Fitzroy wants her back. Desperately. He realises how badly he reacted to the revelation of my birth before she married him.'

She paused, thinking back to the lunch before John's birthday.

'The four of us had lunch together before my half-brother's twenty-first birthday in March. It felt like we were a family.'

'Four of you?'

'My half-brother John, my mother and me, and John's father James.'

'And do you think your mother might go back to her first husband?' he asked.

It was the first he had ever heard of the possibility.

'Well, he hadn't spoken to my mother since they broke up until very recently. I think he realised then how much he loved her and how much he overreacted to finding out about me. He really can be quite charming.'

'It all sounds very complicated,' he said, smiling.

She shrugged.

'Complicated is one word for it. Only time will tell how it will all play out.'

She smiled and relaxed. But she wondered where her relationship with Walter would head now. She reached across the table and put her hand on his.

'I like you a lot, Walter. I want you to know that but let's just be friends. I don't want any scrutiny from our respective families.'

He smiled, disappointed but not surprised by her response.

'I understand completely,' he said as he began to tackle the large plate of seafood in front of him.

It was late, the big house was quiet. Clarence glanced at the mantle clock in his sitting room. It was his habit to sit up until everyone had arrived home and he could lock the main door. He had been reading the latest John le Carré novel but he set it aside, carefully marking his place with a bookmark.

It was ten thirty. He reached for the keys that hung from a hook near the door to his sitting room. He would wait in the entrance lobby in the hope he would not be kept waiting too long.

He had barely sat down again before he heard the familiar throaty sound of the Camaro. He walked to the partly opened door and watched as Walter helped Pippa out of his car.

She smiled at Clarence and wished him goodnight as she headed upstairs. A very short time later, he was relieved to see Joel Tynan put his head around the door.

'You still up, Clarence? It reminds me of how my mother always used to wait up for me when I was a student.'

Clarence smiled. He liked the personable young Australian.

'I hope you enjoyed your day out with Virginia,' he said.

'Yes, I did, Clarence. She was delightful company actually. And she seemed to know a lot of the history of the place. I had an interesting day.'

'And dinner at Gosman's. How did that go?'

Joel laughed. He remembered being told that Clarence sees everything. And knows things even before they happen. But how did he know where they had dined, he wondered?

'Was that just a good guess, Clarence? The food was terrific by the way. I met some of Virginia's friends too although I was warned off by one of the young blokes who said his brother was her boyfriend. I thought he was going to take a swing at me.'

'But he didn't, I hope?'

'Not once I started talking about how I learnt to disarm machete-wielding young men who didn't like their wives being treated by a male doctor.'

Clarence chuckled. It was clear to him that Joel Tynan was no pushover.

'It's been a long day, Clarence. Thanks for waiting up. I'm going to take a shower and then bed.'

And then he noticed Clarence go back to his seat.

'More latecomers?'

He nodded, deliberately choosing not to mention it was Philippe he was waiting for.

Joel headed towards the stairs with a cheery goodnight but not before Clarence's sharp eyes noticed the traces of lipstick Joel had tried but not succeeded in wiping away. The boyfriend would indeed be angry if he had witnessed that, Clarence thought. Very angry indeed.

It was a further half an hour before he heard the crunch of tyres on the gravel. He opened the door to greet his employer as Philippe's new Mercedes sports car slowed to a stop.

Philippe walked up the front stairs quickly and handed his keys to Clarence.

'Get Frederick to put my car away for me in the morning please,' he said. 'Is everybody else in?'

Clarence nodded.

'Good. Time for you to lock up. I'm off to bed. Goodnight.'

Clarence watched him head upstairs aware Philippe had deliberately avoided any conversation.

As Clarence locked the big front door and pocketed the keys, he was left to speculate. Where had Philippe been? He could make one educated guess. He looked at the time. Had Philippe complicated his life further? Or simplified it? He hoped it was the latter.

CHAPTER 9

PHILIPPE WAS ENJOYING his first cup of coffee of the day, flipping idly through the Sunday newspaper but reading little, his mind elsewhere. He was in fact reflecting on the events of the previous evening. He had set out with the intention of simplifying his life. Instead, he knew he had probably achieved the exact opposite. He was pleased to be alone with his thoughts for the time being, except for Clarence who hovered in the background.

Beyond the house, everything was quiet. It was at least two hours to the opening of the gates to the public. And being Sunday, there would be no office staff on the ground floor.

Philippe had abandoned his father's longstanding habit of family meals being served in the vast dining room on the ground floor. Unless Philippe was entertaining, meals were now eaten in the much smaller dining room that had been created from a sitting room on the first floor. Clarence had not entirely approved the new arrangement but he had been overruled. The kitchen staff had grumbled too. Philippe had simply shrugged his shoulders at the small mutiny.

He expected everyone to comply with his wishes and so comply they did.

Not for the first time did Clarence remark Philippe's likeness to his father. He noticed how Philippe could be uncompromising if he chose. In reality, Clarence had been reassured by the speed with which Philippe had established his authority over the house, the family's wealth, his foundation and, by default, the family, which had been his father's express wish, yet he sometimes wondered if Philippe was in danger of going too far. At times Clarence thought he seemed too quick to impose his will.

He pushed back against the thought as he placed Philippe's breakfast in front of him. It was an uncomplicated breakfast. Poached eggs. Toast. Fresh Fruit. Coffee.

'Am I breakfasting alone, Clarence?'

'Your daughter has gone out sailing with Walter. They left just after seven. And Dr Tynan …'

'Is here. Good morning to both of you.'

They both looked up at the sound of Joel Tynan's cheery voice and enthusiastic greeting. He walked to the sideboard and poured himself a cup of tea. Clarence, anticipating his imminent arrival, had ordered a pot of tea from the kitchen with Philippe's breakfast.

'And the same, Dr Tynan?' indicating Philippe's breakfast choice.

'Thank you, Clarence,' he said, enjoying the rare luxury of having someone else prepare his breakfast.

'Did you enjoy the day yesterday with Virginia as your guide?' Philippe asked. It seemed to him it was an invitation totally out of character for Virginia but perhaps he had misjudged the girl.

Joel looked at Philippe and smiled.

'I did as a matter of fact. She knows a lot about the history of Long Island. I was really impressed. She was great company.'

There was something about Joel's smile and enthusiasm for Virginia that made Philippe pause ever so slightly before asking the next question.

'And Clarence says you stayed on to have dinner with her and her friends. How did that go?'

Joel caught the searching look in Philippe's eyes and looked away. He wondered if there was more to Philippe's question than there appeared to be.

'Yes, I had dinner with Virginia and her friends. Virginia insisted,' he said. 'And I enjoyed it. A nice restaurant.'

What more could he say? What more was Philippe entitled to know?

Philippe, hearing Joel's slightly defensive reply, began to wonder if the evening had ended badly. Surely not, he thought, looking at Joel. He seems relaxed and happy.

Before Philippe could say anything more, everyone's attention was drawn to the open doorway of the dining room.

No one had heard Barbara Cox enter the house and climb the stairs to the first floor. But they heard her now as she stood just inside the doorway, her finger pointed in Joel's direction, her voice an agitated, high-pitched screech, her words an incomprehensible babble.

Clarence was the first to move.

'Mrs Cox, please come and sit down and have some coffee. And tell us calmly what's going on. You're not making any sense.'

He held out a chair for her but she did not move towards it. Instead, she moved just a little further into the room, her heavy breathing beginning to subside, her agitated expression replaced by a cold accusing stare.

'I'll tell you what's going on,' she yelled, pointing at Joel. 'That man raped my daughter. He raped her. Do you hear me? He raped her.'

Her words whizzed around the room like unseen bullets hitting their unsuspecting targets one by one. And all the time, she continued to point directly at Joel whose face had begun to register the shock of her terrible accusation.

Then she exhaled loudly as if she had been holding her breath.

She looked from one to the other. From Philippe to Joel and then back again, her anger fuelled by her indignation and by her certainty at what her daughter had suffered at Joel's hands.

For a full minute, no one spoke. Philippe noticed the colour drain from Joel's face. Was he guilty as charged? Surely not. Not rape. Philippe refused to believe it. But he could tell by the look on Joel's face he was not entirely innocent. Had he pushed too far? Had he taken advantage of Virginia?

Philippe pushed back his chair and walked around the table to stand directly in front of Barbara Cox. He was calm. Icily calm. He did not like Barbara Cox but he knew he could not let his personal feelings affect his reaction to her accusation. He needed to gain control of the situation immediately.

His voice was unnaturally calm.

'That's a very serious accusation, Barbara,' he said. 'Very serious. Are you absolutely sure of what you're saying?'

'Of course I'm sure.'

She spat the words at him, her contempt for Philippe in full view.

He was thinking quickly. It was very early. Had Virginia said something this morning? Perhaps regretted something that happened the night before? Had her mother demanded an explanation from her?

'You say your daughter has been raped,' he said, his voice neutral and concerned, as if he was dealing with an hysterical patient he needed to calm. 'Has your daughter been examined by a doctor?'

'No, of course she hasn't,' she said.

'Have you called for the doctor to come? Is she badly injured? Because if she is, that should be our first consideration, don't you think?'

He had wrong footed her and she knew it.

'Tell me about the visible injuries she has,' Philippe said, his voice that of the concerned professional.

He watched Barbara Cox's internal struggle. He knew she very much wanted to go on accusing Joel and in the process undermine Philippe's confidence in him. But he could see she was genuinely concerned for her daughter.

After a few moments, her voice much calmer now, she began to list her daughter's injuries.

'She has some bruising on her body, on her face, around her neck.' She pointed to her own neck and face to illustrate what she meant.

'And she has a split lip where she has probably been slapped or punched.'

Philippe didn't wait to hear more. He turned and motioned urgently to Clarence.

'Call for the family doctor, Clarence. He must come straight away to examine Virginia.'

He turned back to Barbara Cox.

'Those injuries sound serious, Barbara. Go home and wait with Virginia for the doctor. The examination is going to be quite difficult for her. She'll need you with her.'

She hesitated. What right had Philippe to give her orders? And then she turned to go. She didn't want to acknowledge it but he was right. Her daughter needed her. But she took one last opportunity to remind Philippe who was responsible for her daughter's distressing state.

'He did this to her,' she hissed. 'He was out with her until all hours last night. He's to blame.'

Joel stood then, finding his voice at last.

'I promise you Mrs Cox I did not rape your daughter. I would never do such a thing. Ever. I would never hurt her. Or any other woman.'

But she let out a sound that told him she would never believe him.

'You'll pay for this,' she snapped. 'You'll rot in jail because of what you've done to my daughter. She was a virgin. And you've betrayed her trust.'

She turned suddenly and walked out. Philippe hurried to catch her. He was desperate to make sure she did not go on making wild accusations against Joel without proof. He put his hand on her arm.

'Barbara, I ask you not to go making any accusations until we know for sure. Has Virginia accused Joel?'

She stopped and looked him. And then shook her head.

'No, she hasn't,' she snapped. 'Because she was crying. I couldn't get her to tell me anything very much at all. But it was enough.'

He let her go then and hoped the doctor would not be too long. He was tempted to look in on Virginia himself but something told him it would be unwise for him to intervene in that way. He turned and headed back into the dining room.

His next step would be to speak with Joel. He wondered what he would have to say for himself. Would he deny having sex with the girl? Because if he did, Philippe knew he would be lying.

Clarence looked at Philippe as he re-entered the room. He was trying to decide whether Philippe believed the accusations directed at Joel or whether he continued to have confidence in him.

'Clarence, I need to have a private word with Joel. Perhaps you can ring the yacht club and see if we can locate Walter.'

Without a sound or even an acknowledgment, Clarence walked to the door and closed it behind him, leaving Philippe and Joel alone together.

Philippe moved further into the room and then stopped abruptly. He looked at Joel, trying to decide what to say, trying to assess the situation. In the end he chose to ask the one question that was upper most in his mind.

'Tell me, Joel, did you have sex with Virginia last night?'

Philippe waited, his eyes never wavering from Joel's face. Waiting for him to explain. Waiting for him to tell the truth.

After what seemed like an eternity, Joel spoke, his voice quiet but firm.

'Yes, I did have sex with her but, believe me, I did not inflict those injuries on her. There's no way I'm responsible for the injuries her mother described.'

Philippe let out a long sigh, satisfied that Joel hadn't denied having sex with Virginia but disappointed all the same. What was he thinking, Philippe wondered? Did he not understand how inappropriate it was?

'Did she consent to have sex with you? Or did you push her to have sex with you?'

It's like I'm already being cross examined in the witness box, Joel thought. But he knew he had to answer the questions, as difficult as it was for him.

'She did consent, Philippe. In fact, she initiated it, not me. I tried to keep her at arm's length. I really tried.'

'What a pity you hadn't succeeded, Joel,' Philippe said, shaking his head.

'I didn't force her to have sex with me. It wasn't rough or violent. And whatever her mother says, she wasn't a virgin.'

Philippe smiled bleakly for the first time. He guessed her mother would struggle to accept her young unmarried daughter might already be sexually active.

'Did she drop you off here and then drive out our driveway and into her own or did you walk over from her house?'

He shook his head, wondering at the purpose of his question.

'She dropped me here.'

'And how was she when you said goodnight to her?'

He shrugged, remembering how she hadn't wanted to let him go.

'We were on good terms. I kissed her goodnight if that's what you want to know. And she certainly didn't have any bruising on her face or a cut lip or anything like that at that point.'

'Did she say she was going straight home?' Philippe asked.

He wondered if it was possible the girl had gone elsewhere after she dropped Joel off.

'As far as I knew, she was going straight home,' he said.

'Did you notice if her car headed down the driveway to her house?'

'I didn't notice, to be honest. I came straight in and spoke to Clarence before heading upstairs.'

Joel got up then and began to pace the room.

'There is something terribly wrong about all this, Philippe,' he said. 'Terribly wrong. I'm not a violent man. I would never do that to a woman.'

Do I believe him, Philippe wondered? He wanted to trust him, trust his version of events, but he knew so little about Joel.

'I understand your marriage broke up. I have to ask. Were you violent towards your wife? Is that why she left you?'

He knew Philippe was entitled to ask such questions but it did not make it any easier for him to have his private life suddenly exposed in such a way.

'My wife decided she preferred another man. That is why she left me. And as to violence, she threw an artefact at me in our final argument. She was quite volatile at times. Not me. I tried to keep the peace. I never hit her or anything like that, if that's what you're suggesting.'

He pointed to the almost invisible scar on his face.

'Do you think it's possible Virginia regrets what happened last night between you or her mother guessed and she needed to convince her mother she was an unwilling participant?'

It was the question upper most in Philippe's mind.

Joel shook his head.

'Honestly, there was no indication she regretted it at the time. Not at all. I said to her to tell me to stop if she didn't want me to go any further.'

He was remembering back to the tenderness and pleasure of their lovemaking under the night sky on her favourite beach, with the relaxing sound of the waves breaking on the sand. At first, he had been reluctant to touch her. And then she had looked disappointed, asking him why he did not find her attractive. And then he had reached over and put his hand behind her head and kissed her gently. It had been meant as a gesture of reassurance until it became something else. But the catalogue of injuries her mother described perplexed him. He had been gentle with her. And loving.

'And she never asked you to stop at any point?'

He shook his head and managed a smile.

'No, she didn't. I'm sure she enjoyed being with me as much as I enjoyed being with her.'

'Except that somehow she has ended up with injuries consistent with being taken against her will,' Philippe said. 'Do you have any explanation for that?'

He wanted to test Joel's story from every angle.

'I don't,' he said. 'I don't have any explanation at all.'

'Were you more physical with her than you planned to be? Did you hold her down, for example?'

To this point, Joel had endured Philippe's interrogation with good grace but it seemed to him he was being asked the same question over and over, but in different ways. He closed his eyes briefly. For the first time he began to fear for his future. If he ended up being charged, it would be a stain on his reputation forever. And his new career would be over before it had properly begun. He opened his eyes and sighed heavily, looking directly at Philippe.

'No, I was not rough with her, if that's what you're suggesting. I didn't hold her down. I didn't slap her or punch her. I didn't force myself on her. She was willing. More than willing if you must know.'

Philippe nodded. He sensed Joel was quickly reaching the end of his patience. He looked at him steadily before speaking again.

'I believe you, Joel,' he said finally. 'I believe you.'

'Thank you, Philippe,' he said. 'I realise you might reasonably call my judgement into question. Perhaps it wasn't the wisest position to put myself in.'

To his relief, Philippe smiled.

'We've all been there, Joel, myself included. But we need to find out what's to be done to clear up this mess.'

How could he judge a man harshly for doing what he had done himself? Hadn't he pressured Julia just a little to consummate their relationship without thought for the consequences? And Karen? A stronger man would have walked away from her, he thought. But he was annoyed with Joel. He could have chosen any other girl but the tense relationship with Virginia's mother had possibly blown everything out of proportion.

As he was deciding what to do next, he heard a quick knock on the door followed by Clarence.

'The doctor is at the house now,' he said, 'and Walter is on his way back home. I managed to track him down.'

Philippe needed Walter more than ever. He could trust Walter.

'Did you ask him to come here first, Clarence?'

'I did,' he said.

'What did you say to him?'

'That there was an urgent family matter you needed to see him about.'

Philippe nodded. He knew there had been no need to remind Clarence to be discreet. He turned back towards Joel.

'Let's go into my study and wait for Walter. We need to talk to him. And you'll need to be honest with him, as you were with me. And you will need to be calm.'

Joel nodded. And then he thought of Pippa. He knew she wouldn't want to be excluded from what was going on. He was beginning to understand the implications of his actions. He wondered what she would think of him. He found himself feeling completely bereft at the thought she would despise him when she heard his version of events.

Philippe was standing at the window of his study staring at nothing in particular. He might have taken the time to admire the gardens but in fact he was impatient for the sight of a red Camaro. He did not have to wait long. Walter brought the car to a halt in a spray of dust and gravel. He was out of the car quickly, not even waiting to open the door for Pippa. Clarence has certainly managed to convey the urgency of the summons, Philippe thought.

Less than a minute later, Walter flung the door open and walked quickly into the room. Pippa was almost running to keep up with him.

'Philippe, what's up? What's this urgent summons about?'

Walter looked from Philippe to Joel. Both men were unsmiling. Some instinct told him then his sister was somehow connected with the urgent summons.

'Sit down, Walter,' Philippe said.

But Walter declined the invitation, remaining standing part way into the room. Pippa hung further back, uncertain whether she should stay in the room at all.

'Tell me, Philippe, is it something to do with my sister? And Joel?'

He looked towards Joel for confirmation. And then Philippe spoke, choosing his words carefully.

'Your mother came across to see me about an hour ago. She was very agitated. She was accusing Joel of forcing himself on your sister. Your sister has sustained some injuries. The doctor is with her.'

He heard a quick intake of breath from Pippa. But in Walter's eyes he saw cold fury. He turned on Joel, his anger ready to be unleashed.

It was Clarence who recognised the danger. He put himself between Walter and Joel, forcing Walter to swerve around him. He caught Walter's arm in a strong, unyielding grip.

'Wait until you hear what Joel has to say, Walter,' Clarence insisted, his grip remaining strong.

Walter turned on him.

'What, you're defending a rapist now, Clarence?'

Joel took a step towards him. He had known the meeting with

Walter would be difficult. But he hadn't anticipated it would be quite so difficult.

'Walter, I didn't rape your sister,' he said, trying to keep his voice calm. 'The accusation is totally false. She was fine when she dropped me here last night.'

But Walter noticed Joel's uneasiness.

'But you had sex with her, am I right? Maybe you crossed that fine line between what Virginia agreed to and what you did. Is that it? It's just a matter of definition. You probably gave her a couple of slaps to get her to submit to you. Or held her down.'

No one spoke. The clock ticked loudly. The old house creaked as if in protest at the warming sun. Philippe held his breath. He wanted Joel to defend himself. He did not want to be seen to be taking sides.

'Walter,' Joel said, remembering Philippe's advice to stay calm, 'nothing I did with your sister last night was against her will. And she hasn't accused me. It's your mother who's accused me.'

'So, if I'm to believe your story, my sister welcomed your advances and you did nothing that might have caused her injuries. If that's the case, how did she get to be so injured she required a doctor?'

Joel shrugged his shoulders and gestured helplessly.

'I have no idea, Walter, but I certainly didn't leave her battered and bruised. I would never do that to a woman.'

He risked a look at Pippa then and saw the disappointment in her eyes but before he could say anything further, Philippe spoke.

'Walter, I'm convinced of Joel's story but I needed you to hear it from him. I need you to go home and speak to the doctor, to your mother and most importantly to Virginia. We need to know the truth of what happened.'

He began to walk towards the door.

'Walk with me, Walter. We need to have a private word.'

Walter was too stunned by what he had heard to protest so he fell in beside Philippe and they walked down the main stairs together towards the front door.

'How do you feel about this, Philippe? For my part, I think Joel's not being entirely honest.'

Philippe turned to look at Walter.

'I think he was trying to be circumspect about what he said about your sister, Walter, which is to his credit. He told me he tried to keep her at arm's length.'

'Meaning that he's saying my sister put the word on him?'

'I wouldn't go that far, Walter, but I don't think she was unwilling. But it's possible she felt some remorse about what happened last night and in trying to protect herself, Joel became the scapegoat. Or maybe something else happened with someone else? Did she go somewhere else after she dropped Joel here?'

Walter was beginning to see there was more to it than it first appeared. And he knew then he was going to have to act as the intermediary. Was Joel Tynan capable of raping a young woman? He wouldn't have considered it a possibility until now.

'I'm relying on you, Walter,' Philippe said. 'I've already cautioned your mother not to go about making wild accusations. That would help no one, especially Virginia.'

Walter nodded. He understood then his sister was the most important element in the whole sorry saga. And he began to see he had not done enough to take care of her. Because she had been difficult. Because they hadn't got along. But that was no excuse, he thought. I'm her older brother. It's my responsibility to take care of her.

He headed off on foot in the direction of his home, desperate now to understand what was going on and what had taken place. It was time he stepped up for his family. They had all drifted along almost independent of one another since the death of his father. He understood now it was time he put them first. His loyalty to Philippe would have to take second place.

CHAPTER 10

AS WALTER ENTERED the house he shared with his mother and sister, he was suddenly anxious about what he would face. And anxious about how to approach a situation that could be potentially volatile.

Dr Joseph Grey was more relieved than he could say to see Walter at the foot of the stairs as he made his way to the entrance hall.

'Dr Grey, how's my sister? Have you examined her?' Walter asked, not even bothering to greet him.

Joseph Grey paused briefly and then looked around him. He did not want to have a conversation with Walter where household staff might easily overhear what was said. He motioned to a door on his left, which he knew had been Walter's father's study. Or rather his retreat from the world.

'Shall we?' Dr Grey said, motioning towards the closed door.

Walter walked ahead of him and opened the door. The room had barely been used since his father's death. It smelt musty, the air stale. Walter forced up a reluctant window, grateful for the fresh air that flooded the room. The doctor sat, by habit, in one of the visitors' armchairs forcing Walter, reluctantly, to choose the chair that had been his father's. It felt strange, as if he was intruding into his father's private domain. At any moment, he was sure his father might walk through the door and order him out of his chair.

He then repeated his question to the doctor. Was his sister badly injured? For no reason, he had begun to imagine the worst.

The doctor pursed his lips, trying to decide what he should say or how much he should say.

'First of all, I want to reassure you your sister will make a full recovery. She isn't badly injured.'

He noticed Walter relax a little. He went on in his usual serious but reassuring voice.

'Your sister has some of the injuries consistent with what I would expect to see in a young woman who has been forced to have sexual intercourse against her will. She has visible light bruising around her midriff, indicating she might have been held down. There is also some evidence of her being choked and a red mark on her left cheek where I think she's been struck at least once. Whoever hit her is possibly wearing a ring which would account for the split lip.'

He got up to demonstrate, bringing his left hand towards Walter's face as if he was practising his backhand for tennis, the outside of his hand almost hitting Walter. He then demonstrated how she might have been hit with the open palm of a right hand.

He waited patiently while Walter absorbed the information before he continued.

'I can confirm she's had sexual intercourse recently. But it's not possible to say whether it was with one man only. Or with multiple partners.'

He saw the shock in Walter's eyes and hurried to explain.

'Walter, I'm just saying it's not possible to say she's only had one male partner in the past twenty-four hours. That's all. I'm not saying she did have more than one. But there was no vaginal bruising I could see. No bruising on her thighs, which I might have expected if she had been raped.'

'Did she say she had been raped? Do you think she was raped?'

The doctor paused before answering. He was careful in what he said.

'Your sister was clearly upset. That I can say. As to whether she was raped or whether something else happened, I couldn't say. She didn't seem to be able to speak freely with your mother in the room. And your mother refused to leave the room.'

'And what is my mother saying?'

But he didn't really need to ask.

'Your mother's been quite forthright. She's pointed the finger at one of your uncle's employees, Joel Tynan. Have you spoken to your uncle this morning?'

Walter nodded, remembering their tense conversation.

'Yes, I've seen him. My uncle contacted me at the yacht club to come home urgently. And I've spoken with Joel too. He admits to having sex with Virginia but not to forcing her. They were out all day yesterday together and then dinner last night. My uncle believes him.'

The doctor shrugged.

'Is it possible he was just a bit more forceful with her than he says he was? Is he the type, do you think?'

Walter shook his head.

'I wouldn't have said so. He's a doctor who spent years in central Africa helping to bring medical help to some of the poorest people. He seems kind and sincere.'

But none of that information seemed to impress the doctor.

'But you wouldn't know him well, would you?'

'No, we don't know him well. But, as I said, he did admit to having sex with Virginia. He didn't try to lie about that. He says they parted on good terms and that she had no injuries when they said goodnight.'

The doctor considered this information for a few moments. Something didn't add up. It was possible Joel Tynan was being economical with the truth, he thought. If he wasn't, there had to be another explanation.

'All I can say is, someone caused those injuries to your sister. If Joel Tynan didn't, then who did?'

There was one more question Walter knew he had to ask. He had to know.

'Dr Grey, can you tell me. Was my sister a virgin?'

The doctor smiled slightly and shook his head. It was clear to him neither her mother nor her brother was taken into Virginia's confidence.

'No, Walter, I don't think so. I prescribed the contraceptive pill for her a year ago. She told me she didn't want to take any chances and I applauded that. And she is an adult. She doesn't need her mother's permission. Or yours. It's her private life and this is not the nineteenth century.'

Walter smiled, surprised the doctor would feel the need to remind him his sister was entitled to make her own decisions and live her own life.

'You say, though, she will recover?'

'Oh, yes, she's young and healthy. She will recover. The bruising will be gone in a day or so.'

'And how is she in herself?'

'She's more settled. I've left her a sedative if she wants to take it. But I've given your mother a sedative and she's now lying down. She should sleep for a few hours at least.'

And then Walter understood what the doctor was trying to say to him.

'Thanks, Doctor, I'll go up and have a chat with Virginia.'

'Be gentle, Walter,' he warned. 'Be caring and considerate. And don't assume the problem is Joel Tynan. It could be something else or someone else altogether. Build trust with her so she'll confide in you as she wouldn't in her mother. It's quite likely your mother would look on any liaison with an employee of Philippe Duval's with complete distaste so it's possible your mother jumped to conclusions that could turn out to be totally wrong.'

Walter listened carefully to the advice.

'You don't think I should call the police?'

'No, not at this stage. Not until we know more for certain. And remember, if someone is charged with rape in relation to your sister, the defendant's team would be within their rights to examine her sexual history. She would feel as if she was on trial. It would be very unpleasant for everyone.'

'Thank you, Dr Grey,' he said. 'Thank you for coming so quickly.'

He walked with the doctor to the front door and then headed upstairs to his sister's bedroom.

He tapped lightly on Virginia's door and then eased the door open slightly.

'It's Walter. Can I come in?'

He waited and asked again.

'If you must,' she said, trying hard to sound like her usual antagonistic self.

But Walter wasn't easily fooled. To him, she didn't sound quite right as much as she was trying to pretend she was fine.

She was sitting on her bed with her back against the bedhead, her knees drawn up to her chest, still in her pyjamas.

He looked around the room quickly. She was habitually untidy but it was obvious their mother had tidied the room in advance of the doctor's arrival. And then he looked at her. He could see a slight puffiness in her face but she was no longer crying. He noticed the angry red mark on her cheek and the split lower lip. She put her fingers up to her mouth to touch it.

'I must look awful,' she said with a crooked smile that made her wince.

You do look awful, Walter wanted to say, but didn't. Her hair needed brushing too. He sat down on the bed and reached out awkwardly to put his arm around her.

'My poor little sister,' he said. 'Has someone used you as a punching bag?'

She tried to smile again but her lip still hurt too much.

'Are you going to tell me what happened,' he asked quietly. 'The doctor says you'll be over the bruising in a day or two. No permanent damage.'

He noticed the red marks on her throat too now he was closer to her. He wondered if her voice had been affected. He touched her throat gently.

'Does your throat hurt?'

She shook her head.

'No, I kneed him in the groin so he loosened his grip. That's when he slapped me.'

'Who? Joel?'

She looked up startled by his question.

'Joel? Why would you think Joel did this to me?'

'Because our mother has been accusing him of raping you. Didn't you know that?'

She let out a long sigh.

'Is that what she was telling the doctor? I couldn't hear it. Not properly.'

And then she looked at Walter, understanding everything for the first time.

'So that's why he examined me so thoroughly,' she said. 'I just thought he was being an old lech. I agreed to see the doctor because I thought I might have a broken cheekbone or something. I never said I'd been raped.'

'But our mother found you hysterical and in tears.'

She shrugged as if all the fuss her mother had made had been unnecessary.

'And so she jumped to her own conclusions without even asking by the sound of it. Typical.'

He could see her old spirit returning now she was beginning to talk about what happened to her.

'So tell me from the beginning what did happen last night,' he said, encouragingly. 'If Joel didn't do this to you, then someone else did.'

She stretched out and swung her legs to the side of the bed. She felt the need to move, to think about how to start and what parts of the story to leave out. But how could she leave out anything if Walter was to understand fully what happened.

She moved to the window seat which had a view of the driveway and beyond to the gardens of the big house.

'It was that snitch Tom Boyd. He was part of the group at dinner. He noticed how attentive Joel was and afterwards he followed us.'

'To your favourite beach probably.'

She smiled lopsidedly, wincing again.

'To my favourite beach. How did you guess?'

But he ignored the question.

'Anyway, he hid in the bushes and saw us together, Joel and me. And he must have called his brother then. I didn't know Patrick was getting home last night. He'd told me he'd be away all weekend.'

Walter was at last beginning to get the picture.

'Did Patrick intercept you after you dropped Joel back?'

She nodded.

'He was waiting for me and blocked the driveway so I couldn't get down our driveway. He practically dragged me out of my car.'

'And then?'

She shrugged as if none of it mattered anymore.

'He yelled at me. Called me a slut. He wanted to know how many other men I'd been with. He was so angry. And then he pushed me against his car and began to pull my clothes off. I struggled with him. I remember he put his hand on my throat. Eventually I got my leg free and kneed him in the groin. He lashed out then with his left hand across my face, his signet ring caught my lip I think.'

Walter found it hard to sit and listen to his sister describe the assault she had suffered at the hands of her boyfriend.

'Did he stop then? Or did he go on with the assault?'

She thought about her answer for just a moment.

'I think hitting me finally brought him to his senses. He mumbled an apology and got into his car. He left without another word.'

'Did he …?'

Walter couldn't quite think how to frame the question. But she knew what he was asking.

'If you're asking if he raped me, the answer's no. He didn't quite get that far.'

He moved to stand behind her and put his hand on her shoulder in a gesture of comfort. Of reassurance.

'My dear sister, why didn't you come to me for help when you got in?'

She looked at him, tears forming again in her eyes as she was remembering what had happened to her.

'Because I was ashamed. Because I didn't want you to think badly of me. Because I was confused that a man who was supposed to love me could treat me that way. And then he phoned me this morning.'

She nodded towards the telephone on her bedside table. Walter knew she had her own private number so her friends could call her directly.

'What did he say?'

'He said if I knew what was good for me, I wouldn't mention what happened between us last night. It would be my word against his and anyway he'd put it about that Joel Tynan had done this to me if anyone saw my injuries. He'd tell everyone how I was all over Joel and his brother would confirm it. He said I was no better than a prostitute but that I'd obviously decided to refuse Joel at the last minute and he got violent with me to get his way. He told me to stick to the story. Or else.'

Despite her split lip, she managed another lopsided smile.

'Nothing could be further from the truth about Joel. He was lovely to me. But gossip like that could ruin Joel's career. I need to make sure he never hears about this. I can't possibly see him before he goes back to Sydney.'

She pointed to her face.

'Even the best make up wouldn't hide this. And Joel is a doctor. He'd notice.'

'And you're finished with Patrick Boyd, I hope?'

'Oh, I think he's finished with me, don't you?'

He stood looking at his sister for some minutes. How could he tell her their mother had already accused Joel Tynan of rape? Loudly and repeatedly. Viciously even. She had attempted to destroy his reputation without even knowing the facts. All because she hated Philippe.

'There's something else, isn't there, Walter? What is it?'

'Our mother went across to the big house this morning and confronted Philippe and Joel. She accused Joel of raping you. She's put him through hell. Fortunately, Philippe took control of the situation. It was his suggestion to call the doctor when she described your injuries. Clarence called the doctor and then he rang the yacht club to tell me to come home immediately.'

She buried her head in her hands. She couldn't believe what she was hearing. Her day with Joel had been so perfect. And later she had offered herself to him. And then her night had been perfect, lying beside him on the soft sand, his hand caressing her. He had been gentle and loving, tender and sincere. And this is how he had been repaid. By being accused of rape. She threw her head back, her hair falling in a tangled mess, anger replacing desperation.

'Can you apologise to him for me? Go and see him now,' she pleaded. 'Tell him how sorry I am my mother did that. All because she hates Philippe who has never been anything but polite and decent to her. Go, Walter. Please go.'

'Are you sure? I will have to tell him everything.'

'Of course, I'm sure,' she said.

He hesitated.

'I shouldn't ask this …'

He couldn't finish the question. She finished it for him.

'You want to know if I'd had sex previously or if I was a virgin until last night?'

He nodded.

'Does it make any difference?'

'Not really.'

'I've been with Patrick twice. I thought we were going to be getting engaged and all that stuff. We'd talked about it. Looked at engagement rings.'

She sighed deeply. Why doesn't Walter have to explain the women he's bedded, she thought? Why is it different for me? Why do I feel ashamed I'm no longer a virgin?

'And Joel?'

Again, a lop-sided smile. But this time she smiled with her eyes too.

'He was so lovely to me. So sincere. So genuine. He has these beautiful eyes. And long elegant fingers. And he's so much fun to be with. And he's done such amazing things.'

She stopped then, a slight blush colouring her cheeks beneath the red mark where she had been hit hard.

'You couldn't resist him, is that it? Or he couldn't resist you?'

Despite everything, he noticed a look of pure pleasure on his sister's face. He hadn't seen that look before. Her usual attitude was mostly mocking or cynical.

'Go, Walter. Go and tell him I'm sorry. So sorry.'

'I will,' he said, but he knew it would be more complicated than merely apologising. 'Will you be alright by yourself for a short while?'

She nodded.

'I need a shower,' she said, 'and to wash my hair.'

'Good idea.' And then he gave her a quick kiss on the cheek and a brotherly hug.

As Walter headed back to the big house, he knew he would have to tell Joel and Philippe the whole story. And then a decision would need to be made. Could he stand by and let Patrick Boyd go unpunished for what he did? He weighed up the options.

Call the police and get him charged with assault and risk everything coming out. But he knew Virginia's reputation would be ruined in the process.

Or take the other option. He would have to be careful. And patient. And choose his moment. There could be no witnesses. A few sessions in a boxing gym would sharpen his skills. At least sharpen his skills enough to down a smaller guy like Patrick Boyd. Because Patrick Boyd needed to be taught a lesson he would never forget.

Clarence opened the front door to Walter just as he reached the top of the front steps.

'Is your sister OK, Walter? I saw the doctor leaving.'

'She'll be alright, Clarence. A nasty red mark on her face where she's been slapped pretty hard plus a split lip. Some red marks on her throat. It will be a few days before she can show her face in public I would think. Unless she wants to attract comment. And she probably doesn't want to do that.'

Clarence motioned towards the stairs.

'Dr Duval and Dr Tynan are waiting for you in the study,' he said quietly. 'I hope your sister told you what happened? I hope she told you the full story.'

Walter nodded.

'She did, Clarence,' he replied quietly. 'It's a bit complicated but it wasn't Joel who did this to her, I can tell you that.'

Clarence let out an audible sigh of relief. He liked the young doctor.

He would have been very concerned to have misjudged his character to such an extent.

'Thanks for telling me, Walter. That's a relief. Was it the boyfriend?'

'It was, Clarence. A nasty piece of business as it turns out.'

Clarence hesitated. But he had to say something.

'Needs to be taught a lesson if he thinks that's how women should be treated.'

Walter smiled faintly.

'My thoughts exactly, Clarence.'

He noticed Clarence nod slightly. A nod of approval perhaps?

'I'll bring some coffee up,' he said as he watched Walter bound up the main stairs two at a time.

Both Philippe and Joel looked up expectantly as Walter entered the study. They had been waiting for him to return. He glanced around the room and noticed Pippa wasn't with them. He was rather relieved by her absence. He stopped directly in front of Joel.

'Joel, I know you had nothing to do with my sister's injuries. She told me what happened. I can only apologise profusely for what my mother said to you. For what she accused you of. It was an unforgivable thing to do.'

He noticed the look of relief on Joel's face. And on Philippe's too. Philippe was the first to speak.

'Well, that's a relief, Walter, but did your sister tell you how she got the injuries? I assume she's OK? What did the doctor say?'

He looked towards Philippe.

'She'll be fine in a few days. No lasting damage, thank goodness. I spoke to the doctor before I spoke to her.'

'And your mother?' Philippe asked. 'Does she accept it wasn't Joel?'

He smiled.

'The doctor, very wisely, gave my mother some sedatives to keep her asleep for a few hours. It was obvious he thought we needed time to sort this mess out without her help.'

Philippe smiled to himself. A clever man. He knows his patient well.

'But that's only half the story, Walter,' Philippe said. 'Joel may be in the clear but somebody assaulted your sister rather brutally by the sound of it.'

'And we know now who that someone was.'

He proceeded to tell them the story Virginia had told him, omitting nothing. When he had finished, he looked from one to the other to gauge their reactions. It was Joel who spoke first.

'What a bastard to go after a defenceless girl like that when there is no one around to protect her. But I feel responsible. Being with her seemed like harmless fun. Well not harmless exactly but we enjoyed each other's company. Too much as it turned out.'

Walter smiled, remembering Virginia's gushing description of him.

'You weren't the problem, Joel. Patrick Boyd was the problem.'

He looked to Philippe.

'Where do we go from here, Philippe? Do we contact the police and accuse him of assaulting my sister?'

Philippe frowned. Was that the best course of action? He had his doubts.

'Does she want that, Walter? Does she really want that or would she prefer just to put this behind her? He's already threatened her. It would get very ugly. Her reputation would be shredded. So would Joel's. And she might be ostracised by her friends.'

'Don't worry about me,' Joel said. 'It's Virginia we need to consider. What's best for her. What did she say?'

'To be honest she was more concerned about apologising to you than worrying about Patrick Boyd. She's certainly well rid of him. I knew he had a temper. If they'd married, how long would it have been before he was taking to her with his fists? A year? Two years?'

And then Philippe looked at Walter. *He's too calm,* he thought. In his late twenties, he's in the prime of his youth. Tall and fit from years of yachting and outdoor pursuits.

A shoulder injury may have ended his high school football career but somewhere along the way he remembered hearing Walter had been good at boxing.

'Are you thinking of doing something, Walter? Because if you are, my advice is don't.'

He looked back at Philippe and smiled as if to say *I have no idea what you're talking about.* But Philippe was not deceived. He looked at Clarence who had just brought in the coffee tray. Clarence simply raised his eyebrows and Philippe shook his head ever so slightly. Clarence nodded. He understood what Philippe was telling him. *Keep the young hothead under control. Otherwise, the situation will simply go from bad to worse.*

Joel noticed the exchange and instantly understood it. He was not a violent man but he could defend himself. And like Walter, he felt he couldn't stand idly by and let Virginia's boyfriend get away with a brutal assault. No one had asked but he wondered how close her boyfriend came to taking her against her will. He desperately wanted to see her. To reassure her. To comfort her. But he wondered what chance he had of being allowed to do that.

And then the door to the study opened again. Joel was first to his feet when he realised it was Virginia standing at the entrance to the room. As he wrapped his arms around her, he could feel her hair was still damp from the shower.

'I had to see you, Joel,' she said, tears flowing down her cheeks. 'I had to apologise for my mother making those terrible accusations.'

He guided her gently into the room to a comfortable armchair. And then he began to examine her face. The bruising was much as he expected but she had been hit hard and viciously. He looked across at Walter.

'The bastard can't get away with this, can he?'

'No, he can't, Joel. He certainly can't.'

Philippe examined the injury to her face too. He was surprised the force of the blow hadn't loosened her teeth. He smiled reassuringly at her.

'You'll mend, my dear,' he said kindly, his hand on her shoulder. 'But it's a terrible thing for someone to do to you. If he ever comes near you again or phones you, you must tell Walter. Or me if Walter's not around. Or Clarence.'

She smiled her thanks. And then winced with the pain from the split lip.

'My mother's going to be furious I ruined a good marriage prospect.'

Philippe laughed quietly. Wasn't there more to Virginia's life than being hawked around as a marriage prize by her mother?

'I'll deal with your mother,' Philippe said. 'She won't say a word to you, I promise. Besides she'll be more concerned about what he's done to you. She wouldn't want a husband like that for you.'

She smiled at him, genuinely smiled at him, for the very first time.

'You'll do that for me?'

'Of course I will Virginia,' he said. 'I'm not the enemy your mother thinks I am. I'm your uncle, remember. I'm family.'

'But she's so horrible to you. Spreading gossip. Terrible gossip about you.'

Philippe shrugged and shook his head slowly.

'I'm aware of that, Virginia, but there's nothing I can do about it. She has never come to terms with my inheriting the bulk of your grandfather's estate. She really wanted to be mistress of this house.'

Virginia looked around her. She had never spent as much time in the house as her brother but she realised then her mother had spent her entire married life with one burning ambition, to be mistress of Eastbury Hall.

'I know she did. But somehow, we must get her to see beyond that.'

Easier said than done, Philippe thought. But it was a problem for another day.

They all looked towards the door as Pippa walked into the room. She took one look at Virginia and went to her side immediately.

'Oh! You poor girl,' she said.

She glanced at Joel and then Walter.

'The boyfriend,' Walter said quickly. 'Intercepted her on her way down the driveway last night. Blocked her car and then dragged her out. Wanted to teach her a lesson apparently.'

'Boyfriend?'

'Patrick Boyd by name. Quick temper. Quick with his fists,' Walter said, trying to fill in the gaps in Pippa's knowledge without having to repeat the whole story.

'Ex-boyfriend, I hope.'

She looked at Virginia who nodded.

'Definitely ex.'

'You look tired, Virginia. Come and lie down in my bedroom.'

With that, Pippa took her by the arm and walked with her along the hallway to her bedroom.

'Have you taken something?'

She nodded.

'The doctor left me some sedatives. I just took two tablets before I came over.'

'I think they're beginning to take effect,' Pippa said. 'Let's get you into my bed. Sleep is the best thing for you now. Everything will look so much better when you've had a good sleep.'

The girl nodded her thanks. She knew she didn't deserve their kindness. But she was grateful for it. Very grateful.

For the first time in a long time, she didn't feel quite so alone. Nor quite so vulnerable.

CHAPTER 11

IT WAS LATE AFTERNOON. Barbara Cox examined her appearance in her bathroom mirror, vaguely satisfied with what she saw. She reached up and coaxed the last strand of wayward hair into place and applied copious amounts of hairspray. A last check of her makeup, a glance in the full length mirror in her bedroom and she was finally ready.

Everything about her appearance was flawless. Hair. Makeup. Manicure. Dress. She had been summoned to the big house that evening, to the house that should have been hers. At least that's how she had interpreted the invitation.

Walter put his head around the door of her bedroom. He felt as if he had been waiting for her forever.

'Are you ready yet, Mother?'

'I'm coming, Walter. I know you don't want to keep the head of our family waiting.'

She said it with a sneer, her voice devoid of warmth. Devoid of contrition too. But Walter was angry with her, an anger that had not subsided since the morning. He put his hand on his mother's arm as she walked out of her bedroom.

'I think you might do well to adopt a less hostile attitude,' he said. 'You are in the wrong. You need to apologise and then we can all move on.'

'You want me to apologise to the man who stole your father's inheritance? Or apologise to his disreputable employee?'

At that point, Walter exploded. Mostly, he could cajole his mother into a better frame of mind or at least to temper her acid tongue but it was clear to him this time he had failed. He gripped her arm.

'Listen to me, Mother,' he said, his voice raised in anger. 'You are not going to embarrass us. Embarrass me or Virginia. You are going to do exactly what I tell you to do. You are going to apologise to Philippe. You are going to apologise to Joel. And you are going to do it graciously. Do you remember how to act graciously, Mother?'

She let out a long, embittered sigh and shrugged her shoulders.

'If you insist, Walter, but don't expect me to like it. Don't ever expect me to like Philippe Duval. Don't ever expect me to forgive him.'

He wasn't satisfied with her response. He tried again as he had done many times before.

'Philippe never asked for my grandfather's estate to be left to him. It was all my grandfather's doing. You must know that. He had no inkling of it until the reading of the will. He didn't steal anything.'

She shrugged, knowing what he said was true but unwilling to accept it. The prospect of being mistress of Eastbury Hall had sustained her through a marriage to a man she had come to despise. And then that had been taken away from her. And then her husband had died. She had lamented his death less than the loss of the property she had coveted. And now her plans for her daughter were in tatters. Didn't Walter understand that?

She had already begun to plan the big society wedding she would host for Virginia. And then her daughter had spoiled it by letting some penniless Australian take advantage of her. And now everyone would know. And Virginia's reputation would be ruined. Mothers with eligible sons would look elsewhere, despite the Cox wealth her daughter would eventually share.

But she did not try to explain all this to her son. Because she knew how he would react. They walked out of the house together in silence.

There was nothing more likely to irritate Barbara Cox than seeing the man she hated most sitting behind the desk that for years had been the sole preserve of her late father-in-law. He sits there as if he was born to it, she thought miserably. And Clarence fawns over him just as he fawned over the old man. How quickly his loyalties had been transferred from father to son. From father to bastard son.

Philippe looked up as she entered the room with Walter. He got up and came forward to give her a quick peck on the cheek.

'Thanks for coming over, Barbara,' he said. 'It's been a traumatic day in many ways.'

He indicated a visitor's chair. She perched on the edge of it. Uncomfortably. A little nervously even. She noticed the smile of welcome on Philippe's face fade as quickly as it appeared. She heard the soft click of the door as Clarence left discreetly.

Philippe sat opposite her in his favourite chair, his eyes on her, as if he was deciding what to say next. And then he spoke.

'You came to my house this morning and made terrible, unsubstantiated accusations about one of my employees. There was not a shred of truth in what you said so I think you owe me and Dr Tynan an apology at the very least.'

He waited for her to say something. But somehow her lips wouldn't form the words she needed to say to apologise. Instead, she attempted to justify her accusation.

'He was out with my daughter until all hours. And when I saw her this morning, it was natural for me to assume ...'

Philippe interrupted her.

'Natural for you to assume that someone associated with me was capable of the worst possible crime short of murder. That's it, isn't it? You didn't want to wait and hear the truth from your daughter. You were desperate to come over here and accuse Dr Tynan of an unspeakable crime. To get at me.'

She shrugged as if to say *so what?*

'Where's your apology for being wrong, Barbara? For defaming an innocent man. Come on. Say it. Because you're going to have to say it to Joel Tynan shortly.'

She closed her eyes.

'I apologise, Philippe. I was wrong. But he had sex with my daughter. I wasn't wrong about that.'

But for you, I might never have known about that, Philippe thought. But knowing what had occurred between them had undermined his confidence in Joel Tynan just a little. He knew it had been a serious lapse of judgement on Joel's part, despite his reassurances. Not all the damage could be repaired, even with an apology.

'Has it occurred to you they were entitled for that to remain private between them, Barbara? You have no right to know. They were consenting adults.'

She threw back her head and laughed.

'Don't give me that. He pressured her. I'm sure of it. And now Tom Boyd knows. And Patrick Boyd. Her reputation will be in tatters. Her friends will probably stop speaking to her.'

Philippe shook his head from side to side.

'You still don't understand, do you? Virginia enjoyed his company. He did not force her to have sex with him or coerce her. She had sex with him willingly. And if her friends turn their back on her because of Joel, then they're hardly friends, are they?'

It was Barbara's turn to shake her head. When will he understand what a blow this is to Virginia?

'You don't understand, do you? Patrick Boyd won't have her back now after that. She's ruined her chance of a good marriage.'

Philippe could not contain himself. He was out of his chair and standing in front of her. His anger, like Walter's, almost uncontrollable.

'Are you seriously telling me you would want your daughter to be married to a man who, at the first provocation, assaults her? Didn't you see her injuries? Do you understand what he did to her? Walter and I have been talking about having him charged with assault. Is that what you want for your daughter?'

She knew then she had made a serious misstep. She had been thinking only of Virginia's marriage prospects. But of course, he was right. She wouldn't want Virginia to marry a bully. But it had only been the one incident. Perhaps it wouldn't have happened again. She still held out a slim hope they could get back together.

'His mother and I serve on the same committees. What am I going to say to her? We were at the point of starting to think of guest lists.'

Walter rolled his eyes. Would his mother ever, for just a moment, think of what was good for Virginia rather than what was going to be socially acceptable or socially awkward for her.

'The truth would be a nice change, Mother,' Walter said. 'Philippe and I believe his family need to be told but we have decided to do it via our lawyers.'

She turned on her son.

'You have decided? Don't I get a say?'

'No, Mother, you don't actually. You haven't demonstrated you have Virginia's best interests at heart. It will be done quietly via his father, who is known to the firm. Philippe has already spoken with Howard Davis. Appropriate contact will be made.'

It wasn't Walter's preferred course of action. He would have much preferred to mete out his own punishment but Philippe had finally dissuaded him. He knew Philippe was right but that didn't make it any easier for him to accept he could do nothing to avenge his sister.

Philippe sat down again, taking several deep breaths to calm himself. Did he dislike this woman as much as she disliked him? It was entirely possible, he thought.

'So you've taken this decision, have you, Philippe? No consultation.'

'That's right, Barbara. I've taken a decision in the best interests of the family. That's my role.'

There was a finality to his words that she could not think how to challenge.

'And while we're chatting, there is something else I would like to say. My private life is exactly that. Private. I do not appreciate hearing about the gossip you so happily spread about me, some of it highly inaccurate. It reflects badly on the family. You must see that.'

She laughed then. A mix of derision and contempt. Who was he to be so high handed with her? A wife and a mistress at the same time. And who knows what other women. Probably Arabella Courtenay too. She hadn't been the only one to whisper that piece of gossip. Arabella's ex-husband was spreading it too, apparently jealous at how quickly his ex-wife had succumbed to Philippe's charm.

'So it's not true then that your mistress is pregnant with your child? That your charming wife is divorcing you for adultery?'

She listed only those things she was certain of. She knew she was on shaky ground to accuse him of sleeping with Arabella Courtenay.

Philippe stared at her. There was no softness in his eyes. No smile. She couldn't mistake the quiet threat in his voice.

'Those things may be true, Barbara, but I would be grateful if you did not speak about my private life. Just as I would not speak about some aspects of your life you would prefer to be kept private.'

He knew he had hit the target when he saw the colour drain from her face despite her heavy makeup.

'What do you mean? My private life? There's nothing to speak about. I don't know what you're talking about.'

She turned and looked towards Walter.

'Tell him, Walter. There's absolutely no scandal attached to my name.'

But Walter looked confused too. He wondered what Philippe knew that he did not.

'You're a widow now, Barbara, but I'm told you weren't at the time. How long did your affair go on with the husband of one of your best friends? Perhaps you can fill in the gaps for me.'

'How dare you,' she yelled, her face contorted with an impotent rage. 'In front of my son. How dare you!'

She buried her face in her hands, trying to hide her humiliation. He hadn't intended to use the information Clarence had given him but she had goaded him. Annoyed him. Pushed him too far. He knew she was spreading gossip about him and especially about him with Arabella even though she hadn't admitted it. He needed that to stop. He needed to protect Arabella.

'So you don't deny it then? I was in half a mind to dismiss it as idle gossip when I was told. But it's clearly true.'

Was he beginning to demonstrate all the same traits he had glimpsed in his father, he wondered? Perhaps that's what I need to be able to survive in this shark pond.

'I think we can call a truce now, Barbara. You must apologise to Joel and then we won't mention this unfortunate episode again. Remember I expect you to stop spreading gossip about my private life. And about Arabella. If you don't, you'll get a taste of your own medicine.'

She looked at him then. Something about him had hardened since she had first met him.

He wasn't the weak, whining disappointed man her husband had become. He hadn't asked to inherit the Cox wealth but, having done so, he was proving to be a shrewd custodian of it. And he had become a man used to having his own way. A man who had easily and seamlessly taken over as the head of the Cox family, just as his father had wanted. Early on, she had thought he would be a failure.

Now she could see she had underestimated him. Seriously under-estimated him.

She nodded in his direction, not trusting herself to speak and headed towards the door. She was anxious to see her daughter but in no hurry to meet Joel Tynan. Philippe hung back, letting her go.

'Sorry, Walter. I didn't want to have to use that information about your mother but she left me no choice.'

He shrugged. Thinking about it, he wasn't surprised. There had been nothing endearing or lovable about his father for at least a decade. If his mother had sought solace elsewhere, who was he to judge? He hoped it had brought her some happiness.

'It was a surprise, Philippe, but my father was not a good husband to her. They hated one another at the end.'

Philippe nodded, knowing how disappointing it had been for Walter to witness firsthand the collapse of his parents' relationship. Walter and Pippa have something in common, he thought, except he didn't hate Julia. Part of him still loved her.

'On another matter, I think we need to bring your sister into some role with the Foundation,' Philippe said quietly. 'She needs some-thing more in her life than being hawked around in the society mar-riage market to the highest bidder. Arabella would be a good influence on her, I think.'

'That's a good idea, Philippe. A very good idea. I realise I saw another side to Virginia in all this. I hope it's brought us closer together. By the way will you tell Arabella what's gone on today?'

Philippe smiled in the way he always smiled at the mention of Arabella's name.

'Some of it, Walter, but not all of it if I can avoid it. I don't want her getting too deeply involved in family matters. But if she sees Virginia, she'll ask what happened. And I would rather not tell her half-truths.'

Walter looked at him closely. Had he been telling her half-truths about something else? About someone else? Philippe read the unspoken question in Walter's eyes and smiled.

'She knows about Karen if that's what you're wondering. I've told her Karen's pregnant and that I'm getting married as soon as my divorce is finalised.'

What am I supposed to say to that? Ask how she reacted? Say that I thought she'd be disappointed at the news? Walter stayed silent rather than risk an inappropriate comment. And then he remembered he had seen Philippe's car parked in front of the house at seven o'clock that morning. It hadn't been there when he had dropped Pippa off the previous evening. He knew then where Philippe had been. He had been seeing Arabella. And no one had breathed a word of it. Not Pippa. Not Clarence. No one.

And then he realised it was because Pippa didn't know and Philippe wanted it kept that way. And Clarence? He would have been pledged to silence. The loyal offsider being discreet.

Did it mean what he thought it did? Or were they simply good friends? The unanswered questions continued to preoccupy him as he and Philippe walked the short distance to the dining room for what they both hoped would be a relaxing dinner.

Clarence paused in the act of pouring drinks and greeted Barbara Cox as she walked into the room where hours earlier she had made her terrible accusation against Joel Tynan.

'Mrs Cox, a glass of champagne perhaps?'

She accepted the drink without a word and then looked at her daughter who was standing between Pippa and Joel, almost as if they were guarding her. She hadn't seen her daughter since the doctor's visit earlier in the day but she had been told Pippa was looking after her.

'You look better than you did this morning, Virginia,' she said, inspecting her daughter's face. 'A good sleep has done wonders by the look of it. Thanks for looking after her, Pippa.'

For the first time ever, Pippa detected a hint of motherly concern in Barbara Cox's voice.

'And makeup, Mrs Cox. Let's not forget the makeup.'

But the bruising on Virginia's face was still evident as was the split lip. She put her hand up to her daughter's face.

'I never imagined Patrick Boyd could be such a bully,' she said. 'His family isn't going to like it when they find out what he's done.'

'Are they going to find out, Mother?'

She nodded.

'Your brother and Philippe have decided to do so via our lawyers. They're contacting his father. I don't think we want to make it public, do you?'

Virginia shook her head. And then she watched as her mother turned towards Joel.

'I apologise, Joel,' she said, her voice remarkably friendly and contrite. 'I jumped to conclusions. I should not have said what I said. I was wrong, as it turned out.'

There, I've said it, she thought, now can we all move on?

'Thank you for the apology, Mrs Cox,' he said.

He could have said more but he knew it was pointless. He looked at Virginia who smiled at him and slipped her hand through his arm. She was relieved her mother had apologised. Relieved too that it sounded genuine. She wondered what Philippe had said to get her to do it.

Philippe and Walter heard the last few words of Barbara Cox's apology. They were satisfied. She had done what Philippe had asked of her.

'Shall we all enjoy a good dinner now,' Philippe said as he motioned to Clarence to draw a chair out for Barbara Cox. She was seated at one end of the table with Philippe at the other. Virginia sat on Philippe's left with her brother alongside her. It had been deliberate on Philippe's part. He wanted to get to know Virginia better. He realised he had dismissed her as a spoilt rich girl whose interests did not extend much beyond the latest fashion and the juiciest gossip. He remembered it was much the same opinion he'd had of

Karen in the early days of their friendship. He smiled encouragingly at her.

'Does your face still hurt?' he asked.

I'll always be a doctor first, he thought. But then she would have had her fill of doctors today. He knew Pippa has examined her injuries. And Joel too. Just to be sure.

'It's not so bad now, Philippe,' she said, 'but I've taken some painkillers. But I won't go out in public until the bruising has faded.'

'Good idea, Virginia. You should know we're contacting our lawyers to have Patrick Boyd's father told of the incident. We thought his family needed to know.'

'Mother was telling me before you came in. I think his parents will be shocked to be honest. His father is a very mild-mannered man.'

'One more thing. The staff at both houses have been told you've been injured but not how. I left Clarence to deal with it but with the clear instruction if anyone is caught gossiping about you or your injuries, they'll find themselves without a job.'

She smiled and looked at her mother who shrugged. So much had been taken out of her mother's hands, Virginia was beginning to wonder at her mother's silence.

'And when you're better, Virginia, I'll set up a meeting with Arabella. I'm sure you'd find the work of the Foundation interesting. You might like to be involved in some capacity.'

She nodded.

'I'd like that,' she said and smiled.

But Philippe noticed the smile was for Joel, not him. He wondered then if her flirtation with Joel was going to end up being a problem. If it did, he knew Joel would be the one to lose out.

Conversation around the table fell silent as plates of clam chowder were served under Clarence's eagle eye. Clam chowder had become one of Philippe's favourite dishes. He nodded his appreciation at Clarence.

'Good choice, Clarence. And the wine for this evening?'

'Well, certainly not a big Australian red,' Clarence replied.

The cases of Grange Hermitage Philippe had ordered more than six months earlier remained untouched. He wondered if it was a silent rebuke to leave the important matter of wine selection to Clarence who was busy uncorking a well chilled bottle of French chablis.

Thinking about the cases of wine he had ordered reminded him of the dinner with Julia which had prompted the order. Reminded him too of how he had been less than honest with her. And reminded him too of how his personal life had unravelled. But he understood this was not an evening for quiet reflection. It was the night to mend a broken family. The Cox family. He smiled at Barbara encouragingly.

'I hope I'll see more of you, Barbara. We do have things to discuss regarding the family's investment portfolio. You really should be involved to protect your children's interests.'

They both knew it was an olive branch he didn't need to extend. But he did it anyway. He did not want bitterness to divide the family as it had divided father and son, both now dead. There had to be a new chapter. A new chapter in the interests of their children.

'Nice wine, Clarence,' he said as Clarence moved silently around the table filling and refilling glasses.

Clarence smiled and continued to pour the wine and oversee the clearing of plates as the next course arrived. Despite everything, the terrible events of the morning had somehow broken through the silent hostility between the two households. For the first time Clarence could remember, the two households were sitting down together with a sense of pleasure in each other's company.

He was pleased at that. He could almost hear the old man chuckling. What would he be saying, Clarence wondered? But he knew instinctively. *See, I knew it was the right thing to do, nominating Philippe as my principal heir.*

And with each bottle of vintage chablis Clarence opened, the atmosphere at the table became more and more relaxed. He had never thought it would be possible. And yet Philippe had achieved it. And in doing so proven himself a worthy head of the family, just as Walter William Cox the second had predicted.

But Philippe's private life? Better not to speculate, he thought, better not to speculate at all.

CHAPTER 12

Australia—June 1969

JOEL TYNAN STOOD, arms crossed, leaning against one of the new visitors' armchairs watching the telephone technician install the small switchboard on the reception desk of the Foundation's new offices in Sydney.

Initially, there would be a staff of just four. He and Pippa, a secretary and an accounts clerk. The space, which had been completely refurbished, included a meeting room, a utility room and a small kitchen, in addition to offices for himself and Pippa.

Once the office space was up and running, their first task would be to call the inaugural meeting of the Foundation's local board. Then the work of the Foundation could really begin. It had been two weeks since he and Pippa had returned from America.

'I think we'll always be the colonial outpost here, Pippa,' he said, surveying the small office.

She laughed, frustrated at the slow progress of the office fitout. His description was as good a description as any.

'Who knows, we might be able to act as a liaison between research projects here and projects in America,' she said, 'once we get estab-lished.'

And then she noticed the airmail letter protruding from the pocket of his jacket.

'Someone's writing to you then? Someone we both know?'

He smiled and pushed the letter further into his pocket. He did not want to run the risk Pippa would ask to read it.

'It's from Virginia if you must know.'

'You obviously made quite an impression on her. An unlikely conquest if I may say so.'

He shrugged. He wasn't sure how he felt about her but he saw no harm in corresponding with her.

'Despite what you think of her, she is a nice girl,' he said. 'Well, she was nice to me.'

He tried to ignore Pippa's knowing smile.

'Very nice to you, as it turned out,' she said teasingly, rolling her eyes in a way only she could.

'Don't go there, Pippa, please' he pleaded. 'It was enough to endure your father's look of disappointment in my judgement.'

'Sorry, Joel,' she said, still smiling but taking pity on him. 'I couldn't resist it. Does she have any gossip? Anything I might be interested in?'

'Patrick Boyd wrote her a letter of apology apparently, which is good. And she says she's helping Arabella now as an assistant but only on certain projects. She says she wasn't brought up to a nine to five life.'

Despite herself, Pippa laughed. No one would have ever expected Virginia to shackle herself to such an arrangement. She was pleased though that her former boyfriend had been forced to apologise to her.

'She says your father has been very kind to her. And she and Walter are getting along better too. She doesn't mention her mother.'

'I suppose she wants to know when you'll be back over there?'

He smiled and shrugged. She had underlined the question. He was flattered but cautious. He knew in the right circumstances he wouldn't trust himself around her again. Better not to be tempted, he thought. Despite everything, he remembered the pleasure of being with her on the beach under the night sky, just the two of them.

But there were things from the letter he did not tell Pippa. Things he wished Virginia hadn't told him. About Philippe. About Arabella. She had underlined that paragraph too in case he missed it. He was seen coming out of Arabella's house late one evening by one of my friends, she had written. Delicious gossip, isn't it? She had triple underlined the words. *She'll be devastated if he marries his mistress, in my opinion.*

He wondered how relevant the opinion of a young, inexperienced woman was. For all she knows, Philippe might simply have been visiting Arabella for totally innocent reasons. Or dropping her off after a function. Any number of explanations occurred to him.

Pippa looked at him critically, waiting for him to say more. She had quickly come to understand Joel. She could tell instantly when he wasn't quite telling the whole story.

'There was more in that letter than you're telling me, wasn't there Joel? Something about my father?'

'There's nothing I want to share with you, Pippa,' he said quickly. 'Nothing at all.'

He glanced at his watch.

'Don't we have a meeting?'

She nodded, aware they were already running late as they headed out the door, leaving the technician to close the door behind him when he finished his work.

America

Philippe had never previously attended the offices of the law firm that had for years dealt with all the matters relating to the Cox family, preferring, as his father had done before him, for the lawyers to make the trip to visit him but today was different. There were always matters to discuss but the most pressing matter was to look more closely at investment options for the family trust he was now responsible for. Some investments had recently matured which meant cash on hand needed to be reinvested.

He took the time to look about him. The Davis & Dunn offices extended over several floors of an unremarkable Midtown office building. The reception area, which opened out directly from the elevator, was dominated by a large Chesterfield sofa and two matching armchairs. A reception desk of highly polished timber occupied one wall. Behind the desk a middle-aged woman looked over her glasses at him but did not ask his name.

'Dr Duval,' she said, in a polite, slightly condescending voice, 'I'll let Mr Davis know you are here. Please take a seat.'

If he was surprised at the slight hint of condescension in her voice, he did not think about it for long. He knew she would have been familiar with his father and his half-brother as clients of the firm. But he did not know Rosemary Harper had repeatedly expressed her opinion to anyone who would listen how disappointing it was for the firm to have to deal with the illegitimate first born son who should hardly have been entitled to anything at all. And a man of dubious morals into the bargain, she always added, touching the crucifix on her gold chain as if such a gesture would ward off the evil effects of such depravity.

She had read the salacious details of his admission of adultery that had been sent from his Sydney lawyers for his perusal. *His mistress pregnant to him while he was still married*, she had announced in a shocked voice. Well, he wouldn't be married for much longer, she thought. She felt sorry for his wife. A lovely woman apparently. The mother of his daughter.

And then that very day, in the newspaper, a picture of him with his arm around another woman at a fund-raising function. Arabella Courtenay, of course. The gossip had already swirled around the office in advance of Philippe's eleven o'clock meeting.

'It's going to be an interesting meeting with the team from the private equity fund this morning,' she said as she handed over the newspaper column to Howard Davis before informing him his client was waiting in reception.

'Look at him,' she demanded. 'His arm around another woman. Bold as brass.'

Philippe had been pictured standing close to Arabella, his arm around her, her body slightly turned towards him, her bright smile betraying her delight in being with him. Rosemary took the newspaper back and read the paragraph accompanying the photograph aloud as if her boss was incapable of reading it.

Dr Philippe Duval (pictured here with Miss Arabella Courtenay) is, according to our sources, spending more time at his Eastbury Hall estate in East Hampton since he began the process of divorcing his Australian wife. News of his impending divorce comes as no surprise given the frequency with which we now see him escorting Miss Arabella Courtenay, the former Mrs Felix Latimore, to the major fund-raising events being held in this city. We are speculating that he might be hoping to emulate the success of these events in the future for his newly-created Ella Duval Foundation. The name of the foundation honors Dr Duval's mother who brought him up by herself in a modest cottage in Sag Harbor owned by her lover's family.

'At least they missed the worst part of the divorce saga, Mr Davis,' Rosemary sniffed. 'The pregnant mistress in Australia. I feel sorry for the women in his life.'

Howard Davis shook his head. In twenty years, he had failed to curb Rosemary Harper's delight in gossiping about the firm's clients. But she had insisted she only ever did so among the handful of trusted office staff, so he had demurred about replacing her. Anyway, he didn't like change, she knew all the firm's clients and their foibles and, just occasionally, he was amused by her insights.

'That column is wrong on another point,' he said, as if it really mattered. 'Arabella Courtenay isn't the former Mrs Felix Latimore. He hasn't agreed to their divorce yet, I've been told.'

Which caused Rosemary Harper to raise her already raised eyebrows even further.

'So the meeting this morning with the private equity team is going to be interesting, to say the least. Should you warn Dr Duval, do you think?'

He shrugged.

'Surely he knows who Arabella's husband is.'

But Rosemary Harper wasn't so sure.

'It might never have come up. She's probably told him she's already divorced. Or has given him that impression.'

Howard Davis rocked back in his chair and threw his pen on the desk in a rare expression of frustration. He hadn't anticipated these problems when he first met Philippe Duval. He had believed him to be happily married with no interest in other women. He was disappointed to find out he had been wrong. He had seen men brought down by their extramarital interests. He couldn't help but think Philippe Duval was heading down that path. He hoped he was wrong. Yet in the space of a year, he had cheated on his wife and got his mistress pregnant. And now he appeared to be romancing another woman.

He let out a long sigh and got up from his desk to walk the short distance to the reception area. At the very moment he held out his hand to greet Philippe, the team from the private equity fund walked through the door.

Felix Latimore held out his hand to Howard Davis, whom he knew, and then to Philippe. He was meeting Philippe for the first time. He then introduced the other two men who accompanied him before Howard Davis ushered the group into the meeting room and closed the door. A coffee tray had already been placed on the table and Philippe helped himself before he sat down.

Felix Latimore moved around the table and chose a chair directly opposite Philippe. He was a neat man, slim build, mid forties, his greying hair swept back cleanly from his face. He smiled at Philippe.

'I guess you're in unfamiliar territory, Dr Duval,' he said, 'having to deal with the family's investments. No doubt you'd rather be in an operating room than a meeting room.'

Philippe shrugged. It was unfamiliar territory but he felt it would put him at a disadvantage to admit it.

'I'm learning quickly, Mr Latimore. Very quickly. I look forward to hearing what you have to tell me.'

'That's good,' he nodded as he pushed a glossy prospectus across the table to Philippe. He slid another copy across to Howard Davis.

'In any case this is very preliminary today, Mr Latimore,' Philippe cautioned. 'My investment advisors will be going over it for me but I wanted to take this meeting myself.'

'To get your head around this investment opportunity yourself and form your own opinion, I assume?'

Philippe nodded.

'Yes, if you like. There are many things I understand about my new life. Our aim to assist with funding for medical research for one. But making the right investments for the family is quite another responsibility.'

'Then let me take you through what we are offering, Dr Duval,' Felix Latimore said smoothly.

He proceeded then to talk at length about investment options, industries the fund would be investing in and potential returns. He noticed Philippe listened attentively and took notes. At the end of his presentation, he looked across to Philippe.

'Any questions?'

'No, none that I can think of,' Philippe replied. 'It all sounds very impressive but as I said I will run it past my investment advisors so no decision today.'

'I didn't expect one, Dr Duval,' he said. 'Please take your time to think about what I've put before you. We won't take up any more of your time today.'

Felix Latimore stood then. His colleagues, largely silent throughout the presentation, followed his lead. And then Philippe noticed Felix Latimore pause for just a moment.

'By the way, Dr Duval,' he said, with a knowing superior smile, 'please give my regards to my wife. You seem to be on better terms with her than I am.'

He reached into his briefcase and tossed a copy of the morning newspaper on the table. It had been folded to the gossip column. Philippe picked it up and read it quickly. He understood then why the morning newspaper had not made an appearance alongside his breakfast that morning.

'Your wife? Arabella is your wife?'

He had completely wrong footed Philippe.

'Oh, didn't she tell you? The Miss Arabella Courtenay you had your arm around is actually Mrs Felix Latimore. Still Mrs Felix Latimore in fact.'

The smile had completely faded from Felix Latimore's face. He watched Philippe closely. Was Philippe Duval suddenly looking uncomfortable? He couldn't decide. He was a hard man to read.

'I had no idea. Arabella told me her marriage was over.'

Philippe was wary now. Angry too that he hadn't been forewarned. Howard Davis must have known, he thought.

'Well, I can tell you now she told you a lie,' he said, pointing at Philippe, the anger in his voice rising with every word. 'We are still married. And we'll go on being married until I decide we won't be married anymore. I'd be grateful if you would remember that.'

He paused, trying to judge the impact of his words.

'Mind you, I might relent and give her a divorce if I can prove her adultery. I'd prefer to trash her reputation and keep mine intact.

I'm happy to trash yours too if it comes to that. That won't help you get donations for your precious foundation, will it?'

Philippe was silent, refusing to be provoked into responding. But he understood the implied threat only too well. He remembered then what Arabella had told him. *My husband was very controlling towards the end.* A lovely woman like her deserved better. Much better, he thought.

Without another word, Philippe turned and walked out of the meeting room, leaving the prospectus on the table. It was left to Howard Davis, open mouthed, to usher the three men out of the office.

'I don't think you can expect to hear from Dr Duval any time soon,' he said.

Felix Latimore shrugged his shoulders, apparently unconcerned he had lost a potential investor.

'I know all about Philippe Duval's reputation,' he sneered. 'I don't expect to hear from him but he'll be hearing from me if I can prove he's sleeping with my wife, which he obviously is.'

Howard Davis wisely said nothing. A photograph in a newspaper proved nothing and they both knew it. But Howard Davis knew something of Felix Latimore's reputation. A tough negotiator in business. And probably in his personal life as well, he thought. Not a man to cross. But a man who had made his fair share of enemies too.

As the visitors departed, Howard Davis turned to Rosemary Harper, her eyes wide at what she had just witnessed.

'Not a word about this to anyone,' he warned. 'Otherwise, we'll both be in trouble.'

He began to consider what course of action Felix Latimore might take to prove what he suspected. Would he go so far as to hire a private detective to spy on Philippe? Or Arabella? Should he warn Philippe? He was uncertain but he made a note to mention the prospect at their next meeting.

L'Etoile restaurant was busy but not yet packed with lunch trade when Philippe entered. He checked his watch. He was early by fifteen minutes as he followed the waiter to his table, a generous tip ensuring one of the best tables. Everything about the restaurant was modern, perhaps too modern for his taste. But he had been told the food was excellent and he had a weakness for French restaurants.

The events of the morning continued to trouble him as he quickly downed the glass of bourbon the waiter had brought him. Why had Arabella not been completely honest with him? It was a question he asked himself time and again. And then he caught sight of her, smiling as she came towards the table.

'Very modern, isn't it? Too modern for your taste, Philippe?'

He smiled.

'Perhaps,' he replied, looking around him.

He knew interior design trends were at the forefront of Arabella's mind at that particular moment. He had agreed to engage her friend Claudia Rossi to update the décor of his Midtown apartment.

As she sat down, she looked at him. She could tell immediately something was wrong. Something, or someone, had upset him. While the waiter hovered over them taking their meal orders, she said nothing. When he had gone, she reached across the table and put her hand on his.

'What's up, Philippe,' she asked quietly 'What's wrong? Please tell me.'

He smiled at her briefly. There was a hint of sadness, disappointment even, in his voice when he spoke.

'You should have been honest with me, Arabella,' he said finally. 'I was honest with you.'

'What do you mean, Philippe? What have I not been honest about?'

But she knew, of course. She knew what she had failed to tell him. He pulled his hand away from hers.

'You haven't been honest about your husband. I met him this

morning at a meeting with a private equity team who were promoting a new investment to me. You should have told me your divorce wasn't finalised. He tossed this on the table in front of me accompanied by some choice threats.'

She reached out and picked up the newspaper he had pushed across the table towards her. She understood now why there had been no newspaper in the office that morning when she arrived. Clarence had obviously seen to that.

Even in the muted lighting of the restaurant he could see the colour drain from her face. She shook her head slowly from side to side. And then he noticed tears begin to slide down her face. She would have got up from the table but he put a restraining hand on her arm.

'Don't go, Arabella,' he said. 'Tell me the truth. Is your marriage over? Or have you been lying to me?'

'I'm so sorry, Philippe,' she said.

What could she say? How much should she tell him? She took a deep breath. He deserved to know.

'The truth is my husband made my life a misery almost from the day we married. I had to get away from him. The only way I could survive was to move to my own house without telling him where I lived. In my mind, the marriage is over even if legally we are still married. He's been difficult about that. I sued him for divorce on the grounds of his treatment of me but he wouldn't accept that of course. He's concerned about his reputation.'

'And you didn't think to tell me so I could help you?'

She looked at him through her tears and shook her head.

'Why would I want to put that burden on you?' she said. 'I wanted to have a new life, a new job, where none of this was known. Where I could forget about him.

'And then unfortunately he saw this and drew some conclusions about our relationship and decided he could potentially use this against you. Against me. Against the Foundation.'

Philippe tossed the newspaper aside. His voice was gentler now. It wasn't her fault. He could see how much she had been hurt. Emotionally. Physically perhaps.

'Was he violent towards you?'

She closed her eyes, remembering. But not wanting to remember. Why was he asking her? It was in the past.

'A few times. When he got jealous. When he thought other men were paying attention to me. When he was in a bad mood.'

He realised then the potential danger he had put her in.

'Are you sure he doesn't know where you live?'

She shook her head.

'As far as I know, he doesn't.'

But still he was concerned at the fact she lived alone. Would her husband go that far? Would he be a threat to her safety? He would need to confer with Clarence to decide what was best to be done. He smiled encouragingly at her then.

'Don't look so worried,' he said gently. 'I understand now why you didn't want to tell me. I was just taken by surprise, that's all.'

He reached out and touched her cheek, wiping away her tears.

'I'm sorry. I should have been honest with you just as you were honest with me,' she said.

For her sake, he had told her the truth about his private life.

He looked at her closely, her deep blue eyes still glistening with tears. He knew what he really needed if he was to help her was leverage against Felix Latimore. He needed to know more about him. Much more. To Philippe he looked like a man who might already have made some enemies. Were all his financial and business dealings above board, he wondered idly?

And then he thought about another possible line of enquiry, one that might be easier for him to pursue if he revived some of his medical contacts in the city.

'Were you ever examined by a doctor after he was violent towards you?'

She nodded slowly, dragging back old, long buried memories.

'There would be a medical record of the injuries I sustained about four years ago,' she said quietly. 'He was particularly brutal that evening. I was examined by a doctor at St Luke's.'

She heard Philippe's quick intake of breath. He had no idea how a man could do such a thing to a woman. Surely that would have meant the end of the relationship.

'Did you leave him then?'

She shook her head.

'He was all apologetic. Said he would never do it again. I said I would give him one last chance. It turned out to be one last chance he didn't deserve.'

He reached out to her then and held both her hands in his.

'I will take care of this for you,' he said. 'Please trust me on this.'

She smiled, relieved to have his reassurances.

'Thank you, Philippe,' she said.

For the first time in a very long time, she felt she was not entirely alone.

For Philippe, it would mean a trip back to the hospital where he had spent his early years as a doctor. He hoped some of his former colleagues still remembered him. It would make his task so much easier.

Chapter 13

America

SEVERAL DAYS LATER, Philippe Duval headed towards the entrance to St Luke's hospital. It was years since he had last walked beneath its imposing entrance. As he did so, he was remembering the years he had spent there, learning how to be a doctor, later specialising in neurosurgery for which he would become renowned. The hospital appeared little changed in the decade or more since he had left. It was a forbidding structure of red brick, with small rectangular windows symmetrically arranged on each of its seven floors. It was not a beautiful building but its solid architecture was strangely reassuring.

Within minutes, he was being shown into the office of his former colleague Dr Adam Langton. He glanced around him. It seemed so familiar except that the office decor at least had been updated. And then he spotted a patient file on the otherwise clear desk but he could not read the name. He hoped it was what he had come for.

'Philippe, it's good to see you. It's been a long time.'

Adam Langton's friendly greeting on the telephone had reassured

Philippe and his greeting today was no less enthusiastic. Philippe had not been in touch with his former colleagues since his sudden acquisition of wealth which he knew they all must surely have read about. And talked about. It had been an oversight on his part but one for which he had already apologised to his former colleague.

The two men chatted, attempting to fill in the gaps in each other's lives in a few brief minutes. But Philippe was keen to get to the purpose of his visit.

'Is that what I think it is,' he asked, nodding towards the patient file.

Adam smiled, picking it up from his desk and flipping it open.

'Yes, it is. I received it this morning. Your Miss Courtenay, or Mrs Latimore which she was then, received quite a battering at the hands of her husband on one occasion. It's well documented here,' he said but he did not hand the file over to Philippe.

Adam had requested it from the hospital archive on the pretext she was about to become his patient and he wanted to understand her medical history. He could see no reason to hand it over to Philippe but he was prepared to outline the contents.

'That's exactly what I wanted to know, Adam,' Philippe said. 'Her husband is holding up their divorce, denying her claims of mistreatment. He says there's no credible evidence. He's a nasty piece of business.'

Adam read further, flipping the page on the notes.

'A nasty piece of business indeed. Fortunately for her, the injuries were largely superficial except for one cracked rib, obviously where he punched her. The bruising was bad though.'

He read on quickly.

'Of course, you probably know she had an emergency caesarean a few months after the attack. The baby didn't make it sadly. It was premature, perhaps the early labour was brought on by the stress of the attack but it would be hard to make a case that the bashing was the cause.'

Philippe nodded. He was shocked that Felix Latimore had assaulted his wife in the early stages of her pregnancy. He hadn't known she had been assaulted only months before she lost her baby.

Adam looked up from the notes.

'Other than that, there's nothing remarkable about her medical history. Was there anything else you wanted to know?'

'Do you know the doctor who treated her at the time? Do you think he would be prepared to make a statement for my lawyers? I've asked them to take over representing her in her divorce.'

Adam nodded and looked at his watch.

'For a start the doctor is a she and we both know her. And she's due here shortly.'

Philippe looked perplexed, his mind running through the very short list of women doctors he remembered from his time at the hospital. And then he realised who Adam meant. Before he could say anything, a head appeared around the door.

'Jennifer,' Philippe said, getting up quickly. 'It's good to see you.'

She came forward and kissed him on the cheek.

'It's nice to see you too, Philippe,' she said, taking a pace back then to scrutinise him. 'Your circumstances have undergone a marked change since we last met.'

He's aged well, she thought. And the changes in his fortune have been especially kind to him. Everything about his appearance spoke of money. Of wealth. The latest Rolex on his wrist. The beautifully tailored suit. The expensive shirt and tie. But no wedding ring.

Philippe was desperately trying to think how long it had been since he had seen her. Hadn't it been about the time he had received Pippa's letter? The letter from a child that had changed his life. He wondered how much she had gleaned about his life in the intervening years.

'Yes, you're right, Jennifer,' he said, knowing there would be a barrage of questions to follow. 'My circumstances have changed. Changed a lot in the past year in fact.'

'And if the newspaper reports are to be believed, your marriage to your wartime sweetheart back in Australia didn't survive the upheaval?'

He shook his head. What could he say?

'No, it didn't survive, Jennifer. The newspaper was right about one thing. I'm headed for my second divorce. And you? You married again I believe.'

She nodded.

'I did. But he says I'm married to my work. We battle along though. Are you headed to the altar with Miss Courtenay when your divorces are final?'

Adam Langton would never have asked such a question. He remembered how Philippe had been very reticent about his private life. And how surprised he had been to learn Philippe had fathered a daughter during his war service in Australia. The newspaper report of his unexpected inheritance had named her too as a substantial heiress in her own right. The gossip had spread like wildfire through the hospital. But Jennifer felt no constraints about quizzing him about his life. She waited for his answer.

'No, I'm not marrying Arabella, if you must know. She's not the reason my wife is divorcing me. The newspapers aren't always right. I didn't bother to correct the story.'

And then Jennifer remembered an earlier gossip column piece about him.

'Of course, I remember. You had another woman on your arm back in February, didn't you? My husband spotted your picture in the newspaper and pointed it out to me. At a fashion event if I recall correctly.'

They waited for him to say something to fill the silence. Her interrogation of his life was not unexpected.

'You have a good memory, Jennifer,' he said. 'That was Karen Clarke with me. I met her through her uncle who worked with me at St Vincent's in Sydney.'

He noticed her quizzical look as if to say *come on, there's more to this story.*

'I should have been more discreet if you must know. More cautious.'

'Did someone show that picture to your wife?' she asked, curious as to how his wife, who lived on the other side of the world, had seen the picture. Did people read *The New York Times* in Sydney, she wondered?

He shook his head. How much more would he need to reveal about his private life to satisfy her curiosity?

'No, she found out about my relationship with Karen in quite another way. We separated but there was always a possibility we would get back together.'

'But not now? There's no possibility of that now?'

Jennifer knew there was more to it than he was telling them. She was surprised at the revelations. Her marriage to him had ended, not because of his interest in another woman, but because medicine had been his mistress. And she later came to realise there were unresolved issues he had never spoken about from the war. From his time in Australia. He had simply never been present in their marriage. But now it seemed he had the time and money to indulge himself with other women. She wondered what expensive indulgences he now bestowed on his mistress. Or was that mistresses?

He let out a deep sigh and gestured helplessly.

'No. My wife Julia filed for divorce recently. Karen is pregnant with my child.'

A stunned silence settled in the room. Neither of them had expected such a revelation.

'Which means you're going to have to marry Karen Clarke when your divorce is final?'

Jennifer was beginning to piece together his complicated personal life. She began to wonder where he would live with his new wife. His life appeared to her to have become centred on New York again.

'Yes, that's the plan but the baby will be born before that. It's due in October. My divorce is going to take a while.'

And then she asked the question he fervently hoped she wouldn't ask.

'You seem to be taking a great interest in Arabella Courtenay's personal affairs,' she said. 'What's her role in your life apart from being an employee?'

She looked at him directly as she asked the question, a knowing smile teasing the corners of her mouth. Would he answer? She was curious.

Philippe considered his response for some time. What could he say? Yes, she was an employee but that would hardly explain his interest. A friend. She was more than just a casual friend. He answered her after a long pause.

'She's a good friend, Jennifer. A very good friend of mine.'

His ex-wife laughed out loud, enjoying his discomfort. She suspected there was more than mere friendship between him and Arabella.

'Well, well,' she said, with a knowing smile. 'You could be complicating your life even further by the sound of it.'

He ignored the jibe. His ex-wife had always been outspoken and free with her opinions.

'Arabella is a good friend,' he repeated, trying to hide his irritation. 'She accompanies me to a lot of functions. That piece in the gossip column might have rendered her less safe because of her husband. He needs to be dealt with once and for all.'

He noticed Jennifer become serious then. This was her area of expertise, helping women who suffered at the hands of their husbands.

'I apologise, Philippe,' she said. 'I was being flippant when this is really a serious matter. It is important to do what we can if there's a risk he might become a threat to her safety. What do you want me to do?'

'We need a statement about her injuries. If you could provide that to my lawyers, that would help.'

She took the business card he held out to her.

'Do you want me to talk to the lawyers too?'

'It might help,' he said. 'Can I leave it with you?'

She nodded.

'And I'd be grateful if you would refrain from trashing my reputation to my lawyers,' he added.

She laughed quietly. Part of her still admired him. He had been a fine surgeon. She even found herself envying the younger women who aroused his interest.

'My lips are sealed,' she said. 'I promise I won't gossip about you but I would love to see the mansion you inherited out at East Hampton. Eastbury Hall, isn't it?'

He handed her a card with his home number. And then he passed a card to Adam Langton.

'Come for lunch on Sunday,' he said. 'Just give me a call to confirm so I can let the staff know. If I'm not there, speak to Clarence. Bring your better halves. And the rest of the gang too or those you're still in contact with.'

They knew who he meant. There had been a regular group of them who had socialised together on the rare occasions their free time coincided.

'Are you sure?' She counted the potential attendees on her fingers. 'It could be as many as sixteen people.'

He smiled.

'My dear Jennifer, the dining table seats twenty. The cellar is stacked to the ceiling with vintage wine my father was too ill to drink in his last years. And the cook complains the meals I ask for are too simple and that I never entertain.'

'So we just drive up to your big mansion? Will we be let in?'

'There will be a guard on the gate,' he explained. 'You'll be expected. There'll be a list of names. Clarence will see to that. The gardens are now open to the public, so we've had to be a bit more security conscious. The house has a lot of valuable antiques and paintings.'

'And all this from a father you never knew,' she said, still hardly able to believe his good fortune.

'I knew him briefly in the last few weeks of his life actually. But it's a story for another day.'

Philippe looked at his watch. He had promised Arabella he would meet her at his apartment to make some decisions about the redecoration.

'I must go. But thank you for helping me out. For helping Arabella.'

They walked with him to the end of the hallway and waited together for the elevator.

'You should be able to get a cab without too much trouble,' Adam said as he held out his hand to Philippe.

'No need. My chauffeur is waiting for me actually.'

'Ah, the life of a rich man has many advantages, it seems,' Adam said.

'We look forward to seeing how a rich man lives on Sunday,' Jennifer said, giving him a quick hug.

'Until Sunday. And remember, I'm relying on you, Dr Newman.'

She smiled at him and nodded. She would do it for him. For Arabella. Women deserve to live a life free from fear, she thought, yet few had the means to achieve it. Arabella, with Philippe's backing, had a much better chance of moving on from her violent marriage than so many of the other women she had treated. She was happy to play her own small part in making that happen.

As they watched the elevator door close behind him, Adam turned to her.

'Is that a wistful look in those eyes? You should have stuck with him, Jennifer. You'd be dripping in diamonds and designer gowns now.'

But she shook her head.

'And wondering which of his mistresses he was seeing when he wasn't with me.'

'Does that surprise you? That side of him?'

She shrugged. It had in a way. And then again it hadn't.

'He was too busy when I was married to him to be involved with other women but there were always young nurses trying to find excuses to do something for him. Most times he didn't seem to notice but occasionally he flirted with some of them. I think he's making up for lost time, don't you?'

'And how do you think he's going to handle becoming a father at his age?'

She laughed.

'With the nannies and household help he can afford, it's hardly likely to affect his lifestyle, is it? But where will they live? Sydney? Or here?'

'You notice he said marrying his mistress was, what did he say, *the plan*,' he said, thinking back over their conversation.

She thought about it for a moment.

'I suspect he enjoyed having the lady as his mistress. But as his wife? Perhaps he never really thought that was a realistic possibility. She almost certainly trapped him with the pregnancy. He wouldn't have agreed to it at his age. She must be quite a bit younger than him.'

He knew Jennifer was right. Philippe had fallen into the classic trap of a woman who wanted a child and probably his child in particular. He wondered idly if it might be for the money the child would be entitled to? Or was he doing the mother-to-be a disservice? Could Arabella Courtenay decide to try the same tactic? She was thirty-five. Running out of time but not too late.

'And Arabella Courtenay? Is he really sleeping with her, do you think?'

She thought about it for a moment.

'I'm not sure. I think he's attracted to her but would she want to become involved with him knowing he's getting married again. But I know he's worried he's put her in danger from her bully of a husband because of the gossip column picture.'

She paused. Should she say what she was thinking?

'I think he might actually be in love with her, Adam, but I think he's locked into offering marriage to his Australian girlfriend because of the baby.'

'A complicated life, then, for our friend Philippe.'

She shrugged.

'Indeed. But don't feel too bad for him. He's wealthy. And good looking. I would say he could have his pick of a dozen women now. Probably more.'

'So that's what it takes,' Adam chortled, aware his looks had never set female hearts racing.

But still her thoughts were on his relationship with Arabella.

'I wonder if Arabella will be there on Sunday? It would be interesting to see them together.'

'Well, we'd better do some phoning around to see who's available.'

'You mean to say they won't drop everything to be there? I think they'd cancel their own weddings not to miss the opportunity to see the newly wealthy Philippe Duval in his East Hampton mansion.'

He laughed.

'Let's go and make some calls and see if you're right, Dr Newman.'

Together they turned and headed back to his office, the day brightened by the prospect of Sunday lunch at Eastbury Hall.

Later, across town, Philippe sat in his favourite chair in his favourite retreat, his Midtown apartment. He sat quietly remembering back to the day he had sat in that very same chair and read the letter, in Pippa's childish handwriting, telling him she was his daughter. He was remembering too it was the day the final divorce papers had arrived, declaring he was again a free man. Had it been acrimonious between them? Acrimonious enough for Jennifer to move to a job in another hospital, away from St Luke's. He hadn't realised she had returned to St Luke's after he had left.

He remembered now. He had seen her for the final time that day. In the morning when they had met in the hospital corridor. She had accused him of never being there for her, that his career had been the only thing that mattered to him. And she had been right. Until Pippa's letter arrived. It had been strange to meet his ex-wife again so unexpectedly.

'You're deep in thought, Philippe,' Arabella said brightly as she walked in.

She sat down on the sofa opposite him. Her friend Claudia was due to meet her that afternoon to discuss the redecoration of Philippe's apartment.

'How did you get on at St Luke's? Did they find any record of my treatment?' she asked, unable to contain her anxiety.

Her voice woke him from his reverie.

'I don't think you're going to believe this,' he said, 'but the doctor who examined you at the hospital after you were injured was my first wife. Her name is Jennifer Newman. You probably don't remember her.'

He could see the look of surprise, almost shock, on her face.

'And I thought I knew all about you. I thought your present wife was your first wife. Everybody does, I think.'

There's always something new to learn about him, she thought. His first wife. His first love, surely.

'Jennifer and I weren't married very long. Less than two years. I was consumed by my career. And by not knowing what happened to Pippa. The marriage didn't really stand a chance. She married again. Today was the first time I'd seen her since our divorce.'

'I hope she's forgiven you otherwise she might not help me.'

He shook his head.

'Jennifer isn't like that. She isn't someone who would carry a grudge so don't worry, she's going to help you. She'll go and see Howard Davis and make a statement about your injuries. And then the lawyers can resubmit the divorce application.'

'It may provoke him, Philippe.'

He could tell she was anxious.

'I've thought of that. We'll increase the security at your house. I'll get Clarence on to it.'

'Thank you,' she said, although the words hardly seemed adequate. 'I'm so grateful to you. I want you to know that.'

But he waved away her thanks. After all, he wasn't doing it only for her. He did not enjoy hearing the slurs being uttered about her by Felix Latimore. And about himself. He knew he had to put a stop to it for all their sakes. And for Karen's sake too.

But there was no further opportunity for conversation as her friend Claudia breezed through the open doorway in a whirl of fabric samples and design books.

'Philippe, it's lovely to see you again,' she gushed.

Having Philippe Duval as a client had increased demand for her services and she was making the most of it.

'You too, Claudia,' he said, as he got up and prepared to leave.

'Not staying to make decisions with us?'

He shook his head. He was more than happy to leave the two women to decide what should be done. He had been happy with the redecoration of the bedrooms at Eastbury Hall.

'No, Claudia, I'll leave it to you and Arabella. Frederick is waiting for me. Just no modern monstrosities please. No orange plastic lamps or shag pile carpets. Or white fibreglass chairs for that matter. It needs to be elegant and comfortable.'

She laughed, protesting she had never intended to inflict such things upon him.

'And my favourite chair stays,' he said, as he disappeared out the front door and headed for the elevator.

For just a brief moment he thought of Karen. She should be doing this, he thought. And then he began to wonder, not for the first time, how she would ever become part of his life in America. And yet America now felt like his home again.

He pushed the thoughts to the back of his mind. Better not to think about it, he decided. Much better not to think about the future at all.

CHAPTER 14

HIGH CLOUD. A BRIGHT SKY. A gentle breeze. The weather could not have been better as first one car and then another drove up to the private entrance to Eastbury Hall to be greeted by the guard on duty. Names were ticked off. Each of the cars, seven in all, was directed up the long private driveway to the front of the house. The gravel driveway looked as if it had been hand raked that morning. Immaculate hedges on either side of the driveway afforded a surprising level of privacy, separating the private driveway from the public gardens.

'This is what real wealth means,' Jennifer Newman said as she looked around her. It was beyond anything she had imagined.

'Well, you pulled the wrong rein there, didn't you? You should have stuck with him instead of opting for a poor man like me.'

It was a joke Frank Benson had made any number of times since the news of Philippe Duval's unexpected inheritance had become known. It was beginning to irritate his wife who failed to see the joke. He shrugged off her complaints. Besides, he thought, he would almost certainly have traded her in for a younger model by now judging by the gossip. His mind then went to the question of money. That was the real pity of it. The divorce settlement would have set her up. He wondered what the second Mrs Duval was getting. But of course he was being divorced under Australian law which might be kinder to his fortune. Or maybe his estranged wife wasn't interested in his money. But he couldn't conceive of such a situation. She would want to be compensated for the humiliation of his pregnant mistress.

His wife's strident voice brought him back to the present.

'Frank, don't be ridiculous,' she said. 'And don't go asking him personal questions about his divorce. I know what you're like. You'll want to know the ins and outs and offer your opinion.'

He laughed.

'I promise I won't. I know he's represented by one of the hotshot firms in Manhattan. They'll fight tooth and nail to keep his fortune intact.'

'Did you know they're now representing Arabella Courtenay in her divorce too? She was married to the investment advisor Felix Latimore.'

'Is your ex being cited?'

She shook her head.

'No. Latimore was handy with his fists.'

'Not nice,' he said.

In his experience, a battered wife filing for divorce added a layer of complexity he'd rather not deal with. By comparison, he preferred straightforward adultery. There was a lot of it in the divorce petitions he handled. If Philippe Duval had become a wayward husband, he certainly hadn't been with Jennifer, he remembered. His main failing had been his dedication to his career. And not being committed to his marriage. He remembered how he had helped Jennifer unravel her life from Philippe's. And then he had married her.

He brought the car to a halt. Behind him, the other cars made a neat line along the driveway. In all there were thirteen guests.

Monica Brewer had been delighted to be included in the invitation among the doctors and their spouses. Her car was the last in the line. She had worked alongside Philippe as a head theatre nurse. And she had worshipped him from afar. She had been devastated when he had left to settle in Sydney.

Adam and Maria Langton waited for her as she crunched unsteadily along the gravel driveway in her high heels.

'You look terrific today, Monica,' he said, noticing how much effort she had taken with her dress. He was used to seeing her at work, scrubbed up ready for theatre.

She blushed at the unexpected compliment, chiding herself that at forty-five she was too old to be blushing like a young girl. But it was true she had taken extra care with her appearance, her simple dress of deep turquoise blue was new. She had pulled out her mother's treasured pearls from the depths of her jewellery box. She hadn't worn them in years. And she had spent most of the previous day in the beauty parlour.

It puzzled Adam, and his wife too, that Monica had never married. Too busy with work had always been the excuse no one had challenged. Jennifer Newman knew the truth of course. She had seen it in her envious glances. Monica had fallen hopelessly in love with Philippe and no man was ever a match for him in her mind.

If they expected to see Philippe at the top of the stairs to greet them, they were doomed to disappointment. It was Clarence who welcomed them in his grave butler voice. *Dr Newman and Mr Benson. Dr Langton and Mrs Langton. Dr Cameron and Mrs Cameron. Dr Hannah and Mrs Hannah. Dr Horne and Mrs Horne. Dr Moore and Mrs Moore. And Miss Brewer. Welcome to Eastbury Hall. Please come in. My name is Clarence. Dr Duval is waiting for you in the drawing room.*

The group trailed behind Clarence through the marbled entrance hallway, trying hard not to gape at the fineries on display. Several of the women stopped to admire a collection of enamel trinket boxes.

'Is that what I think it is, Clarence?'

The question came from Adam Langton's wife Maria. She worked part-time in a private art gallery and volunteered at the Metropolitan Museum of Art.

Clarence smiled. The lady knows something of art, he thought. She has a good eye.

'It is, Mrs Langton. It is by the great Russian designer Fabergé. Enamel with silver gilt. Circa 1900. A prized piece in the collection.'

'Of how many pieces, Clarence?'

'About fifty I believe. Some are in other rooms.'

She looked around her then, noticing the fine paintings on the walls.

'Does Dr Duval really own all this now?'

'Of course, Mrs Langton.'

Clarence was surprised at the question, yet he understood Philippe Duval's friends had only seen him in the role of doctor. No doubt a well-paid doctor towards the end of his career but not a wealthy man.

'Shall we?'

Clarence urged the group towards the drawing room. They had just passed through a small ante room. Beyond lay the drawing room and the dining room.

As Clarence opened the door, Philippe came forward to greet them all, one by one, saving a warm hug for the woman he described as his *best ever theatre nurse*, which caused Monica to blush again. She had not set eyes on him for more than a decade, yet she would have known him anywhere.

And then Philippe turned towards Arabella and Walter.

'A couple of people for you all to meet,' Philippe said as Clarence busied himself with the important business of making the pre-lunch cocktails.

'I think you know Arabella, Jennifer, but for the rest of you, this is Arabella Courtenay. The executive director of my Foundation. If you're planning on taking up medical research, be nice to her. She might be deciding in the future if your project gets funding.'

He's standing too close to her, Jennifer thought, and his arm around her waist looks slightly too familiar. She's beautiful too now she's not covered in bruises. Her deep blue eyes are sparkling with delight. Most probably delight at being with Philippe, she thought.

'And this is my nephew Walter Cox,' she heard Philippe say. 'I made Walter cancel his plans for today. I thought it would be nice to have an even number at the table.'

'I thought your daughter might be here, Philippe?'

'No, Jennifer, Pippa lives in Sydney.'

'A doctor too I believe?'

'Yes, a doctor but she got tired of the grind. I indulged in a bit of nepotism, I'm afraid. I gave her a job at the Foundation in Sydney.'

'And you Walter?'

Jennifer was curious. He didn't look like a young man harried by the daily grind of having to hold down a job. By her calculation he was actually Walter William Cox IV. Would he be the one to inherit the bulk of the estate from Philippe?

'I help with the Cox investment portfolio, Jennifer,' he said evenly, trying not to resent the inference in her question he did nothing useful. 'I manage the real estate assets and do things on Philippe's behalf when he's not here.'

'When he's in Sydney you mean?'

And then she turned to Philippe to ask the question they all wanted to hear the answer to.

'Are you planning to spend most of your time in Sydney in the future, Philippe?' she asked as she sipped her cocktail. News of Karen's pregnancy had spread quickly among his former colleagues. As she asked the question, she glanced at Arabella.

Trust Jennifer, he thought. She would have made a good prosecutor. It's like an excruciating cross examination. I expect to be found guilty very soon. Even her husband is starting to look uncomfortable.

'That's all for the future, Jennifer,' he said smoothly, hardly looking at her as he replied. She noticed his eyes seek out Arabella who smiled and then blushed slightly, knowing his ex-wife's keen eyes had seen the exchange.

It wasn't only Jennifer who had seen the intimate look that passed between Philippe and Arabella. Walter too caught the interaction and smiled to himself. It was then he remembered what Clarence had said. *She's set her cap at him.* As for Philippe, Walter was still uncertain. Perhaps he's simply enjoying the flirtation and will take it no further. At least that's what Walter hoped as he looked on, dismayed.

The truth of the matter was he envied Philippe. In other circumstances, he would have enjoyed romancing her. His mother had been right. He liked being with older women. He still remembered with pleasure the night he had spent with Karen's friend, Bianca, earlier in the year. And then he tried to banish those thoughts from his mind. He smiled at Arabella and was rewarded with a bright almost conspiratorial smile in return.

Will I be consoling her one day soon, he wondered? Was the child Karen would give Philippe enough to sway the odds in her favour? Was he still besotted with her, as he had been earlier in the year? Walter remembered he had married Julia to give his daughter his name. To Walter, it seemed very likely Philippe would marry again for the same reason, even if his feelings for Karen had cooled. And Arabella? She will be left devastated, just as Karen herself had been left devastated once before. These thoughts preoccupied him until Clarence's commanding voice announced lunch was about to be served.

In arranging the placement of guests at the table, Clarence had left nothing to chance. He did not know Philippe's friends but he had asked a few pertinent questions before deciding the seating plan.

Philippe, of course, was at the head of the table. Walter at the opposite end.

Philippe's suggestion that Arabella be placed on his left was ignored. Instead, she found herself in the middle of the table with Adam Langton on her left and Leon Horne, an orthopaedic surgeon of some renown but limited conversation, on her right. She was grateful when Adam Langton claimed her attention after the first course.

'Have you known Philippe long, Arabella?' he asked, trying hard not to let his eyes drift to the wide neckline of her dress and the enticing swell of her breasts. How lucky is Philippe, he thought? She's beautiful, charming and sexy.

He noticed Simon Moore, on the other side of the table, smile at him and mouth the words *she's gorgeous*. Simon had always been Philippe's preferred anaesthetist. His pretty wife Natalie sat further along the table. She had been a nurse but now she spent her days taking care of the couple's three children. Simon's wandering eye was well known to everyone except his wife. Adam Langton shook his head and mouthed back *you've got no chance* at which his colleague laughed and pulled a face.

Arabella, however, remained blissfully unaware of the interest her presence had aroused.

'I've only known Philippe a few months,' she said. 'I was on the shortlist for the executive director's position. Fortunately, he chose me. But you have known him much longer, haven't you, Adam? You must find all of this quite unbelievable.'

She gestured to the ostentatious room in which they were lunching. The crystal chandelier blazed overhead. The table was set with rarely used Victorian-era silverware. They were eating their lunch from fine Limoges porcelain and drinking from Wedgwood glassware ordered especially by Philippe's grandfather. Despite Philippe's protestations the meal should be simple and casual, Clarence had insisted he should delight his friends with the full display.

'I do find it unbelievable. He was always very reluctant to speak about his early life, except the army. It's hard to believe he has gone on to inherit all this. I remember him being embarrassed at being illegitimate.'

And then he noticed the slight dip in her previously cheerful mood and he cursed himself. Why had he used the word *illegitimate*? She must know about his mistress and her condition. Surely, he's been honest with her. Perhaps Philippe isn't her lover after all. Perhaps Jennifer got it wrong. And then he noticed the sapphire and diamond bracelet on her wrist. Sapphires to match her eyes. He certainly indulges his women. But then he looked at Arabella. Intelligent. Charming. Stunning. She deserves every gift he gives her. Because he won't ever be able to give her the one thing he was sure she would want. A wedding ring.

Through the haze of his thoughts, he heard her speaking again.

'Yes, he is reluctant to speak about his private life,' she agreed, as if to emphasise she knew no more than they did about him. 'He is a very good friend though. I think you know what my ex-husband did to me. Philippe has hired security for my house just in case he decides to seek me out. It makes me feel much safer.'

'That's good,' he agreed. 'That's very good of him.'

He had been shocked reading the medical report of her injuries. He was even more shocked now he had met her. How could a man do that to her? A man should be her slave, he thought. Worshipping her and wanting to please her. Wanting to make her happy. He hoped she was finding happiness with Philippe. He wondered what would happen when he was free to marry. Was he going to have a wife in Sydney and a mistress in Long Island? Would he treat his new marriage with such contempt?

Almost everyone seated around the table was asking themselves the same question. Those who knew Jennifer well had whispered the question to her. Is he having an affair with Arabella?

From the far end of the table, Walter saw the envious looks of the men who cast surreptitious glances at Arabella. And then at Philippe. And he noticed the envious glances of the women too but their envy centred on the exquisite jewellery she wore, everyone assuming the exquisite bracelet and matching earrings to be a gift from Philippe.

Later, as they all sat in the drawing room drinking coffee, Philippe found himself immersed once again in the world he missed. The world of medicine. He was listening with interest to an animated discussion of some of the latest surgical techniques that were being adopted at St Luke's. He was surprised to find he could still make a meaningful contribution to the discussion.

Walter, with Arabella by his side, offered to guide several of the female guests around the reception rooms to show them some of the priceless pieces in the Cox collection.

'A beautiful dagger, Walter,' Maria Langton said, admiring its intricately carved handle. 'Is it Chinese? Or Mongolian perhaps?'

As she put her hand out to pick it up, Walter put his hand on hers to stop her.

'It's bad luck to pick that up, Maria,' he said.

She withdrew her hand quickly.

'I'm sorry,' she said. 'It's obviously got some bad family history.'

He smiled but said nothing further. How could he explain he believed it brought bad luck on those who touched it when, in fact, it was his father who had picked it up with the intention of killing his own father.

It was hardly a story he was going to repeat. And shortly afterwards, his father had suffered the terrible stroke that would eventually lead to his early death. He regarded the dagger as cursed from that day. He was surprised it hadn't been locked away somewhere. He looked around for Clarence.

'I think we should find a more secure place for that, don't you, Clarence?'

His request was met with an almost imperceptible nod of the head.

Walter, his arm loosely around Arabella's waist, guided the rest of the group towards the paintings that Philippe had admired so much on his first visit to Eastbury Hall.

'John Singer Sargent portraits. How fabulous. I've never seen any of his work in a private collection before.'

Maria Langton stood transfixed before the portraits of Philippe's grandparents.

'The Met has his iconic Madame X portrait. The one that caused so much stir in Paris when he first exhibited it.'

Clarence was standing at the back of the group and listening closely. An idea was forming in his head. The Cox collection was in desperate need of cataloguing. Would she be an obvious candidate? He made a mental note to raise it with Philippe at the first opportunity.

And then he smiled to himself as he watched Walter guide Arabella further towards the long gallery beyond the dining room to parts of the house she had not seen before.

If he gets any more familiar with her, he'll be in danger of getting his face slapped, Clarence thought, as he watched them together. But in some ways, he was relieved to see Arabella enjoying Walter's company. And surprised too. Perhaps she's trying to deflect suspicion away from her interest in Philippe in front of his friends? Perhaps she's concerned for her reputation. In the end, he settled on this explanation as he returned to the task of pouring coffee.

Chapter 15

Australia

AS NEW YORKERS THREW open their apartment windows seeking relief from the summer heat, Sydneysiders sheltered under umbrellas, scarcely looking up or looking at one another as they navigated the windy, rain-soaked streets of the city. The harbour, a glorious, picturesque expanse of water on a bright summer's day, huddled under a blanket of thick grey clouds.

'Sydney in the depths of winter. I hate it,' Karen grumbled as she warmed her feet in front of a small heater hidden away under her desk.

Bianca, sitting opposite her, simply shrugged her shoulders. A few more weeks and the worst of the winter would be over for another year. They were thinking about summer anyway, not winter. Designs still had to be finalised for their second summer range. There was a lot to do and Karen was doing less and less. But she understood why.

'How are you feeling today?' she asked. 'Is the baby behaving?'

She watched with only minor interest as Karen opened the latest report from their New York agent, who had been appointed to free

Karen from the necessity of travel. They had already been reassured the department stores were happy with the sales. Not ecstatic. But happy enough to commission a winter range and a summer range for the following year.

'I should have been in New York this week,' she complained.

'Except Philippe put his foot down, didn't he? He doesn't want you travelling in your condition.'

She gestured as if to say *why does he interfere?* But she knew he had her best interests at heart.

'So my blood pressure was up. If he was here taking care of me, my blood pressure wouldn't be up,' she sighed.

Bianca refrained from pointing out the obvious. It was Karen who had decided to get pregnant. And he had warned her he would be away from Sydney for months. But she had conveniently forgotten all of this. Bianca wondered at times if he had ever seriously considered divorcing his wife for Karen. He had only done it finally when she had revealed her pregnancy. Or, rather, his wife had made the move. She wondered how far the divorce had progressed. It was a topic she couldn't raise with Karen.

She sat back looking at Karen who was taking her time reading the sales reports. Bianca knew that was Karen's real value to the business, successfully applying the lessons she had learnt from her father to their business. Bianca was grateful. More than grateful. She wanted to concentrate on design, not financial accounts and sales reports.

Karen was about to put the reports away and then she noticed a newspaper clipping float out of the envelope. It had a short note attached to it. *We thought you might be interested in this*, it said. She expected it to be a promotional clipping. Perhaps their clothes had been included in a department store advertisement. And then she read the paragraph and looked at the picture, which she studied intently.

'Bastard!'

She yelled the word again, this time more loudly, as if once was not enough. Her explosion of irritation reverberated around the office. Heads were raised from worktables. Staff members looked from one to another, their eyebrows slightly raised, but saying nothing, hoping by keeping silent they might hear the reason for Karen's outburst.

Everyone knew her story. Unmarried. Very pregnant with no immediate prospect of a wedding ring. Some felt sorry for her. On the wrong end of the scandal, they whispered. He's treated her appallingly was a common refrain. If he was in love with her, he'd be here with her.

That was the verdict of the hopeless romantics among the women. But the consensus settled on his wealth. He'll pay her off rather than marry her. He's probably already got himself a new lady in New York. Knowing heads nodded as they dissected the single word Karen had yelled. Definitely two-timing her.

Bianca almost wrenched the newspaper cutting from her hand and read it. What could she say? It's nothing, just a picture of him with his employee. But her first instinct had been the same as Karen's. She had to find a way to reassure her friend.

'There's probably nothing in it at all,' Bianca said, in a calm soothing voice.

'You think? Nothing in it. Are you blind?'

She almost spat the words back at Bianca and then she stood up suddenly.

'Where are you going, Karen? Let's go and have a coffee and talk about this.'

But she shook her head.

'I'm going to see Pippa at her office,' she said, as if it was the obvious course of action. She was suddenly desperate to speak to someone who knew Arabella Courtenay.

Bianca could think of no way to dissuade her. Should she forewarn Pippa? She was unsure. How would Pippa feel about commenting on her father's behaviour? She couldn't imagine her being happy about it.

'At least take an umbrella,' Bianca said, pressing one into her hand. 'And take care you don't slip. The pavement is wet outside the office. And don't drive yourself. You should be able to get a taxi in Foveaux Street.'

'I will,' she promised as she stepped into the ancient lift. They had never taken up Philippe's offer to buy them new premises. She wondered if the offer still stood. And the other offer he had made her? She ran her hand over her expanding belly.

'Sorry, little one,' she whispered. 'It looks like you might have to manage without a daddy.'

It's the type of day I don't mind being office bound, Joel thought, as he sat back in his chair, feet up on his desk. He had a view of the rain spattered streets from his office window. If he stood right at the window, he had a glimpse of the grey misty harbour too.

One pile of documents on his desk were the submissions for research grants he had already read and commented on. The smaller pile still awaited his attention. He was surprised at how poorly some of the submissions had put their case for funding. It was his job to prepare recommendations for the board to consider at their next meeting. It came as no surprise to Joel that Pippa's mother had, in the end, declined the invitation to sit on the board. He had met her only once and that had been a very brief encounter. He liked Philippe but he couldn't help wondering how he had let himself be seduced away from a woman as lovely as Julia Duval. He guessed there had been many times when Pippa had asked herself the same question.

He was deeply immersed in these thoughts as Josie Maclean, their newly appointed secretary, put her head around his office door.

'Miss Clarke to see you, Dr Tynan,' she said, in a startled voice.

Joel was startled too. He had not met Karen Clarke. What he

knew of her had been gleaned in small scraps of information from Walter and from Pippa, who had chosen to stay home rather than brave the awful weather.

He stood as Karen entered his office. She peeled off her wet coat and ruffled her long auburn hair, tiny droplets of water landing on his desk. Immediately, Joel's eyes were drawn to her figure. He had delivered many babies in his former post. Seven months along, he thought. Or close to it. And then his eyes moved from her expanding stomach to the long auburn hair and the alabaster skin Walter had described. Despite her pregnancy, he knew immediately what had attracted Philippe. Even in her rain-soaked clothes, he could see she was beautiful. He envied Philippe in that moment. Envied the pleasure he'd had as her lover. But what was she doing here?

She sat down, clearly relieved to find someone in the office to talk to about Philippe.

'You know who I am, don't you?'

He smiled.

'I know, Miss Clarke. Of course, I know.'

She managed a smile at his formality.

'Please call me Karen,' she insisted.

And then she pulled the newspaper cutting from her handbag.

'You no doubt know who this is because Philippe told me you went across there with Pippa at the end of May.'

He glanced at the clipping.

'Yes, I know Arabella. She's the executive director of the Foundation. Philippe appointed her some months back.'

He tried to keep his voice even, being careful not to infer anything with his words. She was watching him intently.

'You might tell me I'm wrong, Joel,' she said, 'but this picture suggests to me that Philippe is involved with her. Am I right?'

He was completely taken aback by the question. He sighed. Why did they allow themselves to be photographed in that way? Indiscreet hardly covered it, he thought.

'Where did you get this clipping, if I may ask?'

He was trying to buy time, trying to think how to frame his answer.

'From our New York agent,' she said, without elaboration. 'You haven't answered my question.'

He gestured helplessly, as if to say, *why ask me, I don't know.*

'I have no idea, Karen,' he said. 'I only know Arabella in a professional context.'

And then he realised his mistake. He should have denied it, called her suspicions silly or unfounded or ridiculous. Any number of words came to him too late.

'Nice try, Joel,' she said with a disappointed smile.

He shrugged. Saying anything further would only make matters worse.

'I think he's sleeping with her. And you do too,' she said, challenging his answer. 'I can see it in your eyes. Deny it all you like but I think the truth is as obvious as this picture.'

He didn't know what to say. He walked around the desk and put his arm around her. He could feel the dampness of her dress where her coat and umbrella had failed to keep out the rain. Her hair too was still slightly damp.

'I don't think you should be jumping to conclusions,' he said, in one final attempt to reassure her. 'Arabella is a very friendly and attractive young woman. I won't deny that. She's used to men taking notice of her. I've seen it with my own eyes. But she doesn't take much notice of it. You'd understand that, surely. A beautiful woman like you. You would turn heads every time you walk into a room.'

She smiled at his flattery. He lacked Philippe's sophistication but he was charming nevertheless.

She was about to speak and then she paused, suddenly clutching her stomach as a sharp pain tore at her insides. Joel knelt beside her. Could this be the start of her labour? He didn't think so but he had to be sure.

'How far along are you?' he asked, trying to keep the anxiety from his voice.

'Six months,' she said, between rapid breaths.

But he shook his head.

'I think you're much further along than that, in my opinion. Is it possible you conceived earlier than you thought?'

It was a delicate question. He had no idea when she and Philippe had become lovers but he realised then it must have been well before he separated from his wife.

She nodded but there were no details forthcoming. He began to try to monitor the intermittent pains. Was she going into early labour or was it a false labour, which is what he suspected? He had seen that happen often enough, women arriving at the clinic expecting to deliver their babies only to be told it wasn't their time.

'Stand up,' he said quietly. 'I think this is a false alarm. The pains could ease if you change position.'

He held out his arm and she lent on him as he walked her through their small office.

'Are you still living alone?'

Pippa had told him previously she was continuing to live in her own apartment, not sharing the harbourside house with Pippa.

She nodded. She hadn't wanted to move out of her apartment. It was home. She was comfortable there. But it worried him she lived alone. And then he remembered her uncle. He had met Robert Clarke at the inaugural board meeting. He sat her down in a comfortable chair in the reception area and headed back to his office.

Within minutes, he was back talking to her gently and checking on her vital signs. The elevated blood pressure worried him.

'Your uncle is coming to pick you up,' he said.

She tried to argue with him but he shook his head.

'No argument,' he said gently. 'You need looking after.'

'He'll fuss,' she moaned.

'Someone has to fuss over you,' he said and then he wished he hadn't. It sounded like veiled criticism of Philippe. She pulled a face. He knew what she was thinking.

'You're a lot closer to delivering this baby than you think. It's better to have someone available to take you to the hospital at three o'clock in the morning when it all happens,' he said, trying to reassure her. 'Babies keep unsociable hours sometimes when they want to be born.'

She held his hand tight as a new wave of pain hit her. She no longer had the inclination to argue with him.

He sat alongside her for some time, regaling her with stories of his time in Africa. Trying to get her to relax. He showed her the scar on the side of his face and told the story of how it had happened. She laughed at his description of his final argument with his wife. It hadn't been funny at the time, he thought, but in recounting the story he could see the humour in it.

And then Robert Clarke strode through the door, hardly stopping to greet Joel, his eyes focused instead on his niece.

'Blood pressure's elevated,' Joel said quietly. 'She needs rest. The pregnancy is much further along than she thinks, in my opinion. She experienced some false labour pains, I believe.'

Robert Clarke nodded. He hadn't seen his niece for several weeks. Looking at her now, he was inclined to agree with Joel.

'Could she have conceived earlier than she believes?'

Like Joel, he wasn't certain when she and Philippe had become lovers but then he remembered their Christmas Eve drinks of the year before. The affair was certainly going then. And then he noticed the slight nod of Joel's head.

'She says it's possible. I'd say this baby was conceived at least a month earlier than she's calculated.'

Joel turned to help Karen to her feet but Robert Clarke put his hand on Joel's arm.

'What was she doing here?'

Joel turned his back so Karen could not see what he was doing.

He pulled the newspaper clipping from his pocket.

'Read this. She was very upset.'

Robert Clarke fumbled in his pocket for his reading glasses. And then he read the piece quickly shaking his head as he did so. He understood why Karen had been upset.

'The bastard. Do you know this woman? Is he sleeping with her?'

For the second time that day, Joel wished Pippa had been there to answer for her father. It wasn't his place to comment on his boss's private life.

'I have no idea,' Joel lied unconvincingly. 'Absolutely no idea. I've only met Arabella briefly. She's very pretty and she turns heads. But I have no idea if Philippe is interested in her in that way. No idea at all.'

Just as Karen had done earlier, Robert Clarke looked at Joel and shook his head.

'I admire your loyalty, Joel. It does you credit. But I think that picture tells me everything I need to know. How did Karen get hold of it?'

'With a report from their New York agents apparently.'

'Some friends they'd be,' Robert muttered as he turned back to Karen and helped her to her feet.

'Can I come and check up on Karen in the next day or two?'

'Please do, Joel. You'd be most welcome. And thank you for taking care of her and for calling me. It was the right thing to do.'

He nodded knowing he had really done little to deserve Robert Clarke's thanks. Were they all reading too much into a single picture? He didn't know but he remembered how Arabella had flirted with Philippe. He remembered Walter pointing out how she only had eyes for Philippe. How many men would turn her down if she made her interest clear, he wondered? He thought about it for a while. The answer he came up with was *none at all*.

As night fell over the city, the rain eased. Joel looked up at the sky as he locked his car and headed towards the front door of the large house of which Pippa was the sole occupant. He noticed the clouds clearing quickly which meant they were in for a clear bone-chilling night. Winter was not his favourite time of the year. He pressed the intercom and heard the click as the front door opened. The warm air of the fully heated house enveloped him as he walked through the hallway to be greeted by Pippa. She held out a glass of red wine to him which he accepted gratefully.

'I'm cooking my pasta special,' she said, leading the way to the kitchen. 'Come and tell me everything while I cook.'

He noticed how much more relaxed she was at home, her blond hair cascading around her shoulders. She was simply dressed in jeans and a light jumper.

'So you met Karen today?'

He smiled to himself at what had been left unsaid in that one simple question.

'I did, Pippa.'

What could he say? *She's stunning*. But he dismissed the idea as soon as it occurred to him. Not the right thing to say to Pippa at all.

'And you say she's further along with the pregnancy than we all thought?'

He nodded.

'At least a month further along I would think.'

Pippa laughed mirthlessly.

'I know when the baby was conceived,' she said, smiling at Joel's look of amazement. 'My mother and I went to a family gathering down at Bowral to celebrate my cousin's engagement just after Christmas. My father pleaded work and only came for the one night. I can tell you now where he spent the rest of the nights. Tucked up in Karen's bed.'

He heard the bitterness in her voice.

'You sound very sure about this?'

'Of course, I'm sure,' she retorted. 'They'd already been lovers for months before that.'

'This must be difficult for you, Pippa,' he said.

He had been sitting at the breakfast bar chatting and watching her cook. Then he noticed the tears begin to roll down her cheeks. She wiped her cheeks with the back of her hand. He got up and walked around to stand beside her, putting his arm around her shoulders, trying to comfort her.

'I should be over it now,' she said, shaking her head and berating herself, 'but if she hadn't got pregnant, he might have gone back to my mother. Now he feels he has to marry Karen but the marriage won't last.'

He didn't know what to say.

'I'm sorry, Joel,' she said. 'You shouldn't be involved in all this. I take it you want me to call him and tell him about Karen.'

He nodded.

'I think it would be better coming from you. I really want to stay out of it if I can.'

'Wise choice,' she said, turning back to the stove top to stir the pasta sauce. 'You haven't told me though why she came to the office.'

He pulled the crumpled newspaper clipping out of his pocket.

'The fashion agent from New York sent this to her apparently.'

He watched Pippa closely as she read the short paragraph and looked at the picture.

'I was afraid of that happening. It's probably just a fling. Karen is going to give him grief over it. Serves him right really.'

'The question is, Pippa, should we tell him she's seen that?'

She shrugged.

'He'll ask why she came to our office, I guess. That would be the only reason to tell him she's seen the clipping.'

'It's agreed then. You will call him?'

She nodded. She agreed because she didn't think it was fair for Joel to be dragged into the mess her father's private life had become.

Later, after he helped her clear away their plates from dinner, they sat together on the sofa listening to music and sipping wine.

'Your father's choice in music?'

She nodded.

'He's always loved jazz. He has an extraordinary collection yet he doesn't get to spend much time here to listen to it.'

He looked around him. It was a luxurious house. He wouldn't have used the word *home* though. It lacked the warmth of a house that truly was a home. And the people.

'It's a big house to be in all by yourself,' he said. 'I thought you might opt for your own apartment.'

'I will if Karen moves in here. I think I'd be surplus to requirements, don't you?'

He put his arm around her then and drew her closer to him.

'That's a sad way to see yourself, Pippa,' he said softly.

It was as if the painful episodes of her life had begun to haunt her again. He had heard about her early life on the long plane flights they had taken together. The shadow times of her life, he recalled thinking at the time. Being given away as a baby. Losing her adoptive parents. Finding her real parents. And then having their marriage break down so publicly. He understood then why she seemed so unwilling to let her guard down.

She settled herself comfortably next to him. He had half expected her to pull away from him. But he sensed she was lonely and in need of comfort. He could at least offer her that as a friend. They sat together in companionable silence listening to the music for some time until the record finished.

'Do you want me to put on more music?' he asked.

'Please,' she said, indicating the cupboard where the albums were neatly arranged by artist. His knowledge of jazz was limited but he recognised the name Miles Davis. She nodded approvingly.

'Can I ask a personal question,' he said tentatively, as he sat down alongside her again. 'Are you and Walter an item?'

Instead of answering, she countered with a question of her own.

'Are you and Virginia still an item?'

He laughed.

'Touché. But I asked first.'

She shrugged and curled her feet up on the sofa, leaning against his chest and enjoying the comfort of his physical presence.

'I like him but I couldn't see a future with him. Besides it would be geographically complicated.'

'Meaning that you don't fancy spending the rest of your life in America with the odd trip back home?'

'Pretty much,' she said. 'And I have to think about my mother. If she had still been married to my father, things might have worked out. Besides, all my mother's family are here in Australia. Living up north. I love to visit them. My uncles and my cousins. I prefer Sydney anyway, except when it's cold. And now it's your turn to answer.'

'I think I would describe my encounter with Virginia as a moment of madness really,' he said.

'Brought on by the intoxicating mix of a willing young woman and the soothing sound of the waves breaking gently on the beach.'

He realised she was making fun of him but he accepted her teasing with good grace.

'Pretty much the way it was,' he said, echoing her words. 'Anyway, I've written back to her in the past few days. A friendly letter but not encouraging.'

'You're a coward, Joel Tynan. Tell the truth. You just don't want Barbara Cox as a mother-in-law.'

He laughed. He couldn't think of a less suitable wife for himself. A girl younger by more than a decade. And a rich girl used to a rich girl's life. It wouldn't last six months.

'This is nice,' he said, ignoring her jibe, 'being here with you like this. It feels good.'

He bent his head and kissed the side of her cheek. He expected her to sit upright and push him away, except she didn't. Instead, she turned her head to look at him.

'This is probably not a good idea,' she murmured.

'No, it isn't,' he agreed as his free hand began to explore beneath her jumper, 'but then sometimes bad ideas turn into good ideas.'

'My bedroom has a wonderful harbour view,' she said, standing and holding out her hands to him. 'You should come up and see it.'

'I'd love to,' he said.

They walked up the stairs together. In her bedroom, all thoughts of the view were forgotten as he made love to her for the very first time. He had never thought it possible or even likely she would be attracted to him.

Later, as she lay in his arms, he wondered where it all might lead. But at that moment he was delighted to be with her, to be her friend, and to be her lover.

Chapter 16

Australia

For the final time that evening, Robert Clarke sat on the bed now occupied by his niece, having checked her blood pressure for the third time, satisfied that it had settled to a much more acceptable reading. The pains had been false labour pains, just as Joel Tynan had predicted. But he was cautious, nonetheless. She would celebrate her thirty-ninth birthday soon. She was an older first time mother and that fact made him even more cautious.

'Bianca called,' he said. 'I told her you were in good hands. She was relieved.'

She smiled. Her uncle was fussing just as she predicted but deep down, she was pleased to have someone concerned about her.

'I've called your father too. I told him you'll stay here until you have the baby. If you're up to it tomorrow, Anita can help you get some clothes from your place. She's off tomorrow.'

She closed her eyes then. She was tired.

'Sleep now,' he said as he pulled the blankets around her, 'but call out if you need help. We'll take care of you.'

She smiled her thanks. He had always been good to her, never criticising her for her behaviour. Or for the choice she had made in being with Philippe.

As he turned out the light and shut the door behind him, he did not head along the hallway to his bedroom. Instead, he headed to his study. He checked his watch. Ten-thirty. He calculated the time difference. Early morning in New York. He picked up the telephone to make a call he wished he didn't have to make.

America

Clarence paused in the act of pouring Philippe a second cup of coffee as he sat alone at the breakfast table.

'Something the matter, Dr Duval?' he asked. 'Was there bad news in the telephone call this morning?'

Philippe shook his head.

'Not bad news exactly, Clarence. That was Karen's uncle. She's had an episode of what we call false labour pains. And she has elevated blood pressure. She's staying with her uncle now until the baby is born.'

'It's still a few months until the baby is due, I believe,' Clarence said, seeking confirmation.

'Actually, it's sooner than that, Clarence,' he said. 'It seems she mistook the date of conception.'

'Does that mean you'll be bringing forward your trip to Sydney?'

'It does, Clarence. I'll travel at the end of next week most likely. We're due to have a meeting of the Sydney board around then, so that should work in well.'

'Serious faces this morning?' Walter looked from one to the other as he strode into the room. 'Not bad news I hope.'

Philippe shook his head.

'Karen's uncle called me this morning. She had a scare with her pregnancy, that's all. Some quite severe false labour pains. That's all.'

'Her uncle, the doctor? She's in good hands then. I hope she's OK?'

He waited for Philippe's nod of confirmation.

'Any chance of breakfast, Clarence? Philippe and I are going to look at some potential real estate investments this morning.'

It was an aspect of the family's portfolio that Walter was taking a serious interest in. He liked what he called the bricks and mortar part of investing. Something he could see. Something he could touch. He hoped, as Philippe's confidence in him grew, he would be prepared to fund their own property developments.

As they watched Clarence head out the door to organise their breakfasts, Walter turned to face Philippe.

'You seem distracted,' he said. 'There was more to that phone call than you've let on, wasn't there?'

Philippe sighed. Was Walter getting to know him too well?

'Karen's uncle has never been short of an opinion where my private life is concerned,' he said quietly. 'Apparently someone at the fashion agents helpfully slipped in a newspaper clipping with the latest report of the department store sales they sent to Karen. I had to listen to yet another brutal assessment of my character from Robert.'

'You mean she was sent the picture of you with Arabella? That was a bit of bad luck. It could certainly be misinterpreted.'

Philippe smiled bleakly.

'That's one way of seeing it,' he said. 'And apparently Karen drew the very same conclusions on seeing it that others have.'

'Others?'

'Her husband for one.'

'How do you know this? Did he confront you? Is that why you're helping with her divorce? Going to such lengths to prove his mistreatment of her. Because otherwise he's looking for other evidence?'

He almost said other evidence involving you but he stopped short. Suspicions were all very well but he pulled back from accusing Philippe of having an affair with her.

'Felix Latimore is a nasty piece of business. He pitched an investment opportunity to me recently. I didn't know who he was until after the meeting but apparently he's been at some of the same functions Arabella and I have attended together but she didn't tell me. My presence has, in some ways, kept her from awkward encounters with him.'

'And if you're not here in the future to go with her to these gala events she's so keen on?'

'Maybe it would be a good idea if you went with her, Walter. She's wonderful company. You'd enjoy it.'

'Happy to do so,' he said, his mood improving at the prospect of a legitimate reason to be Arabella's partner. 'And Karen's uncle. What did you say to him?'

'Denied it, of course. What else would I do?'

'Did he believe you?'

Philippe smiled to himself at Walter's earnestness.

'I hope so. I didn't want Karen being upset.'

'And Arabella? Are you going to tell her?'

'No, of course not. There's no reason to discuss it with her.'

'But she knows about your situation with Karen?'

'We're friends, Walter. That's it. And, yes, of course she knows.'

Walter sat back in his chair then as Clarence placed his breakfast in front of him. For some minutes, he attacked the meal in silence.

Philippe got up and threw his napkin on the table.

'I'll be downstairs in ten minutes, Walter,' he said. 'I'm interested to see what you have lined up for us. And remember, not a word to anyone about what we discussed this morning. That conversation is closed.'

Walter looked at Clarence as Philippe headed back to his bedroom. Clarence simply shrugged his shoulders. What his boss did was not something he was ever going to comment on but he saw the angry look in Walter's eyes.

'He's just using her, Clarence. Arabella imagines she's in love with him. And probably imagines that he's in love with her. But he's going to leave her devastated.'

Clarence said nothing, simply smiling to himself as he busied himself clearing away the breakfast plates. He was sure he knew the reason for Walter's outrage. It can be summed up in one word, he thought. Jealousy. But would Walter offer her more than Philippe could? Would he be prepared to offer her marriage?

Clarence began to wonder what the future would hold. For Philippe. For Karen. For Walter. And for Arabella. Was she the innocent in the middle of it? Only to be used and discarded when it suited the men she chose? Or was she a manipulative and cunning woman out for what she could get, using her charm and beauty to her best advantage? He hadn't yet decided which role she would ultimately fulfil.

But he disagreed with Walter's assessment of Philippe's interest in her. He was sure there was nothing insincere about it. He had seen the way he looked at her. He rather suspected it might be Philippe who would end up being disappointed.

It had been another hot day. Too hot really for the hours they had spent negotiating the baking hot streets of Manhattan and the nearby boroughs.

As the heat finally lost its grip on the day, Walter sat alone in Philippe's study, glancing through the information he had gathered on the real estate deals being proposed to them. He sipped the beer Clarence had just poured for him as he read through the information again.

'How's Karen?' he asked as Philippe reappeared. 'I take it you managed to get through to her.'

'She's fine, thanks, Walter.'

'That's it, she's fine?'

'Yes, she's well. She's taking it easy. The entire household is running after her, she says.'

'Did she give you a piece of her mind over the picture in the newspaper?'

He knew Walter wouldn't be able to resist asking the question. He had been right.

'I made light of it, Walter,' he said. 'I told her she was jumping at shadows. I reminded her that when I first knew her, I often acted as her escort to parties. Just as her friend but people jumped to conclusions about our relationship then.'

'And she believed you?'

'I think so. I certainly hope so. She has nothing to worry about in that regard.'

Did Philippe always have the ability to sweet talk the women in his life, he wondered?

And then, just as it had with Clarence, the realisation hit him. Walter is jealous, he thought. Jealous of my friendship with Arabella.

'What's your opinion of the opportunities we saw today, Walter? Which one is going to be the best investment for the Cox family?'

'Honestly, I think the older building in Manhattan is the best prospect. It's on a prime corner site. In ten years' time we could look at redeveloping it. If the building next door should come up for sale, which it very well might, we should buy that too.'

Philippe nodded. He had quickly come to the same conclusion himself.

'Over to you now, Walter, to do the negotiations. But your grandfather would have said it was overpriced so I think we should look to get a bit knocked off the purchase price, don't you?'

'You want me to handle it?'

'I do, Walter. You said the real estate portfolio was your special interest. I'm happy for you to make the running. But remember we'll always spread the risk. No single investment should ever comprise more than ten per cent of the total value of our investments. Anyway, we should be borrowing to buy it to allow us to leverage other opportunities.'

'Right, I'll get on to it tomorrow,' Walter said, surprised he didn't have to make the case to back his choice.

'That's good, now let's go and eat or Clarence will be annoyed with us for spoiling the dinner. And that would never do,' Philippe said with a smile. 'That's certainly not something I could deal with tonight.'

'How's the weather over there?'

Philippe was delighted to hear his daughter's voice on the other end of the phone. He missed her. There were many times he wished she would spend more time with him at Eastbury Hall. He was fully aware the past few months had created a tension in their relationship that hadn't quite eased. He hoped they would get beyond that but he continued to worry she might never accept Karen as his wife. The jury is still out on that, he decided.

'It's hot and uncomfortable,' he replied. 'Like Sydney in January. I suppose you're going to tell me it's unbearably cold in Sydney?'

'Cold. And wet. Until yesterday. Now it's just cold.'

'A particular reason for the call?' he asked. He had his suspicions but he would wait for her to tell him.

'It's Karen. She came to the office yesterday. She was pretty upset according to Joel.'

'You didn't see her?'

'No, the weather was wild. I decided the office could do without me for a day. Joel dropped in last night to tell me.'

'I know what happened,' he said, pre-empting a potentially long explanation. 'And I know Joel called her uncle and that she had some false labour pains. I've spoken to her already. She's fine.'

'Then you know she was angry with you about the newspaper photograph of you and Arabella together.'

'I know,' he said, hoping to cut that particular discussion short. 'I explained it all to her. That she has nothing to worry about.'

'And you are still going to marry her? There's a lot of doubt in her family that it will ever happen.'

He smiled to himself at the irony of Pippa taking up the cause for Karen when she had tried so hard to get him to end the affair.

'Well, your mother has agreed to the settlement I've offered her. It's all about to be signed off. And the application for our divorce is about to be filed to the court. It just depends on how long that takes but the Sydney law firm is well placed. Hopefully they can exert a bit of pressure. How is your mother by the way?'

'She's fine. She's renting an apartment in Sydney for the time being, until she decides what she wants to do. We're all due down in Bowral very soon for Paul and Nancy's wedding.'

'Ah, Bowral,' he said, not needing to say more. It had been where everything had begun to unravel between him and Julia. But the past was the past. He had lamented the loss of his marriage but there had been no way to repair it. Not completely. Not when Karen became pregnant. And even if she had not been pregnant, had he deluded himself he could go back to Julia and be happy with her? For a long time, the answer to that question had eluded him. But not now. He knew his marriage to Julia belonged to his former life. He felt as if his life had been completely reset by his sudden wealth. He had a new life with new opportunities and possibilities. And he had changed too. And Karen? Perhaps she really belongs to my old life too, he mused.

'Ah, Bowral,' Pippa said, echoing his words. For her, the revelations from that weekend had been eye opening, catapulting her from a daughter who thought her family life was perfect to a bitter young woman disillusioned with love and marriage.

'I'm coming back to Sydney at the end of next week,' he said, trying to move the conversation along.

She noticed he didn't say home.

'We should plan the board meeting then to discuss the funding applications.'

'I think that's a good plan,' he said.

'How long will you stay?'

'Certainly, until the baby is born. Robert thinks it's a maximum of six weeks away.'

'And then?'

'Who knows? We'll see.'

'Do you want Karen to move in here when the baby is born? If so, I need to get myself a new place.'

She left unsaid the words she really wanted to say. *I don't want to play nursemaid to your mistress and your illegitimate child.*

'I think her parents are keen for her to live with them when she has the baby. I'm fine with that. That's what she told me on the phone. The nursery's already been decorated apparently.'

'Tell me, how is this marriage going to work? You want to live at Eastbury Hall. She wants to live in Sydney. Have you thought of that?'

He paused. It was a good question, one he couldn't answer.

'We'll find out in due course, won't we?'

'I guess so,' she said, wondering if that was really the way for him to plan his future married life.

'On another topic, I have to think about how the Cox estate is left after my death. I have a plan I need to tell you about.'

She noticed he didn't say *discuss*.

'If it's that you want to make Walter your principal heir, I'm fine with that,' she said. 'I'm assuming you won't leave your daughter penniless.'

But he caught the bitterness in her voice.

'Someone has to take on the task of managing the Cox legacy in the interests of all those who stand to benefit. Walter. You. Virginia.'

'And don't forget the new baby,' she said quickly.

'And the new baby of course,' he said.

He tried again.

'It makes sense, Pippa. Walter is here. The assets are all American based. And he is the eldest of his generation.'

'Of course it makes perfect sense,' she said as she hung up the phone.

She couldn't help but feel Walter had usurped her position. She envied him his growing closeness to her father. She hadn't even been offered the opportunity to work alongside him managing the family's wealth.

But that meant a life in America. She couldn't do that to her mother. And to her mother's family who had welcomed her so warmly. And to her half-brother John. The ties were too strong. Too deep now to turn her back on. Too important in her life. She had felt the warm embrace of the family at Prior Park and loved it. Loved being part of them. And her flirtation with Walter? A part of her past too now.

CHAPTER 17

Australia—August

'HOW'S KAREN? How's the baby?'

Pippa was looking out over the harbour, cup in hand, trying to pretend it was warm enough and calm enough to enjoy her morning coffee on the terrace. She did not look at her father when she asked the question but she had heard him slide the door onto the terrace. Would she even go and see Karen and the baby? She hadn't decided yet.

'The baby is well. And so is Karen,' he said, wondering exactly how much detail she really wanted to know.

'A long labour, was it?'

'Not overly long for a first baby although telling her that wasn't much comfort at the time.'

'Boy or girl?'

'A bouncing boy as I think you predicted. But not a redhead. He's dark haired, like me.'

'Have you agreed on a name yet?'

'Louis-Philippe Duval.'

'With a hyphen no doubt.'

He laughed.

'Yes, with a hyphen.'

'It's very French.'

'So is Philippe. I wanted to maintain the link to my French heritage.'

She pointed to the newspaper she had been trying unsuccessfully to read, the wind regularly ripping the broadsheet out of her hands.

'There'll be no birth notice though.'

She turned to look at her father. He looked tired. She remembered it was the way he used to look when he'd just completed a long and complex operation.

He shook his head.

'No, I'm afraid David Clarke is going to be denied the pleasure of gloating about his grandson. But he seems pleased. A bit put out that the child will have my name. Until I mentioned he'll also have part of my fortune. Without my name, that might be challenged.'

'Who by? Me? Walter? Virginia? I don't think so.'

'But he's not to know that, is he?'

She laughed then. It all seemed so surreal.

'Have you talked about the wedding?'

'Briefly. Hopefully in the first part of next year. Her parents want to host it at their house. Just a small wedding.'

'You know his birth date is very lucky in Chinese culture. The eighth of the eighth.'

'I didn't know that but I hope he has a fortunate life. I feel a bit old to be a real father to him.'

She wondered what sort of a father he would have been to her as a young child and he a much younger man. She remembered her adoptive father as a cold, distant man with little interest in her. Her adoptive mother she remembered with love and gratitude. And a deep sense of loss she could not share with anyone. They had loved one another unconditionally. Mother and daughter. She recalled how they had inhabited their own special world when she was small. Just the two of them. And her real mother? Bruised by everything surrounding her birth, she had tried hard to make up for the lost years. But it had never been quite the same. As if she always tried too hard to make amends, Pippa thought. Tried too hard to right the wrong she had done me.

'How long are you going to stay?' she asked.

There had been constant late night telephone calls. A growing list of things demanding his attention. A growing list of decisions only he could make, it seemed. Documents only he could sign.

'I'm off next week,' he said.

'Have you told Karen?'

'I did.'

'And her reaction?'

'A bit disappointed but she understands.'

'Have you bought her a gift to celebrate the birth?'

She was curious.

'I did actually. I had the diamond pendant I gave her last year remodelled to include both our initials. She loved the idea. The jeweller fussed over it. Fortunately, he was discreet enough not to enquire after your mother. He's obviously kept up with the gossip.'

She laughed then. She remembered the stunning pendant Karen had worn almost everywhere. It had been a talking point. And unbelievably indiscreet of her father. The gossip about his affair with Karen had then gone into overdrive. But perhaps that's what he'd intended all along, she thought. A subtle way to get it out in the open.

'Are you going to go and see your new brother?' he asked.

'Do you want me to?'

'Of course, I do. You're not a child, Pippa. You have to understand some relationships run their course.'

'You mean like your relationship with my mother?'

'Yes, of course I mean that. What did you think I meant?'

She shrugged. She wouldn't be drawn into answering.

'I'll go during visiting hours this afternoon. And I promise I'll buy a gift before I go.'

'Thanks. I'd appreciate it. So would Karen. Take Joel with you.'

She was unable to hide the look of surprise on her face.

'Did you think I didn't know?'

'Well, I'm not trying to advertise it,' she said. 'We're keeping it very low key.'

'And Walter? I thought you were keen on him?'

Again, she shrugged, as if his questions were unnecessary.

'I like him but the geography doesn't work. I prefer to live in Australia. He doesn't have a choice, does he? He's your understudy. He will take over from you some day. He has to live in America.'

'I'm relieved actually. I like him but he's very much the all-American boy. I don't think you would suit one another. And you're right. The geography would end up being a big issue.'

'Well, right now, after my cousin Paul's wedding fiasco, I don't think marriage is high on my list of priorities.'

She had given him a brief account of the events that had culminated in her cousin Paul Belleville's marriage not going ahead.

'Your friend Nancy must have been devastated. And her mother too.'

'They both are. My mother and I are going up north in a couple of weeks' time. Uncle Richard's marriage is apparently on very shaky ground from the fallout.'

'Paul's behaviour is not his fault surely?'

'Kate's son Tim doesn't quite see it like that. He hates Richard for taking his mother away and the way in which he did it. He's seeing in the son the same behaviour he witnessed in Richard. Wants his mother back at Berrima Park, apparently, minus her husband. And wishes his sister had never set eyes on Paul.'

'Oh, tricky situation. So you're going to meddle in someone else's private life instead of mine for a change.'

'I don't meddle in your private life. When have I ever meddled?' she retorted.

'Well, perhaps censured me would be a better way to describe it.'

'I'm done with censuring you,' she said quickly.

She was about to say you can sleep with whichever woman you want but she hesitated. She didn't want her relationship with her father to deteriorate further. For some reason, the tension between them had escalated during this latest visit. Was it her disappointment in him? The lingering disappointment of his failed marriage to her mother. Or the realisation he appeared capable of becoming involved with another woman when he was committed elsewhere. I have to stop judging him, she thought. Stop judging his behaviour.

'I'm pleased. I admit I haven't always made the best choices.'

'Meaning?'

'I'm not going to spell it out, Pippa.'

'And your future life with Karen? What plans have you made?'

He shook his head.

'Karen is focused on the baby right now, as she should be. Not on me. We can discuss our future when I know the divorce is close.'

'And until that time?'

'I'll be at Eastbury Hall most of the time, doing all those things my new life demands of me.'

'But not seeing your baby son?'

'I'll see him in a few months' time. I'll spend Christmas here. He'll be christened then. Now I'm off to call Clarence to tell him about the baby.'

And who's going to tell Arabella? The question formed in her mind but it remained unasked as she watched her father head towards the telephone to call Eastbury Hall with the news that a new heir to the Cox estate had been born.

Karen's hospital room resembles a florist shop. Or maybe a teddy bear shop. Those were Pippa's first thoughts as she entered the private suite at Crown Street Women's Hospital to meet her new half-brother for the first time. But first she kissed Karen on the cheek, said how well she looked and added her own bouquet and teddy bear to the display.

Behind her, Joel greeted the new mother warmly.

'See, I said you were much further advanced with your pregnancy than you thought,' he said, holding her hand and kissing her on the cheek.

She pulled a face.

'Well, he was early too don't forget. But I'm happy to get it over with if I'm honest, Joel,' she said. 'How women go through that time after time, I've no idea.'

'So, that's it then. No sister for Louis-Philippe?'

She smiled and shook her head.

'No. I think Philippe might spend all his time in America if there were more children,' she said. 'Besides, I'm too old now. Have you looked at him? He looks exactly like his father.'

They both dutifully peered into the cot alongside her bed. The baby was sleeping peacefully.

'I'm disappointed,' Pippa said lightly. 'I hoped he would be a ginger top.'

Karen pulled a face at the suggestion.

'No, please no. He's going to grow up to look exactly like his handsome father.'

And probably grow up in the image of his handsome father, Pippa thought. He'll grow up wealthy, privileged and entitled. When I'm middle-aged, she thought, I'll be watching him charm the women he wants. And censuring him like my father claims I censure him now.

She let the thought drift away. She wasn't her father's keeper. Nor her brother's if it came to that. Except she had been named as his guardian in relation to his share of the Cox wealth. Until he turns twenty-one, she'd been told. A responsibility she couldn't escape.

'My parents are hosting drinks to wet the baby's head next Friday afternoon at their house. You both must come.'

Pippa was about to roll out an excuse but Joel answered for them.

'We'd love to, Karen,' he said. 'Will Philippe still be here?'

She shook her head.

'No, he won't.'

She glanced at Pippa then.

'My parents feel it's easier to have their friends for a drink without Philippe in attendance,' she said. 'It makes it easier for them.'

'Which is exactly the reason I shouldn't go,' Pippa said.

But Karen reached out and grasped her hand.

'No, that's not what I meant, Pippa,' she said. 'You know that. I want you to get to know your little brother. I don't care about not being married to your father. It's only my mother who feels a bit strange about it. They'll be happy when we can be married and then she won't have to go into lengthy explanations.'

Pippa shrugged.

'She shouldn't try and go into explanations at all, really.'

'But she does, Pippa, and then gets herself tied in knots. Whereas my father is just delighted to have a grandson. He's already ordered him a miniature car like the one Prince Andrew was given. He's going to spoil him like crazy.'

'Lucky Louis,' Joel said with a laugh. He remembered the meagre collection of toys he'd had as a child. This baby is going to grow up surrounded by a level of privilege he'll take for granted, he thought.

'Say you'll both come. Please.'

Pippa relented.

'Yes, of course. Now, get some rest.'

As they turned to leave, the baby gave a whimper.

'The backdrop to her life for the next few years,' Pippa said quietly to Joel, who grinned and nodded.

'Except I bet she's already got a nanny lined up.'

Pippa laughed.

'Of course, she has. And my father's paying for it.'

'And a whole lot more besides I would imagine.'

'Serves him right. He's discovered there's a price to pay. In more ways than one.'

He wasn't quite sure what she meant so he let the remark go.

'Fancy an Italian dinner?'

'Sounds good,' he said. 'Let's go and we can talk about babies and stuff.'

She laughed at him in mock horror at the suggestion.

'Really? Do I look like the sort of girl who wants to talk about babies?'

'Actually, no you don't, which I'm very relieved about to tell you the truth.'

'Well, you can tell me over dinner why you're so relieved.'

He slid into the passenger seat alongside her. Was this the time for more revelations about his own life? Or should he just let the opportunity slide? He was in two minds. He had hoped never to revisit the most painful episode of his life. But something told him he could not keep it locked away forever. Not now. Not from Pippa. He let out a long quiet sigh as the story formed in his mind.

Pippa looked around her as they settled at a table in her favourite Italian restaurant.

'You look unhappy about something, Pippa. What's up?'

Joel had noticed the dip in her mood as soon as they walked into the restaurant.

'This is where we had our last dinner as a family. My father, my mother and I. Six months ago. He was twenty minutes late. We both knew where he had been.'

Joel didn't need to ask where he had been. He knew by looking at Pippa's face.

'We could go somewhere else,' he said, 'if this brings back bad memories.'

She shook her head slowly, her blonde hair drifting across her face.

'No, I need to forget about him. Or at least forget about what he's done to my mother. I actually feel sorry for Karen now.'

'Why? She doesn't look like a woman who wants you to feel sorry for her. She seems very confident in her relationship with your father, I would say.'

She shrugged and turned her attention to the menu.

'She wouldn't be confident if she knew the truth about Arabella.'

'Which is what exactly? Or is it just that you've taken the idle speculation to another level?'

'Walter all but confirmed it to me. I called him a few days ago.'

'And the evidence? I doubt he's caught Arabella upstairs in your father's bed.'

She laughed at the absurdity of such an idea.

'No, but my father's car is often left in the driveway late at night for Frederick to put away the next day. And she's been showing off new jewellery and a new car. Walter says she has unlimited accounts at some of the best fashion boutiques. He's seen the bills on my father's desk awaiting his approval.'

He let out a low whistle.

'There could be another explanation. It could simply be part of her employment package because she has to attend a lot of functions. Did you think of that possibility?'

Pippa shrugged her shoulders.

'Really, Joel? Is that likely?'

He nodded.

'She did say she had very generous allowances.'

She laughed, snorted almost.

'And the jewellery?'

It was his turn to shrug.

'Probably not,' he conceded.

'I think my father is relying on the fact that Karen won't want to travel for a few years until little Louis is manageable on a long flight.'

'And that could be a very long time. Kids and long haul flights are a terrible idea in my opinion.'

'Enough about my father,' she said, as she put her menu down on the table. 'Tell me why you're so relieved not to have to talk about babies with me? It was an unusual thing to say.'

He sat back in his chair, trying to remember the way he had rehearsed the story in his mind. Where to start? At the end? At the beginning? He opted for the end.

'I told you my wife Colette divorced me,' he said quietly. 'I've told you too about the final argument. But I didn't tell you what the argument was about. Not all of it anyway.'

'Was it something bad, Joel?'

'Not bad, Pippa. Devastating. We had a three-year-old daughter, Chloe. She was delightful.'

'What happened to her, Joel?'

'Nothing happened to her, Pippa. It's what I found out about her. I came home early one day, quite unexpectedly. We had our own quarters in the compound where aid agency workers lived. I walked in and found my wife's lover on the floor holding his arms out to my daughter and saying, *come to Papà, Chloe.*'

Pippa could think of nothing to say. She let him go on with the story at his own pace.

'I'd loved that child as mine for three years. My wife never said a thing to me. Her lover was a visiting eye surgeon who donated several weeks of his time a couple of times a year. I don't think Colette was quite sure who Chloe's father was. Not until Chloe got a little bit older and then it was clear. She looked nothing like me. There was very little of her mother in her features. She looked exactly like Marco Morselli who desperately wanted Colette to leave me and become his wife. He'd been asking her for years apparently. He redoubled his efforts when he discovered our daughter was his.'

Pippa reached across the table and put her hand on his. She wondered how he had managed to recover from such a loss.

'That must have been terrible for you,' she said.

The story had moved her to tears.

'It wasn't just me who suffered. My mother lost a granddaughter. When I arrived home, I discovered she'd thrown out all the photos of Chloe, of Colette and I together, of the three of us. All those photos she'd proudly shown friends and neighbours. All she was left with were my school photos, my graduation photo and the usual young doctor with stethoscope photo. It was so sad.'

'Had she met Chloe? Or was she a long distance grandmother?'

If she had met the child, it would have been so much worse for her, she thought.

'We had come home once when Chloe was eighteen months old. That's how I know how difficult it is to travel long distances with small children.'

She smiled sympathetically at him.

'That would have made it so much worse for her.'

'It did. I can tell you it did.'

'And has she been badgering you to get married again and have another child?'

He shook his head.

'She was so devastated by what happened she can't even bring herself to ask me if I have a girlfriend now.'

But Pippa understood. Joel was an only child. His mother was a widow. She had no doubt looked forward to Joel returning with his wife and child to live in Sydney. And then that dream had been snatched away from her in the most unexpected way.

'I'm pleased you told me. All this baby stuff with Karen has obviously brought back some sad memories for you.'

'It has,' he said, more perhaps than he was willing to acknowledge. 'But I must learn to live with it. Just like you have had to learn to live with your history.'

He turned his attention to the menu again, desperate for a distraction.

'You know this restaurant. I'll leave you to order,' he said.

She signalled for the waiter and ordered the pasta special of the day. And then she looked at the wine list. Without thinking, she ordered the same wine her mother had ordered six months earlier.

'You know you can talk to me anytime, Joel. Any time at all if it helps.'

'And you can talk to me anytime, Pippa. I know you've been through a lot, particularly this year.'

She nodded.

'Particularly this year, Joel. I don't know if my father remembers, but it's a year ago when his life changed. And he changed too. Inheriting the wealth he did changed him in ways I hadn't anticipated.'

'But he's still your father, Pippa. He's still your father. And I can see how much you mean to him. Remember that.'

'I'll certainly try to, Joel,' she said. 'I'll certainly try.'

She sat back for the waiter to pour a glass of wine for her.

'Now, let's enjoy the meal,' he said, 'and talk about anything but your father.'

She smiled.

'Agreed.'

CHAPTER 18

America

ON THE FIRST FULL day of his return, Philippe spent the morning locked in discussions with his lawyers, only this time they had resumed the habit of coming to Eastbury Hall. His right hand had begun to ache from the number of times he had to scrawl his signature at the bottom of documents, some of which he merely glanced at.

For Howard Davis, it seemed strange to be congratulating a man on the birth of his illegitimate son but he did it anyway. He hoped the stain of illegitimacy would be removed as soon as Philippe's divorce became final.

The most important matter for the morning was the signing of Philippe's will. The lawyer was pleased that, like his father before him, he had chosen one person to control the bulk of the family's wealth.

After much persuasion, Walter Cox had finally acquiesced to the proposal he become responsible for taking care of the family's wealth on Philippe's death.

Philippe signed the will, initialling each page, with a swift decisive signature. It was finally done when the witnesses, first Howard Davis and then his senior associate Charles Cameron, added their names and signatures.

Philippe sat back, satisfied with the morning's business.

'Walter says we raised a loan for the building purchase without trouble.'

'Of course, Dr Duval,' Davis said. 'Your liquidity and your assets meant we had financiers falling over themselves to offer you finance.'

'That's good. Walter seems to be enjoying this part of the work. One thing, though, I suppose he will need to make a will too. You will need to discuss it with him.'

But Howard Davis was already ahead of him there.

'We've discussed it and a will has been prepared.'

It was unthinkable but what if Walter met an untimely death, who was going to step up, he wondered? Pippa? Virginia? It had to be one or the other. Until the family added more heirs. It would be decades before Louis-Philippe was old enough to participate.

'He's proposed joint control between Pippa and Virginia,' Davis said, answering Philippe's unasked question.

Philippe thought about it for a few moments. There seemed to be no other option really.

'Has he signed that yet?'

'No, I said I would run it by you first.'

'I'm fine with it.'

'Then I will seek him out this morning if he is around. We have the document with us.'

'Good idea, Mr Davis.'

His relationship with the lawyer had never reached the informality of first names.

'And on the matter of your divorce, Dr Duval. Your Australian lawyers seem to be progressing it quite quickly.'

He shrugged. He already knew that.

'It's a well known firm with some leverage, I believe. My wife has agreed to the settlement. It's happening more quickly than I might have expected. I believe it will all be final by early next year.'

Part of him had been disappointed not to see Julia during his most recent trip. But then he reminded himself how awkward it would have been. There were still times when he missed her. Missed her companionship. Missed their shared history. He was brought back to the present by his lawyer's next question. Always questions, he thought. They always want decisions from me.

'And your next marriage? Shall we prepare a pre-nuptial agreement and send it out to your Australian lawyers?'

He thought about it for a short while.

'We probably should.'

Howard Davis was relieved. He had expected to have to mount an argument in favour of such an agreement.

'The standard arrangement?'

'Which is?'

'A cash settlement and to keep the marital home, meaning the home in Sydney you occupy together plus any gifts she receives during the marriage. And support for the child, of course.'

'How is the cash settlement calculated?'

'An advancing scale, depending on the years of the marriage. The more years, the more money.'

Would Karen sign such a document, he wondered?

'I guess it's an important part of protecting the family's wealth, Mr Davis, so please go ahead. I'll discuss it with Karen when I'm in Sydney next.'

'I take it the marriage will take place in Sydney, not here?'

'Yes, so we have to consider Australian law. But I don't think I need to tell you your business, Mr Davis. Have the Australian lawyers look over the agreement. But stipulate it must not be seen by Nicholas Gleeson in the firm.'

'Your wife's lawyer? Would he have an interest in it?'

'He's not only my wife's lawyer, Mr Davis, but David Clarke's lawyer, Karen's father. I don't want anyone looking at it before Karen. If she wants to consult Gleeson for advice, she's welcome to. But it won't be an ungenerous offer. I'd rather our marriage not descend into legal wrangling about a pre-nuptial agreement.'

'Understood, Dr Duval. Very wise.'

'Just one more thing before we finish up. Arabella Courtenay's divorce? Any progress?'

Davis nodded. He had known to expect the question.

'His lawyers have accepted the filing on the grounds of mistreatment without the medical evidence being included. We're keeping that in reserve in case they change their mind.'

'How quickly will it all be resolved?'

'Hopefully by the end of the year, I believe.'

'And she knows this?'

'Yes, she does. And is very relieved if I may say so. It wouldn't have happened without your intervention.'

Howard Davis was about to say something more and then thought better of it. Was it necessary to say he'd had to apply pressure not to have a counter filing of adultery against Arabella Courtenay, citing her employer Dr Philippe Duval? Still, he needed to warn his client. He chose his words carefully.

'There were mumblings from his lawyers about pressing for a divorce on the grounds of adultery. They claim they have proof.'

He paused, looking directly at Philippe to gauge his reaction.

'Really? They're bluffing, Mr Davis.'

'That's what I thought too.'

'I hope you told them that?'

'I did although not in quite those terms. I reminded them I have a medical report from a respected doctor at St Luke's detailing Miss Courtenay's injuries. That by itself is significant leverage and Felix Latimore's lawyers know it.'

'It is indeed.'

'The only possible problem with the report is that Dr Newman was your first wife. I hadn't known that until she told me. I don't think the other side know about the connection though.'

'Well, it's better we don't tell them, don't you think? Besides, Jennifer examined Arabella years before I met Arabella. Remember that.'

'Certainly. And there's nothing to link you and your first wife now. No children, for example.'

Howard Davis began to return the various papers to his briefcase.

'I think that's everything covered for today, Dr Duval.'

He motioned to his colleague Charles Cameron.

'I'm making sure Charles is fully across everything related to your legal matters. A precaution, Dr Duval. I'm not getting any younger. At some stage in the next few years, I will retire.'

Philippe nodded. It was a sensible approach.

'Good idea, Mr Davis. Very much in the same way I've made Walter my understudy.'

He looked at his watch. He had spent nearly three hours ensconced with the two men.

'Let's go and have some lunch,' he said. 'Clarence has organised lunch for us in the small dining room. I think Walter is joining us.'

Philippe led the way out of his study, pleased to be finished with business for the day. He had begun to feel tired. As frequently as he did it, he was still unaccustomed to the long haul travel between Sydney and New York.

By contrast, Walter, full of energy, took the main staircase two at a time, almost colliding with Philippe and Howard Davis at the top of the stairs. As he recovered his breath, he put his hand on Philippe's arm.

'A moment,' he said quietly.

Philippe hung back while Clarence ushered the two lawyers into the small dining room.

'Congratulations on the birth of your son by the way,' Walter said. 'I hope mother and baby are well.'

It was the first time he had seen Philippe since his return.

'Thanks, Walter. Yes, mother and baby are well. He was a few weeks premature but there doesn't seem to be any repercussions from that. Was there something else?'

'Only that Arabella was hoping to see you this afternoon after work.'

Philippe smiled at Walter having assumed the role of messenger.

'By the way I take it you told her about Karen having the baby as I asked.'

He nodded.

'I did.'

'Have you been acting as her escort in my absence?'

Walter smiled. It had not been a difficult task. He had done it willingly.

'Yes, of course,' he said, 'but let me tell you, she can hold her own. Her ex decided he would try and embarrass her in front of a group of people at the latest function we went to. He obviously could see you weren't around, so he walked right up to her and in a loud voice asked her if you had dumped her, if you had grown tired of her being your *expensive whore.*'

Philippe was furious. Angry with Felix Latimore. Angry even with himself for having exposed her to such slanderous gossip.

'What did you do, Walter?'

He was worried Walter might have set back her divorce negotiations.

'My first instinct was to hit him so hard he would never get up again. But Arabella stopped me. She turned to the wide-eyed group gathered around her and smiled sweetly. *It's amazing what stupid things men will say to cover their own shortcomings. Dr Duval and I have an excellent working relationship. Nothing more. Anything else is a figment of my ex-husband's overactive imagination.*'

He paused to take a breath.

'And then she paused and looked Latimore up and down before

delivering her coup de grâce. *It's OK, Felix. I got over the beatings you handed out to me. I'm fully recovered thanks for asking.* He was speechless. You could have heard a pin drop.'

Philippe threw back his head and laughed, delighted at her display of spirit. He guessed she had felt confident in calling out her ex-husband in public because she wasn't dealing with him on her own now. She had his backing. And the backing of a respected law firm.

'Shall I tell her it's OK for her to come up and see you later this afternoon?'

Philippe nodded.

'Of course,' he smiled. 'Now, let's go and have some lunch. No doubt the lawyers' clock is still ticking away. And they have your will to sign too.'

'Are you OK with what I proposed?'

'Yes, of course. It's just a precaution in case you come to grief within a short time of me. But time may change it all. When you get married and have the next Walter Cox perhaps.'

He laughed.

'I'm not going down that stupid naming path. My son is going to be Daniel or Paul or Michael. Anything but Walter.'

'You know Pippa's seeing Joel Tynan? Are you disappointed by that?'

Walter smiled. Did anything escape his notice? He doubted Pippa had told him.

'I like your daughter but we had a chat and we both agreed the geographic problem was insurmountable. Better to remain just good friends. I think she's realised the problems it has potentially created for you.'

He did not elaborate. He didn't need to.

'She's right about that. But I'm taking my life as it comes at the moment.'

'Good plan,' Walter said, wondering what that really meant, as they walked together into the small dining room to join the lawyers for lunch.

Late that afternoon, Arabella knocked and opened the door to Philippe's study slowly. He was standing by the window looking out over the gardens. She wondered if he had heard her knock. And then he turned to greet her as she entered but he did not move towards her.

She smiled at him, her eyes lighting up, but she was uncertain all the same. His mistress had now given birth to his son. Walter had hinted his divorce was closer to being finalised.

'Walter tells me you gave your ex-husband a good set down the other night. I would have loved to have seen his face.'

'I did,' she said, laughing at the delicious memory. 'Maybe I'd had one glass of champagne too many. It gave me false courage. But it did the trick. He walked away, very embarrassed by what I said.'

'That's good. He deserved it. Much more effective than Walter being charged with assault. Anything else of interest happen during my absence?'

Was he not going to speak about the birth of his son, she wondered? Or of his plans? Was this a cue to restrict their conversation to business matters only? She couldn't decide.

'We've closed off the applications for our first funding round,' she said. 'I've visited a few of the projects that have applied for grants. Virginia has come with me too on some of the visits.'

'That's good to hear. Anything of particular interest?'

'There's a project looking for funding to begin research into brain function and brain dysfunction. I thought you might like to visit them.'

'Sounds interesting,' he said but she could tell he was preoccupied. And then he held out his hand towards her.

'Let's get out of here. I've been cooped up in this room most of the day. And it's a lovely summer's evening outside.'

'I'd love to but Claudia is expecting to see me this evening,' she said apologetically.

He slipped his arm around her waist and guided her towards the door.

'Go downstairs to your office and call your friend. Tell her something's come up. You need to take a rain check. I'll meet you out front in fifteen minutes.'

'Let's go out and enjoy the summer evening,' he added, as he held the door open for her.

He simply wanted to be with her. To enjoy her company. To hear her laugh. He had missed her. Missed her more than he should have. More than he wanted to acknowledge.

As he headed out the door of his study, he called for Clarence to have his car brought around before heading to his bedroom to change from his business suit.

'This is wonderful. We don't do enough of this,' he murmured.

Philippe stood beside Arabella. Together they were taking in the last of the daylight as the golden rays of the setting sun glistened off the bay. A gentle breeze soothed the heat from the day.

'Aren't you concerned we'll be noticed?' She looked around nervously.

She was concerned, not for her sake, but for his. He shrugged.

'I'm not concerned. Are you?'

He did not hear her reply as the waiter arrived to take their meal order. She had said *perhaps you should be concerned* but her words were lost on the breeze.

'I know I shouldn't be seeing you like this when I'm promised elsewhere. But I enjoy being with you. I look forward to our time together and I'm not going to pull back from it. But if you want to, you only have to say so.'

He paused, trying to judge the effect of his words on her.

'I've always been honest with you,' he added quietly. 'I can offer you nothing but friendship.'

For a moment, he noticed a fleeting look of disappointment in her eyes and then she brightened. She reached across the table and put her hand on his.

'Philippe, I understand that. I've always understood that.'

He smiled slightly at her earnestness. He knew it was his fault for the awkwardness that now existed between them. But she's not entirely blameless, he thought. She hadn't tried to hide her interest in me. But, of course, I could have ignored her.

But these thoughts remained unspoken as he contemplated the prospect of having to distance himself from her.

'I understand if you want to end our friendship now.'

She shook her head, the breeze catching her blonde hair.

'No, I don't want to end our friendship,' she said finally. She noticed the deliberate choice of words. Was he suggesting she resign?

'If Karen had not been …' He gestured helplessly, choosing not to finish the sentence.

Was I really about to say I would choose her over Karen, he wondered? Am I capable of such disloyalty? Isn't Karen the woman I've been in love with for a decade? But another thought began to take hold in his mind. Karen belongs to my previous life and I don't feel part of that life anymore. But he would not allow the thought to take hold. His future was bound up with Karen and with their baby son.

Arabella sat very still, not knowing quite what to say, afraid to push him to explain. Did he mean he would have offered marriage if Karen hadn't trapped him? But he hadn't said so, she reminded herself.

Why does my life lurch from one crisis to another, she wondered? First, a whirlwind romance that became a tortured marriage. And now? A relationship that never had a future. How can I go on working with him? Seeing him every day. And then eventually seeing him with his wife and young son.

But she knew, ultimately, the child Karen had borne him had determined his future and hers. Karen's been clever, she thought. She knew he wouldn't allow his son to be brought up as an illegitimate child as he had been.

'Let's enjoy being together,' he said finally as he called to the waiter to bring champagne.

'Are we celebrating something?' she asked. It seemed to her as if there was nothing to celebrate. At least, nothing for her.

'We're celebrating our friendship, my dear sweet Arabella,' he said, using the endearment for the first and only time. 'I think we should enjoy our dinner and let the future take care of itself.'

She smiled at how easily he could charm her. How readily he could gain her confidence again. She relaxed. He was right. She had to let the future take care of itself.

As the daylight faded, they laughed together, sharing food from one another's plate and drinking champagne, until the darkness enveloped them and it was time to go. As Philippe held the car door open, his mind was consumed by one thought: how am I ever going to deny myself the pleasure of her company? Will a wedding ring on my finger be enough when I'm back here for weeks and months at a time by myself?

He pushed those thoughts to the back of his mind as he settled himself into the driver's seat and tried not to think of the future.

Chapter 19

Australia—January 1970

KAREN REACHED UP to brush the confetti from her hair and from Philippe's suit coat. For just a moment she held some of the tiny pieces of paper in the palm of her hand, remembering her father's reassuring words from months before. *Think of the day confetti lands in your hair. The day the champagne corks pop. The day he slides that wedding ring on your finger.* And now that day has finally come, she thought.

For her, there was a sense of unreality as they stood together on the steps of the beautiful little sandstone church perched high above the harbour on a cloudless day, the blue sky overhead, a gentle breeze whipping at her long auburn hair. How long had she waited for this moment? A decade at least.

She looked at her left hand, at the plain gold band that now nestled alongside the diamond ring. The ring she had begun wearing on her right hand before transferring it to her left hand.

She looked around her. It was a small wedding. Only the very closest family and friends. Bianca fussed about her dress which had been the most important project in their workroom for weeks. Classically sleek. Slightly off white. No long wedding veil, just a simple circle of flowers in her hair. The diamonds of her pendant sparkling in the sunlight.

Philippe bent his head close to hers and whispered.

'How do you feel, Mrs Duval?'

'Wonderful.'

She smiled. And then well-wishers surged forward to offer their congratulations.

'Well, the wedding has finally happened, brother. Are you relieved? Or surprised?'

David Clarke sipped his glass of champagne before answering.

'Both, Robert,' he said quietly. 'Both relieved and surprised if I'm honest. But it was the child that tipped the balance in Karen's favour, I've no doubt of that. And there's no doubting who his father is.'

Robert Clarke followed his brother's gaze. Across the room, Louis-Philippe Duval, dark eyed with a shock of dark hair, looked on perplexed from the safe arms of his nanny at the unfamiliar movement and noise going on around him.

'He's a fine looking child, brother.'

'I take it there are no worries from his being premature?' The question had been niggling away in the back of David Clarke's mind but he could not ask his daughter.

'No, he's fine.' His brother was quick to reassure him. 'I'm told he's passed all his milestones. He'll be running around in no time. I guess it's possible you'll be more of a father to him than his own father in his early years.'

He found the prospect appealing as if Karen's child might somehow compensate him for the loss of his own son.

'I don't know how that's going to work out, to be honest. How is a marriage supposed to work if one partner spends the bulk of their time away?'

'Time will tell, brother. They'll have to work that out themselves,' Robert said. 'But if I was Karen, I wouldn't leave him to his own devices in America for weeks and months on end.'

David Clarke smiled knowingly at his brother's words.

'You didn't believe his denial then about the woman he was pictured with?'

'Did you, brother?'

'Well, let's put it another way. He's a man by himself, lord of the manor so to speak, and a delicious piece of womanhood crosses his path. And falls for his flattery and charm. Not to mention the expensive gifts. Hopefully he's ended it. And if he hasn't, I hope Karen never finds out.'

'Amen to that, brother,' Robert said, looking around the room and spotting his daughter Anita with Pippa. 'I wonder how Pippa feels about today?'

'Bloody devastated, I would think. She tried hard to get Karen to give him up.'

David Clarke was not without sympathy for Philippe's daughter. He knew she had witnessed the collapse of her parents' marriage and, with it, the end of the fairy tale that had framed her life for the past decade. Everyone knew her story.

'I hope she makes a go of it with Joel Tynan,' Robert said unexpectedly. 'He's a good guy. I'm trying to convince him to become a proper doctor again. He'd be an excellent addition to an emergency department with his background. I promised to put a word in for him if he's interested. He was really good with Karen.'

'Do you think he'll toss in his role at the Foundation?'

'He's thinking about it. He knows Pippa can run the Foundation now.'

'Any money in his family?'

Robert almost laughed out loud. It was exactly the question he had expected.

'No, a modest working class background I've been told. But if he marries Pippa, that won't matter, will it?'

David Clarke smiled.

'No, it won't matter. Except her inheritance got a little bit smaller a few months back.'

'Is it likely to get smaller again? Will Karen try for another baby?'

'She says not but you never know with her. Her maternal grand-mother had babies well into her forties. Perhaps she can too.'

'So you'd like a granddaughter as well, brother. You're getting greedy. I don't think Anita will ever give me grandchildren.'

'Well, you need to introduce her to a few eligible young men for a start.'

'And how well did that work for you, brother, introducing Karen to young men?'

He laughed.

'You're right. Maybe we're not good matchmakers for our daughters. I certainly wouldn't have chosen Philippe Duval for Karen.'

'Exactly,' Robert said as he walked away in search of his wife.

Ian and Angela Dixon stood alongside Patricia Clarke as Robert approached and shook hands with Ian.

'I have a strong sense of déjà vu being here.'

They all nodded their heads, each one of them remembering a wedding they had attended almost a decade earlier. So much had happened in the years since.

'Well, Karen finally got her man,' Ian said. 'That's what I call determination. I feel sorry for Julia though. I know Karen's your niece but Julia deserved better treatment.'

'Does anyone know what Julia is up to these days? Pippa hasn't said much to Anita.'

But no one could offer up any news of her except that she had sold the house she had shared with Philippe and was renting an apartment while she decided what to do.

'I guess we have an American visitor in our midst,' Ian Dixon said, nodding in the direction of a tall young man none of them could recall seeing before.

It was Robert Clarke who provided the answer.

'That's Walter William Cox the fourth, according to Anita. The son of Philippe's half-brother. He works alongside Philippe, I understand. I guess managing the wealth the Cox family accumulated and the Foundation in Philippe's absence is a full time job, more or less.'

'And he seems to know Bianca Ferrari, Karen's business partner, quite well.'

Angela Dixon had been the first to notice Walter slide his arm around Bianca's waist and kiss her on the cheek. He did not release her immediately, continuing to hold her in a friendly embrace until she pushed him away gently.

'He probably met her when she and Karen went across there last year to launch their fashion business in the New York market,' Robert said. He didn't really need to say more. They all knew it was after that trip Philippe's marriage to Julia had begun to unravel.

Across the room, Walter turned towards Karen as she approached, slipping his arm around her and kissing her fully on the lips.

'My only chance,' he said as he released her. 'It's the only time I won't get my face slapped.'

She laughed at him. Should I remind him of how much he disapproved of me when we first met, she wondered? She let the moment slide.

'Maybe Bianca will be doing the face slapping tonight?'

But Walter shook his head and looked at Bianca.

'I don't think so, do you?' he said as he raised Bianca's fingers to his lips.

Philippe saw the exchange and laughed quietly to himself. Walter certainly had a penchant for women older than himself. And then an unhappy thought occurred to him. Walter would feel free to romance Arabella now. Would she be interested in him? He didn't know for sure.

'You look as if a ghost just walked over your grave,' Walter said quietly.

'Thinking about something I shouldn't be thinking about,' Philippe said, making sure no one was close enough to hear what he said.

Walter's raised eyebrows were eloquent acknowledgement.

'I'd think about something else if I were you.'

'Yes, you're right, Walter. By the way you should meet my father-in-law, David Clarke. Let's have a little fun with him.'

Philippe guided Walter across the room to David Clarke who was benignly overseeing the reception on which he had spared no expense. As they approached, he extended his hand towards Walter.

'David, meet my nephew Walter William Cox the fourth,' giving him his full name. 'He's my heir.'

Walter smiled. He knew what Philippe was up to.

'And what about your children. My grandson in particular, Duval,' he growled.

'Don't worry, Mr Clarke, what Philippe means is that I will have charge of the family's wealth for the benefit of all the heirs, Louis-Philippe included. I'm the eldest child of the next generation.'

'And when you're sixty years old, that means it should be Louis who gets nominated. He'll learn everything he needs to know about business from me, I can tell you that now.'

Walter smiled, suddenly feeling sorry for Philippe's baby son at what lay in store for him.

'Unless, of course, I have a son myself soon,' he said.

Philippe smiled to himself at Walter's provocative answer. He moved off in search of his daughter, not waiting to hear the unsolicited advice David Clarke offered Walter.

'Well, if you want a son, I'd look around for someone younger than Bianca Ferrari. There's a bit of free advice for you.'

Walter laughed quietly. Did Karen's father, like Philippe, see everything? He opted to change the direction of the conversation to more neutral ground.

'I understand you have car dealerships, Mr Clarke? I really love cars. I have a beautiful red Chevy Camaro at home.'

He guessed rightly that Karen's father was more than happy to talk about the car business.

'Happy to show you around my dealerships if you're interested, Walter. I haven't delved much into American cars, mainly European and British cars, but we've got some nice models coming through.'

'So that's where Philippe's preference for Mercedes-Benz comes from?'

'Ah, yes, my daughter twisted my arm to give Philippe a substantial discount on his first Merc. He doesn't need a discount now though. By the way, does he drive a Mercedes on Long Island?'

'He does,' Walter replied. 'The latest Mercedes sports in fact. It's a nice car. And there's also the chauffeur-driven Mercedes saloon if he doesn't feel like driving himself.'

And then an image came unbidden to Walter's mind. The image of Philippe's car standing overnight in the driveway after his late night returns from Arabella's house. Not something that would please his new father-in-law. Nor his new wife.

'He has a good life there by the sound of it.'

'He does. But he's pretty busy. Lawyer and investment advisor meetings practically every week. There's always someone putting up an investment proposal. Then there's the Foundation board to chair. And he's also sitting on a hospital board and on the board of a research foundation. With his medical background and his wealth, he suddenly became an attractive proposition to be invited to sit on boards.'

David Clarke listened to all this, understanding then that Philippe's life was never again going to be centred in Sydney. And he knew his daughter had said she had no interest in living in America permanently. He wondered then if the marriage really had a future.

'Tell me, Walter. I believe there's a very attractive young woman heading up this Foundation of his. I hope Philippe's relationship with her is a strictly professional one. Someone kindly sent my daughter a picture of them together, his arm around her. It was in a newspaper gossip column, I'm told.'

There was a long moment of silence broken only by the quick intake of Walter's breath. *Why did I talk about the Foundation?* He began to berate himself silently. *It gave Karen's father a chance to ask the one question Walter wanted desperately to avoid.* And then he thought quickly. What better way to deflect attention than to declare his interest in Arabella?

'Well,' Walter said with a smile as if he was sharing a deep secret, 'I'd be pretty unhappy to find out his interest in her was anything other than professional. Very unhappy indeed if you get my meaning. I'd be having a heart to heart with Arabella myself.'

David Clarke let out a long sigh of relief. He'd been told Philippe had claimed he had simply been her escort and he hadn't believed it. His face was wreathed in smiles at Walter's confidences.

Across the room, Walter caught Philippe's eye. Should he tell him? At first, he decided against it. But he was in no doubt Karen would hear it soon enough from her father, so he motioned to Philippe to meet him on the terrace.

Walter was leaning on the railing taking in the wonderful view of the harbour he had only ever heard about as Philippe came to stand alongside him.

'What's up? I hope you got David Clarke's measure. He annoys me at times.'

Walter smiled to himself. He wasn't surprised at Philippe's comment.

'We have a common interest. Cars. He's offered to take me around his dealerships, which would be interesting. But that's not what I wanted to tell you.'

'He didn't ask about Arabella, did he?'

Walter nodded.

'He did but I gave him the impression I'm the one involved with her. To deflect suspicions. It will no doubt make its way back to you.'

He put his hand on Walter's arm.

'Thanks. That's helpful. How was she when you left, by the way?'

'Putting on a brave face if I'm honest. I think she really fell in love with you.'

'I know, Walter. I didn't mean for that to happen.'

'And you?'

Walter knew it was an inappropriate question, especially on Philippe's wedding day, but he asked it anyway. He had to know for sure. Suddenly, Philippe's answer had assumed a level of importance he hadn't anticipated.

'I enjoyed her company, Walter. We were friends, that's all,' Philippe said, evenly. 'Anyway, it's hardly the conversation for my wedding day, is it?'

In that moment, Walter understood. Turning his back on Arabella had been a difficult choice for Philippe. He noticed too the fleeting look of disappointment in Philippe's eyes as he turned away to rejoin Karen, who guided him back to the bridal table where fresh glassware had been set out ready for the toasts.

Joel stood alongside Pippa on the terrace, taking in the magnificent view of the harbour. Even as he absorbed the wonderful view, he was left wondering if the people in the houses that ringed the harbour had any idea of the life in the suburbs beyond where he had been brought up. Yet it was probably those very people from those working class suburbs who performed the work that produced the wealth that bought the homes so there was a connection. A connection they didn't see of course, he mused. To him, it was another world to which he'd only recently gained access.

'The speeches were mercifully brief,' Pippa said as she sipped a glass of champagne.

'Thank goodness,' Joel replied. Like Pippa, he had no taste for flowery wedding speeches. And, like Pippa, he was cynical about marriage. 'Tough day for you though.'

'Yes, I keep thinking back to when he married my mother. I was so excited. So delighted. Delirious with happiness. My name had been changed to Duval. I thought my life would only ever get better from that day on. And for years it was fine. And then Karen came into view again and he couldn't resist her. And now she's finally got what she always wanted.'

Behind her, Walter stood listening to their conversation. For the first time, he really understood the depths of Pippa's disappointment. But he too had been disappointed by his family life. By his father's bitterness and hatred for his own father. And his mother's relentless social climbing and snobbery. For all Philippe's faults, he still admired him as a person. He enjoyed his company. And he was gratified by the confidence Philippe had displayed in him.

'Beautiful view,' Walter said.

Pippa turned around, momentarily startled. She had not known he was behind them.

'It is beautiful, Walter. Now that I'm surplus to requirements in my father's house, I'm going to buy my own apartment with a harbour view.'

'Not a house with a big family in mind, Pippa?'

She shook her head.

'No, Walter. I'm going to leave that to you. You can have the kids to keep the family going. Or maybe Virginia. I hear she has a new boyfriend.'

Walter smiled. Her sources were good.

'Yes, sorry Joel, she got over you very quickly. She's dating the eldest of the Grenville boys. Matthew Grenville. His family is in transport. And my mother's happy again. A good match, she says.'

'I'm pleased, Walter. Very pleased. Your sister is a nice girl who deserves a nice husband.

'She does. And she's quite enjoying helping Arabella too. A better way to spend her time than just shopping and gossiping with her friends. But did I hear a whisper you're thinking of moving back into real medicine, Joel?'

Joel smiled at the emphasis on the words.

'I'm thinking about it. Robert Clarke wants to set up a couple of interviews for me. Pippa can run the local office of the Foundation now. It's probably time for me to move back into the practical work before I lose all my skills.'

Walter agreed. He could see how Joel would be more valuable as a practising doctor.

'Talking about people leaving, Walter, will Arabella stay on, do you think?'

She had asked the question quietly, not wanting to be overheard.

'Not sure this is the day for that question, Pippa,' Walter said. He too had lowered his voice. 'She enjoys the job. She's good at it. And she's well liked. It would be a shame to see her move on.'

'And when my father's back there for long stretches by himself?'

She didn't need to spell it out. Both Walter and Joel knew what she was trying to say.

'He says they are nothing more than friends, Pippa,' Walter said finally, 'and I believe him. He did acknowledge he was aware she had feelings for him though.'

She smiled to herself. Was he telling the truth? They had all just assumed Arabella and her father were having an affair.

'Friends? That's it?'

Walter shrugged.

'That's what he said, Pippa, and I believe him.'

'Well, let's hope so, Walter. Let's hope so.'

But would he admit it to any of them? Especially today. Unlikely, she decided. She upended her glass of champagne and reached for another.

'There's only one thing for it today and that is to drink champagne and enjoy the view,' she said as she turned back to look at the harbour sparkling below them. Because she could not bear to turn around and look at her father, his arms around Karen, her eyes sparkling with delight, her smile triumphant as she revelled in the day she thought might never happen. And then her thoughts went to her mother.

'You're thinking about your mother, aren't you?' Joel asked quietly. She nodded.

'She headed up north for tea and sympathy with her family. It's the day she finally has to move on from him.'

'And you, Pippa? Is it the day you finally move on from what he's done to you and your mother?'

'Yes, Joel, it is. It has to be.'

He said nothing more. It was as if she was locking away the memory of the family she had once enjoyed. Her father. Her mother. Herself. He understood how much it had hurt her.

He still thought of little Chloe as his daughter. Except she wasn't. He too had been betrayed. He put his arm around her and they stood together without speaking for some time watching the sun sink in the western sky.

CHAPTER 20

America—January 1970

Arabella appeared to be totally absorbed in the Saturday edition of *The New York Times* as her friend Claudia Rossi pulled out a chair and sat down at the table opposite her. But Claudia was not so easily deceived.

'I was watching you. You haven't turned a page in minutes.'

Then she looked at the page her friend was reading. It was the report of a recent wedding. A radiant Josephine Benz, now Mrs Thomas Carpenter, looked back at them from the pages of the newspaper.

'Someone you know?'

Arabella shook her head.

'No. I've never met her. She looks lovely though, doesn't she?'

Claudia understood then. She looked at her watch. It was one o'clock in New York. In Sydney it would be very early Sunday morning. She knew exactly what Arabella was thinking about. Philippe would now be a married man again.

'I did warn you, my dear girl,' she reminded her.

'You did. All my friends did.'

Their words echoed in her mind. *He's a womanizer, Arabella. Whatever you do, don't fall under his spell.*

'But you didn't take any notice, did you?'

Arabella shrugged. What could she say? Had she been especially vulnerable after the way her ex-husband had treated her? *Was I like a mistreated puppy,* she wondered, *responding to his kindness and misreading it?*

'He warned me too. He said he could offer me nothing but friendship.'

'Well, that's to his credit at least.'

Claudia noticed then a stunning diamond and gold link bracelet on her friend's right wrist.

'That's new. That's no family heirloom bequeathed to you by a doting grandmother.'

Arabella smiled and twisted the bracelet. It had been Philippe's final gift to her.

'He left it in the drawer of my desk before he left for Sydney.'

She smiled at the memory of discovering it the next day. Would she ever get a chance to thank him?

'And what happens when he gets back from Sydney? Surely there'll be no more dinners out, just the two of you. Will Walter partner you now at the events instead of Philippe? How's that going to work? Have you thought about that.'

Claudia was curious. Would his wife and child return with him? She tried to calculate how old his baby son would be. Not very old. Perhaps they would remain in Sydney until the child was old enough to travel.

Arabella shook her head.

'I imagine it will be a very businesslike relationship in future. In fact, I've thought about resigning. Going back to England.'

'But you enjoy the job, Arabella. Anyway, where would you live? You'd have to create a career for yourself all over again.'

Claudia knew the struggle Arabella had faced to gain a career foothold in America. Having to do the same again in England seemed like a step backwards.

'My mother is pressuring me to come back to live with her now that my sister Elise is engaged. She said she doesn't want to be rattling around in the house all by herself.'

Her friend laughed. She had met Arabella's mother, Lady Gloria Courtenay. She couldn't imagine Arabella willingly falling in with her plans. She knew the bare facts about Arabella's family. Her mother, a nineteen-year-old debutante, had fallen in love with a married man, fifteen years her senior. He had left his wife and eventually married Arabella's mother. But his extended family had disowned him, preferring instead his first wife and their two sons, the elder of which had inherited the bulk of his fortune, as Arabella had always known he would.

'She moves in the right circles, doesn't she? Perhaps she can help you get a job.'

'She's already suggested it but I want to be chosen on merit, not because my mother can sweet talk a couple of old men on a board of directors.'

Just then as she looked towards the door, she was surprised to see Jennifer Newman walk into the restaurant.

'Someone you know?' Claudia asked, turning to follow her friend's gaze.

'That's Dr Newman,' she said.

'Philippe's first wife?'

Arabella nodded as Jennifer Newman caught sight of her across the restaurant and headed in her direction.

'Arabella, it's lovely to see you. Fancy running into you like this. How are you?'

Arabella greeted her and turned to introduce her to Claudia.

'By the way, do you know when Philippe will be back? I want to ask him to give an after-dinner speech at an alumni dinner we're having in early summer. But I need to finalise the program quite soon.'

She waited for Arabella to respond but she hesitated. Did Jennifer know he had just got married again?

'I don't know, Jennifer. He wasn't sure how long he would spend in Sydney. He went just before Christmas.'

And got married yesterday, she wanted to say, but she did not. She couldn't bring herself to utter the words.

'It's alright, Arabella. I shouldn't have asked. I know he got married yesterday.'

She reached out then and patted Arabella on the shoulder in an uncharacteristic gesture of reassurance.

'Not all our hopes and dreams work out the way we want them to, but I do know he cares a great deal about you. He was very concerned about what your ex-husband did to you.'

'I know he was, Jennifer. He's been a true friend helping me with my divorce, which became final last week you'll be pleased to know.'

'That's good. You can put that part of your life behind you now. And perhaps it's time to put another part of your life behind you too.'

Arabella smiled bleakly.

'I know, Jennifer. I know.'

'If you need to talk at any time, come and see me,' Jennifer said, handing her a business card. 'I was in love with him once too. But I got over it.'

Arabella was curious. Would there ever be a better time to ask why their marriage had failed?

'Why did your marriage fail if you were in love with him?'

'Because he wasn't in love with me. I realised very quickly there was no foundation for our marriage. And later, I came to understand how he needed to find the daughter he'd left behind in Australia. But he never told me. Never told any of us. Even when he married Julia and had dinner with some of his former colleagues when they were on their honeymoon here, he never mentioned he had fathered one of her children.'

'Did you see him then? That must have been strange.'

'No, but one or two others did and they told me later. I think keeping his private life to himself was a habit he couldn't break.'

Jennifer then noticed the bracelet on her wrist.

'A parting gift?'

'No. It's a Christmas gift,' she said. There was no way she would acknowledge it was a parting gift.

'I noticed the exquisite jewellery you were wearing at the lunch last year. He's generous I'll give him that.'

Arabella laughed out loud then.

'Do you mean the bracelet and earrings I was wearing? They weren't gifts from Philippe,' she said, amused they had all jumped to the wrong conclusion.

'Before she died, my maternal grandmother, the Dowager Countess of Dantrey, divided up her jewellery between my mother, my sister and me so my uncle's wife, whom she described as *vulgar*, couldn't get her hands on it.'

They all laughed.

'Good on your grandmother, I say,' Jennifer said, knowing that everyone at the table had assumed the jewellery had been a gift from Philippe.

As she turned to leave, she paused.

'Walter would make a good husband,' she said unexpectedly. 'I noticed he seemed very eager to please you at the lunch.'

With that, Jennifer was gone and Arabella and Claudia were left to speculate on what her short marriage to Philippe had really been like. And who had done the leaving.

'So what about Walter?'

Arabella smiled slightly at Claudia's unexpected question.

'What about Walter? We're good friends, that's all. Besides I'm years older than he is. And don't forget, he can probably take his pick from among the daughters of New York's social elite. Anyway Virginia told me he's seeing a girl whose older brother is one of his good friends. She's only twenty-four. A more suitable age for him, don't you think?'

'You're probably right,' Claudia conceded. Yet she was sad there were going to be no neat solutions for her friend.

'I think we're both destined to be spinsters,' Arabella declared.

'I think you're right,' Claudia laughed, as they clinked glasses and bemoaned the lack of suitable men in their lives.

❋❋

Walter's news on his return from Sydney that Philippe would travel back to America in February seemed to raise the spirits of everyone at Eastbury Hall, including Clarence, who felt the house needed Philippe's presence to come alive.

But for Arabella, the news was unsettling. In the time he had been gone, he had not contacted her at all, preferring instead to relay any news or instructions via Walter. She knew why, of course.

She had listened politely to Walter's brief description of the wedding on his return. What else could she do? But she had the sense he had been careful about what he had said.

It was Friday afternoon and Walter had been back home for only a few days. He sat perched on the edge of Arabella's desk, watching her sign a bundle of letters her secretary had prepared, her last task for the week.

'Nearly finished?' he asked.

She smiled.

'Finished,' she said, finally laying aside her pen and handing the letters to her secretary.

Walter waited a few moments until they were alone together.

'There's something I wanted to tell you about Philippe's return. I didn't tell you before but Karen and the baby are coming with him.'

He wasn't deceived by the casual shrug of her shoulders. The news had come as a surprise to her, as it had to him. No one had expected Karen would want to travel with the baby just yet.

'And a nanny and a nursery maid too, apparently,' he added, with a chuckle. 'Clarence is now in a pickle as to how a nursery can be got ready in just a couple of weeks. Not to mention rooms that haven't been used for decades.'

'Well, I'm not asking Claudia if that's what you're suggesting. And I'm not doing it,' she said, her voice sounding harsher than she intended.

'That's not what I was suggesting,' he said gently. 'In fact, I was going to suggest you don't have to be here, if you don't want to. Why don't you take some time off and go back to visit your family in England?'

'Run away, you mean?'

'No, I didn't mean that. But I know it's not going to be easy for you. I know you had a very close relationship with him. Besides, I think Karen is only staying a couple of weeks, from what I understand. She has some fashion business to attend to.'

How could he tell her it had been Philippe's idea that she return to England for a couple of weeks?

I don't think I need to spell out why, Philippe had said.

No, you don't have to spell it out, Walter had been about to say but thought better of it. He had seen Karen with Philippe. And he had seen her possessiveness. And he had seen Philippe with Arabella. He knew instinctively Karen had finally claimed the prize she had long coveted. And she was determined to hold onto that prize.

Walter held out his hand towards Arabella.

'Let's go out and enjoy a nice dinner together,' he said, hoping to cheer her up. He wanted to see her eyes sparkle again. He wanted to see the colour return to her pale cheeks. And then he stopped and looked closely at her.

'Are you OK? You do look a bit tired and a bit pale.'
She shook her head.
'I'm fine. And dinner would be lovely.'
She glanced at her watch. It was five o'clock.
'Can I meet you somewhere? I'd like to go home and change.'
'I have a better idea,' he said. 'I'll pick you up at seven.'
'And disturb my neighbours with your noisy car?'
He laughed.
'They'll get over it,' he said as he headed out the door. 'I'll see you at seven.'

'Do you ever get lonely living by yourself?'
Arabella shook her head.
'Not really. I'm getting used to it.'
But of course that was a small lie. She was living alone because there was no other choice.
'It was a lovely dinner, thank you,' she said, as she handed him a glass of wine. It was so similar to her routine with Philippe she could almost imagine he was Philippe for just a moment. But he was very different from his uncle.
'I hope I didn't bore you with my chatter about the America's Cup,' he said, his enthusiasm triggered by a private visit to the boat-yard building the Australian challenger while he was in Sydney. 'It's being held in Newport in September. You should come with me.'
She shrugged. A lot can happen in eight months, she wanted to say.
'Virginia told me you were seeing Diana Fisher. Wouldn't you want to take her with you?'
He smiled and shook his head.
'That only lasted a couple of weeks. She turned out to be a very silly young woman.'
He could guess why his sister had told Arabella.
'I think my sister was just making mischief in telling you about

Diana,' he said. 'I took her out a couple of times as a favour to her brother. I'd rather be with you, Arabella. Much rather be with you.'

His declaration had surprised her. He put his arm around her and drew her down onto the sofa beside him.

'I'm hoping I might get a look in now,' he said.

By now, she knew he meant now that Philippe is married.

He bent his head to kiss her and fold her into an embrace.

It was at that point she made a split-second decision that would change the trajectory of her life. And Walter's life.

She got up and held her hand out to him. He followed her to the bedroom, surprised at her invitation. But delighted too. He had been jealous of her preference for Philippe. But he was convinced by Philippe's assurance they were nothing more than good friends. And now it appeared she was determined to put the infatuation behind her. It was in that moment he realised he loved her. And that he had loved her since the moment he had set eyes on her.

'Mrs Duval, welcome to Eastbury Hall.'

Clarence was at his imperious best as he greeted Karen, who was crossing the threshold of Eastbury Hall for the first time as Philippe's wife. For just a moment, Clarence was transported back to the day he had first met Julia Duval. So much had happened in that time. And some of it disappointing, he thought. He noticed how Karen's eyes sparkled with mischief. And delight.

'Thank you, Clarence,' she said, smiling broadly. 'Slightly different circumstances from when we last met.'

He nodded. Was a comment really necessary? It was almost exactly a year earlier that he had met her at the Plaza Hotel in New York with her business partner Bianca. He knew instinctively then trouble lay ahead for Philippe's marriage. And so it had proved.

Behind her, Philippe carried his baby son, asleep in his arms.

'I'd introduce you to Louis-Philippe, Clarence,' Philippe said, 'but we won't disturb him. I've developed a knack of getting him to sleep when he won't settle down for anyone else.'

He turned then.

'This is our nanny, Dorothy Long, and Rose Parker, who helps in the nursery. I hope you've had time to open up some of those long-forgotten rooms, Clarence. I don't suppose they've been used much for decades.'

It had been a frantic time for Clarence, overseeing the quick refurbishment of long unused bedrooms and having the nursery repainted and new furniture installed. But it had been achieved.

As they entered the foyer, Philippe handed the sleeping child over to the nanny who was now being taken in hand by the housekeeper, Mrs Anderson. She was clearly very keen to assert her authority over the new additions to the household staff. But she had been warned by Clarence. 'We all liked Julia Duval but he has a new wife now. And a new baby. And they are to be treated with the utmost respect. He won't tolerate anything less.'

As they moved upstairs, Philippe looked around him. There was one thing missing. Whenever he had returned in the past, Arabella would invariably greet him, smiling brightly, claiming his attention, eager to bring him up to date with the latest developments at the Foundation. And eager to see him. Just as he had always been pleased to see her.

'And Arabella? Is she around?' he asked Clarence, his voice barely above a whisper. He hoped Walter had been able to convince her to take time off. But part of him wanted to see her too.

'Off this afternoon, Dr Duval,' he said quietly. 'At a medical appointment, I understand.'

Philippe nodded, surprised at the news.

'Has she been unwell?'

'A little off colour, I believe. A little paler than normal. She looked tired too but I don't think it's anything serious. Walter may know more.'

He wondered then if she had been seeing Walter. Would that be a good thing? He was in two minds. At times he hoped she might move on, out of his life altogether. Wouldn't that be easier for both of them? But at other times the prospect of not seeing her at all depressed him.

Then he heard Karen's voice cutting through his thoughts.

'Our bedroom is wonderful,' she said. 'You had a decorator with very good taste. I approve.'

She was remembering the first time she had entered the room. He had surprised her with a beautiful mink coat, but the room had been depressing and very much in need of redecoration.

He smiled to himself but made no comment. For just a moment, he pictured Claudia and Arabella, heads together, choosing from a vast collection of fabric and carpet samples and then carefully guiding his choices away from the dark and masculine colours he might have chosen to the light, neutral tones and luxurious upholstery that now adorned the room. At times it had seemed to him as if Arabella was decorating the bedroom with herself in mind.

'And Louis? Where's the nursery?'

Karen followed him out the door, marvelling as they walked along the main bedroom wing, at the size of the house. As they turned the corner at the end of the corridor, Philippe gestured to the rooms, long unused, on either side.

'This was the nursery wing, according to Clarence. It was never filled with children. There was only ever one child from each generation. My father. And then Walter's father. But don't worry, the rooms have had a quick update.'

He had been along the corridor only once, when he and Julia were first given a grand tour of the house.

She was delighted with the nursery for Louis. All baby boy blue and white with a freshly upholstered armchair which she tested out.

'Very comfortable,' she said.

Philippe had quickly learned that Louis was not a good sleeper.

Karen would get up to him during the night to relieve the nanny of the responsibility. And if all else failed, he would get up. And Louis would settle almost immediately. And they would laugh about it the next day, Karen insisting he had magic powers.

It had been only a month since they had married. For Philippe, life was different. Julia had, in many ways, been undemanding, fitting her life around his, but he discovered Karen expected more. He knew now she expected her needs and her commitment to her business to rank equally with his commitments. And his house in Sydney, once quiet and empty, at times overflowed with people. People from the fashion industry mostly. Or Bianca who always came with bundles of fabric swatches and sketch pads full of her latest designs. And, on any pretext, doting grandfather David Clarke would drop in and spend time with his grandson.

Philippe had heaved a sigh of relief at returning to Eastbury Hall with its calm and ordered household, overseen by the ever watchful Clarence, who missed nothing and said little.

But of the few things he needed to tell Philippe on his return, he kept one piece of information to himself.

It was his habit to do a final check of the Foundation offices before shutting the house for the night. The day before, he had been surprised to see Dr Jennifer Newman's business card on Arabella's desk. He had dropped the card into the top drawer of her desk and was about to leave her office but he couldn't resist the temptation to flip open her appointment diary. Friday 6 February 2.00pm. Jennifer.

He had closed the diary quickly, careful not to leave any sign of a disturbance, but the appointment puzzled him. Why go all the way to New York to consult Jennifer Newman? He could find no answer at all to that question.

CHAPTER 21

America

'GOOD MORNING, PHILIPPE. Good to have you back,' Walter said, as he held out his arms to Louis-Philippe who eyed him suspiciously for a moment until he decided the new person was acceptable to him.

'He's wary of strangers,' Philippe said, surrendering his baby son, who had been sharing his father's scrambled eggs until he decided he didn't like them and, without warning, spat out the offending food. But Philippe had been alert to the possibility and quickly wiped his son's messy face.

'I didn't expect to find you *holding the baby*, so to speak,' Walter said as he looked around. 'I thought I might see Karen with you.'

Philippe shook his head.

'Still asleep. The difference in time zones is difficult to adjust to. And the nanny and her helper are downstairs having breakfast with the other staff. I offered to take care of Louis for a short time.'

'Mrs Anderson will be in her element. More staff to boss around.'

Philippe smiled and nodded.

'I've learned not to interfere there. Besides Karen is only here for a couple of weeks. Hopefully I won't have a mutiny of nursery staff in that time.'

As Walter pulled a chair out and attempted to sit down, Louis let out a howl of protest.

'Once he's up, he likes to keep moving,' Philippe said, which forced Walter to remain standing while Philippe finished his breakfast.

'Anything of interest happen while I was away?'

He lowered his voice then.

'Did you have any success in suggesting Arabella take a vacation? I wondered if she would be heading off next week.'

He did not ask about her medical appointment, hoping Walter would instead volunteer the information.

Walter spoke quietly, glancing repeatedly at the doorway. He did not want Karen to catch them unawares deep in discussion about Arabella.

'She hasn't been well for a few days. I phoned her last night. Just the flu, she said. The doctor has suggested she rest for a few days. She's going to do that. I told her not to come in on Monday.'

He could see Philippe was relieved it was nothing more serious.

'She needs to be quite well before she comes back to work, otherwise everyone will get it. And I don't want to expose Louis to unnecessary risks.'

'He looks healthy enough,' Walter said.

'He is,' Philippe agreed. 'He's very robust but babies are very vulnerable. Anything to report on the property investment side? Have you been keeping your finger on the pulse of everything?'

'I've been looking at some more Manhattan property but nothing firm yet. And I think Arabella left you a list of things needing your attention. Nothing urgent, I'm told, except she said to remind you that you have a hospital board meeting this coming week.'

He nodded. He was beginning to regret accepting so many board appointments but he had done so to get his name and therefore the name of the Foundation more widely known.

'Karen's got some meetings and a range to present to one of the retailers. She's going to be busy.'

'Motherhood hasn't slowed her down then?'

'No, Walter, motherhood hasn't slowed me down,' she said laughingly as she breezed through the doorway, kissed Walter on the cheek and reached out for her baby son.

Immediately behind her, Clarence glided silently into the room.

'Can I get breakfast for you, Mrs Duval?' he asked.

'Thank you, Clarence. That would be wonderful. Fresh orange juice perhaps. Some eggs. Perhaps some fruit,' she asked hopefully.

'Certainly, Mrs Duval. And tea?'

'Yes, Clarence, always tea at breakfast. Thank you. Are you breakfasting, Walter?'

He shook his head.

'Just coffee thanks, Clarence.'

'And have you convinced your mother to come and meet me tomorrow, Walter?'

'Of course she's coming to lunch. Do you think she'd want to miss the opportunity to inspect Philippe's new wife at close quarters?'

She laughed.

'And your sister Virginia?'

'Yes, of course. She's very interested in fashion. She wants to hear all about your work and see the latest designs.'

Karen smiled broadly. It would be easy common ground for the two of them but Walter's mother might present a tougher challenge, she thought.

But the wedding ring on her finger had given her a new confidence. Her life with Philippe was everything she had dreamed it would be, her only challenge being to get him to stay longer in Sydney with her.

If there was a slight nervousness on Karen's part at the prospect of meeting Barbara Cox, she would have been relieved to know the nervousness was mutual.

Virginia sat on the edge of her mother's bed and watched the discarded clothes become a small heap beside her.

'If you keep going like this, you'll have nothing left in your closet,' she said, looking on in dismay. Unless her mother made a choice very soon, they would be late and Walter would be annoyed with them.

But her mother was not in the mood to be cajoled.

She's always like this when she gets invited to the big house, Virginia thought, shaking her head. Angry. Envious. Embittered. But she knew better than to tell her mother to calm down.

She glanced at her watch.

'Walter will be waiting for us downstairs,' she said finally.

Which elicited a deep sigh from her mother and a resigned look. Finally, she slipped a simple dress over her head and turned her back towards her daughter to zip her up.

'This old thing will have to do,' she said.

'It's fine,' Virginia reassured her. 'The colour suits you. Just keep the jewellery to a minimum.'

She handed her mother a simple gold chain necklace she had chosen from amongst her mother's jewellery collection.

'This with the matching earrings will do nicely.'

Finally, she acquiesced in her daughter's choice. Perhaps simple is best, she thought.

Downstairs, Walter looked despairingly at his watch but he was reluctant to intervene. He had tried that once before and lost his temper with his mother.

And so it was, on a frosty Sunday in February, the three of them headed over to the big house, each consumed by their own thoughts.

For Barbara Cox, being invited to the big house was a reminder of what she had been denied; for Walter it was a reminder of how life changes constantly. As much as he liked Karen, seeing her with Philippe would always be touched by a sense of sadness, knowing she had usurped Julia.

For Virginia, there was a sense of anticipation because she had come to realise she had no real interest in the philanthropic work of the Foundation. It was fashion that interested her. It was fashion for which she had a flair. She was excited to meet Karen. Already the seeds of a new direction in her life were being sown. But first of all, she needed to know how the fashion industry worked. And she hoped Karen would share that knowledge with her.

After a tense conversation, Philippe had finally agreed to host the lunch in the main dining room downstairs.

It's just family, he had said but that argument had failed to persuade Karen.

I don't care, she had replied, *we are having lunch in the main dining room.*

Clarence had quickly learned to stand aside from the small domestic disagreements that marked Karen and Philippe's relationship. He knew Karen would always get her way. He knew instinctively she had her heart set on the one opportunity to use the main dining room during this first visit.

And so he had spent the better part of a day retrieving the dinnerware and glassware from storage for the lunch that became far more formal than Philippe had in mind, but it was exactly what Karen had in mind.

It was, however, Clarence who offered the solution of seating the group at one end of the table, which was really too large for the small group.

To Barbara Cox, the whole thing was surreal. Across the table from her, she eyed Karen enviously. Young. Beautiful. Her husband clearly captivated by her. Yet her natural Australian charm broke down the barriers more quickly than anyone had ever thought likely.

'Philippe tells me you have important meetings next week to show off new designs.'

'Yes, Walter, I do,' she replied.

And then she turned to Virginia.

'You should come with me, Virginia,' she said. 'I could really use someone to model a couple of pieces for me. You would be about the right size, I would think.'

Virginia had already spent the better part of the lunch quizzing Karen about her business. Looking at her, Karen had noticed a real sense of style in the way she dressed.

'I'd love to, Karen,' she said excitedly. 'I'd love to.'

And in that moment, Walter felt a new sense of appreciation for Karen, for her gesture towards his sister. It's strange, he thought. My mother set out to dislike her. Probably my sister too. And I still feel angry about the way Julia was treated. But, for all that, she is very hard to dislike. Impossible in fact, he decided.

Philippe risked a glance at Clarence, who was hovering with wine ready to refill empty glasses and smiled.

The lunch was going much better than anyone expected. And it was all down to Karen. Even Barbara Cox had managed the occasional smile and had contributed to the flow of conversation.

As they finished lunch and headed to the drawing room for coffee, Louis-Philippe, wide-eyed and cautious, was brought in to meet his extended family. He gurgled happily as his mother held out her arms to take him.

'He's wary of strangers,' Philippe explained.

Barbara was the first to remark his likeness to Philippe and with it, the likeness to the men of the Cox family.

'He looks just like you, Philippe. In fact, he looks just the way Walter looked as a baby,' she said.

Philippe nodded.

'Do you think so, Barbara? My daughter predicted he might end up with red hair like his mother.'

There was silence for a moment, each one wondering how Pippa was dealing with the birth of her half-brother and her father's quick remarriage.

'Speaking of your daughter, how is she?' Barbara asked, as if she was genuinely interested.

'She's well, Barbara. She's taking over running the Foundation in Sydney. Joel Tynan is taking a job as an emergency department doctor. It was time for him to get back to practising his profession.'

As he mentioned Joel's name, he glanced in Virginia's direction. Surely it had been a short-lived romance. He was relieved to see her smile briefly as if remembering a delightful interlude.

Barbara wondered then if Pippa's main job had really been to console her mother as her life unravelled. But looking at Philippe's baby son, she was reminded too of the threat he represented to the succession plans she had for her own family.

She had been content, finally, when she heard her son Walter would be Philippe's key beneficiary and would take over as head of the family. But could that change in the years ahead? She had a new worry now. Philippe might easily live to see Louis-Philippe turn twenty-one. Would he make the change then, disinheriting Walter in favour of Louis-Philippe?

Walter must marry soon, she decided, and have a son himself. A son who can contest any arrangement that privileges Philippe's son.

No one knew what thoughts were going through her mind. If they had, they might have remarked how her plotting was worthy of a royal court.

Let them all think I'm reconciled to the situation but nothing is going to be allowed to get between Walter and his inheritance, she decided. One illegitimate child inheriting the bulk of the Cox wealth would torment her forever. The prospect of another one following in those footsteps was intolerable. Heirs, that's what Walter needs she decided. And quickly.

She did not know her wish was going to be fulfilled much more quickly than she ever imagined. But not in the way she hoped. Not with any of the girls she had begun, mentally, to assemble as a future wife for Walter and mother to Walter William Cox V.

As Philippe and Karen farewelled the small family group, he put his arm around her.

'You did very well, my darling,' he said. 'You had them eating out of the palm of your hand.'

She put her arms around him and laughed.

'I told you I could do that. Now you believe me. Make a fuss of Barbara, show her how important she is by having lunch in the main dining room. And make a friend of Virginia. That bit was easy.'

'And Walter?'

'Walter likes me but he doesn't like me if you understand what I mean. A part of him will always be loyal to Julia.'

He smiled at how perceptive she was.

'You're right. He got on very well with Julia,' he admitted.

'As did Clarence, I suspect.'

But he wouldn't be drawn further into discussing his former wife. Even he had times of deep melancholy knowing how he had hurt her. He knew very little about her life now and how she was coping, because Pippa refused to discuss her mother with him. But he felt reassured by the knowledge of her close family at Prior Park. He was sure the Belleville family would continue to be the anchor it had always been in her life.

'That went well,' Walter said, as they all stopped to remove their coats and scarves in the hallway. 'I told you Karen was very nice.'

'Well, she's certainly got Philippe under her thumb,' his mother said. 'He seems very calm about fatherhood at his age.'

Walter laughed out loud.

'I don't think he had a choice, Mother,' he said. 'I'm pretty sure having a baby was Karen's decision.'

'And speaking of babies, Walter,' she said, seizing the opportunity, 'it's high time you got married and had a baby. Hopefully a son to succeed you in running the estate. We don't want Philippe getting any ideas he can flip it back from you to his new son. He'll feel more contented if you have an heir who is being brought up in America. We don't want some half breed Australian taking over the Cox legacy.'

He was aghast at what she had just said.

'Mother, that's a terrible thing to say. So he may be brought up in Australia, but he is still Philippe's son. Philippe can do what he wants with the legacy. If the time comes and he wants to nominate Louis-Philippe in my place, I'll just have to accept it. But that's a long way off. The baby is less than a year old.'

But his mother was not convinced by his argument.

'Be that as it may, if you have a son, that will be a more natural progression,' she said. 'I've stayed out of your life because we always end up arguing but I had hoped to see you married by now.'

And then he smiled.

'Well, Mother, hopefully you'll get your wish very soon.'

'What do you mean? Get my wish very soon. I didn't know you were dating anyone seriously.'

He shrugged his shoulders. Should he tell her? Would there ever be a better time?

'I'm about to ask a woman to marry me. Keep your fingers crossed she'll accept me.'

'Who are you going to ask, Walter? Why don't I know about this?'

'You don't know about this, Mother,' he said quietly, 'because it's Arabella Courtenay. I'm in love with her. I believe she's in love with me.'

For just a moment, it was as if the power of speech had deserted Barbara Cox.

Beside her, Virginia smiled. So she's switched from Philippe to my brother, she mused. Can't he see she's after a meal ticket? But underneath it all, she liked Arabella. She quickly began to warm to the idea of Arabella as a sister-in-law. But there was no way Barbara Cox would warm to the idea of Arabella Courtenay becoming her daughter-in-law.

'You cannot be serious, Walter,' she spluttered. 'She's too old for a start. And she's nobody. She's an employee. You'll be shunned by all the families who matter.'

'She isn't nobody, Mother. She's the woman I love. And what if she is too old to have children? We can leave it to Virginia to continue the Cox dynasty.'

With that he donned his coat again, deciding it was time to visit Arabella and pop the question.

Arabella greeted Walter with a cheery smile and hustled him into the living room where a fire blazed in the hearth. The afternoon had turned very cold with the occasional snow flurry.

As he warmed himself by the fire, he turned to look at her. He noticed with relief she seemed to have regained her colour and spirit.

'I have something important to ask you, Arabella,' he said, struggling to find just the right words. 'You don't have to give me an answer straight away.'

She said nothing, waiting instead for him to ask the question she hoped he would ask.

'I want to marry you, Arabella. I love you. Will you be my wife?'

There, he had said it. When she did not respond immediately, he sighed deeply.

'I've blown it, haven't I?' he said, losing his nerve. 'I've made a complete hash of this. It should have been champagne and flowers. I'm sorry.'

She crossed the floor and put her arms around him. It was suddenly important to her to know his true feelings. Had he simply got carried away and would later regret it?

'Walter. It's the perfect proposal but I thought I was just a fling for you. Just another girl in your long line of conquests. I wasn't expecting it, that's all.'

But still he would not be convinced he hadn't handled everything badly.

'It should have been different, my darling,' he said. 'More romantic. Not with both of us shivering with the cold.'

His arms closed around her.

'You don't have to answer me now, right this minute,' he said. But of course he wanted an answer.

'Yes, I will marry you Walter,' she said finally. Was this the right thing to do, she wondered? Did she love him enough to make the marriage work? Only time would tell. Did he love her enough to bridge the age gap between them? She hoped so. 'But I would prefer to make it official when I get back from England. I left a message with my secretary to pass on to you and Philippe that I will be away for a few weeks. My sister has decided to bring forward her wedding. I'm leaving for London tomorrow.'

Just for a moment, he considered the prospect she might never return. And then he dismissed the thought. She wouldn't do that to him. Or Philippe. Or to the job she valued.

'I'm delighted,' he said. 'By the time you get back a sparkling diamond will be waiting for you. A late spring wedding perhaps?'

She smiled.

'In England, with my family, perhaps?'

'Of course. Wherever you like.'

'And where will we live? Please don't say *with your mother.*'

He laughed.

'Certainly not,' he said, pulling a face. 'I'll start looking for a house before you get back.'

For Arabella, it had solved an emerging problem. But in solving one problem had she simply created another? In accepting him, she had ignored the misgivings deep in her soul. Because she knew in marrying Walter, she would begin her married life with one big lie.

She hoped and prayed it would never be exposed. In that, she was relying on one woman who had agreed to help her.

It was several days before Walter had the chance to catch Philippe alone in his study. An absence of two months had meant a pile of paperwork needing Philippe's signature and accounting and investment reports demanding his attention and approval.

As Walter approached his study, Clarence nodded.

'He's by himself finally, Walter. Mrs Duval is in New York at a department store meeting. The baby is having his afternoon nap. And the lawyers and accountants have finally left. Time for your good news, I think.'

Walter smiled.

'Thanks, Clarence. It is good news, isn't it?'

'It is, Walter,' Clarence agreed, despite his reservations which remained unspoken. And would always remain unspoken.

Philippe looked up from his desk as Walter strode into the room.

'Sorry, Walter, I haven't had time to sit down and catch up with you on business matters since I got back but I have to say you've done a good job of keeping everything on track in my absence.'

'Well, as good as I could. Unfortunately, there are some things only you can sign or approve.'

'We'll change that over time, Walter,' he promised as he moved to sit in his favourite armchair. 'Clarence hinted you have something important to tell me.'

He smiled broadly.

'I've been desperate to tell you that Arabella has accepted my proposal of marriage. We'll be married in England in the spring,' he said.

Philippe stood and held out his hand to Walter to congratulate him.

'I'm delighted, Walter,' he said. 'She will be a wonderful wife to you, I'm sure. She deserves some happiness after what her first husband put her through.'

As Philippe was speaking, Clarence appeared with a tray of fresh coffee.

'It really should be champagne but it's a bit early for that,' Philippe said. 'I take it you know Walter's good news, Clarence?'

He nodded and smiled.

'I think possibly you are the last to know, Dr Duval. The staff of both households have been bubbling with the news for days, although there's disappointment we won't be hosting the wedding.'

Philippe laughed. He knew there were times there were things going on in the house he knew nothing about. But no one suspected for a moment that Philippe had known for days.

At the very moment Arabella had been boarding the plane for England, a letter had been hand delivered to him by her secretary.

In the short time he took to read it, he allowed himself a few moments of wistfulness. Of regret. Of disappointment. Of jealousy. But ultimately all these emotions were tinged with relief.

'We must have an engagement party when she gets back from England to announce it,' Philippe said, as Karen bounced into the room, full of news of the successful presentation of her new line.

'What's this about, Walter? Did I hear the word engagement?'

'You did, Karen. Arabella and I are getting married in the spring.' She hugged him.

'That's wonderful news. I'm sorry not to meet her this trip.'

'There'll be other opportunities, I'm sure,' he said. 'She didn't want to miss her sister's wedding, which was rather sprung on her at the last minute.'

'Of course not,' Karen said.

And in that moment, Philippe breathed a sigh of relief. There would be no eruptions of suspicion from Karen. Had the months he spent enjoying Arabella's companionship been his summer of madness, he wondered? Is that how he should see it? Whatever it was, she had made it very clear. That part of their relationship now belonged in the past. Firmly in the past. And would never be spoken of between them.

✳✳

There was almost nothing about Arabella's and Walter's wedding day that pleased Barbara Cox.

'Mother, it's what Arabella wants that's important,' he had said for the last time as she fussed over his wedding suit.

His mother refrained from correcting him. *It's what Lady Gloria Courtenay wants*, she wanted to say. She knew, as far as Lady Gloria was concerned, if she couldn't snare an English aristocrat for her daughter second time around, then a young, good-looking American with a considerable fortune awaiting him was the next best thing.

So it was that Walter and Arabella made their vows to each other in a local guildhall surrounded by a small group of family and friends before returning to her uncle's country home in Dorset to celebrate in the tepid warmth of an English spring.

Arabella had hidden her expanding waistline under a careful layering of satin and lace. But of course everyone knew. And everyone knew Walter was delighted. And if the wedding wasn't exactly what Barbara Cox had planned for her only son, the impending arrival of the baby she was convinced would be a boy was more than adequate compensation.

But there were notable absentees from the celebrations.

At the last minute, Karen had fallen ill with a bad case of flu so they had not made the trip, news Arabella had received with a small sigh of relief.

CHAPTER 22

America—September 1971

BARBARA COX HAD REPEATEDLY expressed her disappointment that the one-year-old whose fingers were now covered by sticky icing from his birthday cake had not been named Walter William Cox V.

Despite her pleadings, Walter had stood firm. Little Sebastian Courtenay Cox was, of course, totally unaware of his grandmother's misgivings about his name. What everyone remarked, however, was his likeness to his cousin, older by exactly thirteen months. Louis-Philippe Duval eyed the birthday cake from across the table with a mixture of suspicion and eagerness.

Walter was delighted at how much his son favoured his looks and how quickly the child had overcome his slightly premature birth, according to Arabella's doctor. The fact Arabella had chosen Philippe's first wife Jennifer to attend her had only caused him mild surprise. But he knew Arabella trusted her implicitly.

Barbara Cox at least had achieved one victory. She was hosting the first birthday party which was less a children's party and more an excuse to open the best champagne and show off her beautiful grandson to her admiring friends.

Amongst the chatter and laughter of the child's birthday party, only Arabella noticed the whispered conversation taking place in a quiet corner of the room.

For Arabella, there was a fleeting frisson of anxiety in watching Philippe deep in conversation with Jennifer Newman.

'It was good of you to attend Arabella,' Philippe said quietly. 'I think she was worried the child would not survive. I'm grateful. It's not in your normal line of medical work.'

Jennifer smiled.

'I was pleased to help her out. She was worried, you're right. But it all went smoothly this time.'

'If a little prematurely?' Philippe asked.

There was a pause—too long a pause—before she answered.

'Yes, a little prematurely, certainly,' she said finally, 'but he's passed all his tests so far so there's no worry there. He's perfectly healthy.'

She was silent then, but privately she berated herself. *I should have known he would ask some probing questions. I should have been better prepared.*

'Was Walter content with the … ?'

'Yes, he was,' she said, cutting him short. She knew what he was about to ask.

'Good,' Philippe said, nodding slightly.

'You look relieved,' Jennifer said gently.

'I am,' he said.

He was going to leave it at that but he saw the look of stern rebuke in her eyes.

'For a while there I was bewitched.'

He hoped that small admission would be sufficient explanation. It was not a conversation he wanted to pursue. But he knew Jennifer would not let it go at that.

'And now?'

He looked across at Arabella, who was busy wiping little Sebastian's messy face. And then his gaze shifted to Karen, who, champagne glass in hand, was attempting to coax from a determined Louis-Philippe a paper napkin he had chewed to a soggy mess.

'Karen is good for me,' he said finally.

'I can see that,' Jennifer said unexpectedly. 'She's got a tough, independent streak, I'd say. And she has her own business too. Your life together isn't just all about you, is it?'

He laughed then.

'No, it isn't just about me,' he said, seeing how much satisfaction that knowledge gave Jennifer.

He paused for a moment. He was remembering his brief marriage to Jennifer with some embarrassment.

'I'm sorry. I know I treated you very badly,' he said, unexpectedly.

'You did,' she agreed. 'And you never apologised either.'

He was chastened by her accusation.

'You're right. I'm very sorry for the way I treated you but I hope I'm a better man now,' he said quietly, 'although the events of the past few years might give the lie to that statement.'

'What can I say,' she said with a quiet chuckle and an exaggerated roll of her eyes. 'I'm sure I'm not the only woman you disappointed. I hope you apologised to your second wife.'

He was wistful for a moment, remembering Julia. Remembering her with love. Remembering how he had broken her heart. He understood, in the cold light of day, Karen had forced him to end his marriage to Julia.

'I did apologise to Julia. In the end I had no choice but to walk away from her. For Louis' sake.'

Jennifer nodded, knowing he could never leave his son to be brought up without a father.

'And now you must be a good husband to Karen,' she said, as if laying down the terms of her complicity.

'Yes, I will be. She'll have no reason to doubt my commitment,' he said finally as if they were setting the seal on their bargain.

It was a bargain never spoken aloud, but a bargain nonetheless. Only three people would ever know the truth about the son Walter had happily claimed as his own. And of those three people, none would ever speak the truth.

Later that day, when the one-year-old star of the day lay fast asleep in his cot, Walter put his arms around his wife.

'Thank you for letting my mother have her moment of triumph,' he said. 'I think it went well.'

'Your mother's society friends were keen to get a close look at me,' she said. 'I wonder if they approved?'

'Of course they did,' he reassured her. 'Who cares anyway?'

Walter had been surprised at Arabella's anxiety to please his mother, as if she wanted to prove to his mother she was worthy of being his wife.

'Your mother cares, Walter. It's important to her.'

'You're too kind, my darling,' he said. 'I hope she's nice to you. That's what's important.'

She smiled.

'Of course she is. Did you expect anything less?'

'Oh, I think she had plans for me that began with a list of her friends' most eligible daughters.'

'And I wasn't on the list, was I?'

He shook his head, remembering his mother's reaction to the news he was about to propose to Arabella.

'Her main objection was she thought you were too old to have a child.'

'Really? Well I proved her wrong,' she said. And then she paused. Was this the right moment to tell him? 'And I'm about to prove her wrong again.'

She heard Walter's quick intake of breath and then his face broke into a broad smile.

'Are you sure? Are you absolutely sure? When is it due?'

'Yes, I'm sure,' she said calmly. 'I think the baby's going to be a wedding anniversary present.'

'Maybe we'll have a daughter this time,' he said.

She could see he was delighted by the news.

'I think that's in the lap of the gods, don't you?'

He looked at her carefully then.

'I'll have to look after you,' he said gently. 'No stress. You need to take it easy. Don't work so hard. Philippe will understand.'

He had been amazed how successfully she had juggled motherhood and managing the Foundation. He sighed deeply.

How happy can a man be, he wondered? At twenty, he had been wild and irresponsible. Now at thirty, he was settled—a family man—and slowly but surely beginning to shoulder some of the responsibilities of guiding the Cox family's wealth, a role his father had never imagined he would be capable of fulfilling.

And then he thought about his marriage. It was loving and warm. He had been right to choose Arabella. A second child will complete our family, he thought. And her previous close friendship with Philippe no longer troubled him. He was satisfied there was only one woman in Philippe's life. Karen, delightful and demanding, had made sure of that. He smiled to himself.

'Something's amused you?' she said, as she noticed the smile flit across his face.

'Nothing really, just thinking that perhaps Philippe has met his match in Karen.'

She laughed, understanding exactly what he meant.

'She keeps him on his toes, that's for sure,' she said, 'but I have to say she seems to be genuinely in love with him.'

He nodded.

'I think she is,' he said. 'But then so was Julia.'

And then an uncomfortable thought came unbidden to Arabella's mind. *So was I* but it was something she could never confess. Not to Walter. Not to anyone. Instead, she put her arms around him.

'So what will we name a daughter if we have a girl,' she asked. 'I named Sebastian. It's your turn.'

He thought for a moment.

'Allana,' he said. 'I like Allana.'

'Then Allana it will be,' she said. 'It's a lovely name.'

And she knew then another baby would put the final seal on their marriage as if, in her mind, it was some fragile thing that might founder without the certainty of having a child fathered by Walter. As if, at any moment, her terrible secret might spill out into the open and shatter the life they had built together. And there would be nothing to hold onto. But a second child would change all that.

1995

BRIDGING THE YEARS

ACROSS THE SPAN of twenty-four years, much has happened in the Duval/Cox family.

As 1994 turns to 1995, Philippe and Karen are approaching their twenty-fifth wedding anniversary. Karen's fashion business has flourished just as their marriage has flourished as they split their time between Sydney and New York.

Their son, Louis-Philippe, has grown into a good-looking young man, not only full of confidence but confident of his place in the world. Privilege and wealth have settled easily on his shoulders, as have the business lessons his maternal grandfather, David Clarke, insisted on teaching him.

Yet it is clear his grandfather's passing seven years earlier has left a void in the young man's life. Now graduated with a Bachelor of Commerce degree, he feels ready to take on the business world. And agitate for his rightful role as the heir to the Cox estate after his father.

Pippa, now middle-aged, surprised her parents by secretly marrying Joel Tynan and surprised them even more when she presented them a year after her marriage with a granddaughter, Jessica. She has a special relationship with her grandfather, who indulged her shamelessly throughout her childhood. Every time he looks at her he sees the strong likeness with her grandmother, Julia.

Walter and Arabella will celebrate twenty-five years of marriage too. Walter has proved himself an invaluable understudy to Philippe in managing the Cox family wealth, especially with his real estate developments while Arabella, mother to Sebastian and Allana, has been kept busy as head of the Ella Duval Foundation.

Walter's wilful sister Virginia, who developed her own fashion label under Karen's guidance, married Matthew Grenville. The marriage produced two daughters, Mia and Sylvie.

To everyone's surprise Barbara Cox found a new role in life—doting on her grandchildren—but especially on Sebastian whose birth fulfilled her wish for Walter to have a son to succeed him.

As Philippe contemplates the future for the Cox family inheritance, he looks to the younger people—Louis, Sebastian, Allana, Mia, Sylvie and Jessica. A span of only six years separates them.

He worries especially that Louis will begin to press harder to be named his heir. Or at least to be named the principal heir to Walter. He can foresee a future where the rivalry between Louis and Sebastian might undo the unity he has been able to bring to the Cox family.

As Philippe's eightieth birthday approaches, the family is gathering to celebrate.

Eastbury Hall has come alive. Little used dinnerware and glassware is being retrieved from dusty storage cupboards. The chandelier in the dining room has been meticulously cleaned. The highly polished table is glowing.

Everything is being made ready to celebrate …

CHAPTER 23

America—January 1995

PHILIPPE LOOKED UP, slightly startled by the sound of the door to his study being thrown open with some force.

'Sitting in the dark again, old man. That's no good. You're doing too much of that lately.'

Philippe smiled to himself as he watched his son Louis buzz around the room turning on the lights until the room was brightly lit. A child of Australia. Of bright days. Of blue skies. Of the sun high overhead. That's what he is, Philippe decided. He's not a child of the gloomy winter days of New York.

'It's a day for reflection, Louis,' Philippe countered, as he looked closely at his son.

Was there anything of his mother Karen in his son's features? If there was, he failed to see it. Dark hooded eyes looked back at him from a face remarkably like his own. There was a slightly arrogant set to his lips which disappeared when his son laughed. But often there was a cynical edge to his laughter. And a swagger to his movements. Philippe dismissed these thoughts. Simply the over-confidence of youth, he decided. Or perhaps an over-confidence born of the wealth and privilege in which he had been raised. Just like his cousin Sebastian, Philippe thought. Just like Sebastian.

And even as the name came to Philippe's mind, Sebastian appeared as if from nowhere.

Side by side, the two young men looked alike. Both were tall with the same athletic build. The set of the mouth and the hooded eyes spoke of kinship. It was only the light brown hair and fairer colouring that set Sebastian apart. His mother's looks had not been completely eradicated by the Cox genes.

'Pippa and Joel have just arrived,' he announced. 'And Jessica too of course.'

The family had been expected the day before, but their flight had been delayed in Honolulu with engine trouble.

Philippe remembered how he had been surprised when Pippa had announced she was pregnant only a matter of months after she had shocked her parents by marrying Joel Tynan in a ceremony to which no one had been invited. Now, each time he saw his granddaughter, he was reminded of her grandmother. Of the young girl he had loved in wartime Australia.

Even as he was thinking these thoughts, Jessica burst into his study, blonde hair flying as she threw her arms around her grandfather.

'I thought we'd never get here in time,' she said, breathlessly. 'Happy birthday, Grandpa. You don't look a day over eighty.'

He laughed good-naturedly as she hugged Louis and Sebastian in turn.

'My beautiful niece,' Louis said, as he embraced her. He had become an uncle at the tender age of six.

'My delightful uncle,' she said, responding in kind. 'And my delightful cousin too,' she said as she kissed Sebastian on the cheek.

'Are these two annoying you, Grandpa? Do you want me to get rid of them for you?'

Philippe laughed. She knew she was special to him. Having been deprived of the opportunity to be part of his own daughter's young childhood, he had enjoyed being involved with Jessica. There were times he had thought Louis was jealous of her.

'No, my dear,' he said laughing. 'I think they're here to remind me I need to get ready for the big birthday dinner tonight.'

'As if you need reminding,' she scoffed. 'I'm sure Karen's been talking of nothing else for the past week.'

He smiled. She was right. Organising the dinner had been Karen's major preoccupation for the past week or more.

'Before you go, I have something to give you from my grandmother,' she said, her tone suddenly more serious.

Philippe tried to hide his surprise. He had seen Julia only a few times in the years since their divorce. It had, in fact, been Jessica's birth that had brought them together again. Neither of them had been prepared to miss her christening or her first birthday. Or many subsequent birthday celebrations. He was grateful to Karen for diplomatically absenting herself from these landmark occasions. But he had insisted Louis attend with him.

Jessica held out a carefully wrapped box.

'Do you know what's in it?' he asked

She shook her head.

'I don't but my grandmother said it's something you would remember. Fondly, she hoped.'

He read the accompanying card in silence.

P, Do you remember the day you took this photo? And the day you invited me into the dark room to see it? Bittersweet memories for me. Happy birthday. J xxx

He pulled back the tissue paper to study the framed photograph of Julia, nineteen years old, her face partly in the shadow, the light perfect. He had been proud of the photograph. And he had been enraptured by the beautiful young girl.

He sat back in his chair, his mind no longer focusing on the present. He was, instead, remembering the day he had taken the photo. The war in the Pacific not yet won. His life a day-to-day proposition. He remembered how meeting her had been a wonderful antidote to the war and the day-to-day grind of being an army medic.

And later, in the dark room, he had taken advantage of her shamelessly, but always with the intention he would propose marriage. Except that he had been posted. And her well-meaning but controlling mother had intervened. And Pippa had been given away for adoption.

As the entire history of what the photo represented played out in his memory, three young people stood transfixed, watching him closely. Watching his face. His emotions exposed more than they had ever seen before, as if a veil was being lifted.

Gently, Jessica took the photo from him and they all looked at the image.

'Your grandmother, Jessica?' Louis asked.

She nodded.

'Yes, that's my grandmother,' she said, 'but I've never seen the photograph before. It must mean something special.'

She picked up the card that had dropped from the tissue paper. And then she understood.

'It's about the two of them. Where their relationship began.'

And then she looked at Louis.

'You are the reason my grandparents split up,' she said, not meaning to sound unkind but she had to blame someone. Like her mother, she believed her grandparents should still be together. That her grandmother had never quite recovered from the disappointment of being divorced by her grandfather.

Louis shrugged. What could he say except the obvious?

'My father loves my mother,' he said, defending his father's actions. 'They have a very good marriage.'

'But he loved my grandmother. And she loved him. But he wouldn't allow his son—you—to be illegitimate so he had to give up my grandmother.'

Philippe listened to the discussion, marvelling at how easy it was for his granddaughter and his son to discuss his relationships as if he was no longer capable of giving his opinion or of defending himself. But what could he say in his own defence? Jessica was right. Karen had forced his hand. But he could not lay the blame anywhere but at his own door, if it was blame that needed to be apportioned. Did that mean he regretted the birth of his son, Louis? How could he do that? Yet part of him would always regret the circumstances of his divorce from Julia. But the two events could not be separated. Could never be separated.

And now, just as he had predicted, tensions were beginning to emerge with his son. He had always known the day would come when Louis would no longer be content to be passed over as his primary heir in favour of Walter. How many times lately had Louis pushed the case to be his primary heir? Philippe was losing count.

And in those moments, Philippe saw the unmistakable influence of his grandfather, who had doted on the boy. To everyone's surprise, David Clarke had lived long enough to see Louis graduate high school. And on Louis' twenty-fifth birthday the previous year, he had assumed control of his grandfather's final legacy to him. He now controlled a fifty percent share of the Clarke family's car dealerships alongside his mother Karen who, despite his protests, remained as the company chair. It was a part of his son's life from which Philippe was largely excluded.

As he sat thinking about the way his life had evolved, he looked at Sebastian. Each time Philippe witnessed the closeness between Walter and his son, he was quietly pleased. Pleased that Arabella, all those years ago, had decided on a course of action that had secured her child's future. It was something he had never discussed with her. It was, for both of them, a forbidden topic.

He shook his head then as if to dismiss the thoughts, as if even remembering that period of his life was dangerous. He remembered the brief note Arabella had written him before she married Walter.

I have accepted Walter's proposal of marriage. I am determined our marriage will be successful. But for it to be successful, you and I must put the past behind us. I ask for your discretion. But I will always cherish the time we spent together.

What I am doing in marrying Walter is in everyone's best interests. But there will always be a corner of my heart that belongs to you.

A xxx

And even now he wondered if a corner of his heart still belonged to Arabella. Just as a corner of his heart still belonged to Julia. Was it possible to love only one woman? It was a question to which he could never find a satisfactory answer.

'You're deep in thought, Uncle,' Sebastian said, watching him closely.

'Across eighty years, there's a lot to remember, Sebastian,' he replied. 'A lot to remember. It seems like the right day to be looking back over my life. Was there something you wanted?'

Sebastian shrugged.

'A couple of questions I wanted to ask you. But they can wait,' he replied, indicating they were matters he would rather discuss privately.

Philippe nodded.

'Another time perhaps, when I'm not the centre of attention,' he said.

Sebastian laughed.

'But you're always the centre of attention,' he said. 'The entire family revolves around you. It's as if everyone wants to please you. Or impress you. Or is worried about what you will think.'

Philippe let out a short derisory laugh.

'That's not how it looks from where I sit, Sebastian,' he said.

And then he remembered his father. He knew, in his last years, his father had dominated those around him. And not in a good way. He hoped he wasn't being accused of doing the same thing.

'How does it feel to be eighty?' Pippa asked as she glided into the room with Joel close behind her. 'Happy birthday. I wish you'd been born in June and not January.'

His Sydney family had all grumbled at the prospect of leaving summer behind to fly to a snow bound airport in New York.

'What's this?' she asked as she picked up the framed photograph that lay on the coffee table in front of him.

'Jessica brought it with her. It's from your mother,' he explained.

She studied the photograph intently.

'When was this taken?'

'1943, not long after I met your mother.'

'Did you give it to her before you left Australia?'

He smiled, remembering Julia's delight at the photograph.

'I invited her to see it being processed. I set up a dark room in the hotel we were billeted in. It was the most perfect photo I'd ever taken. And then a month or so later I was posted to Hawaii.'

Pippa looked up from her intense study of the photograph.

'And left my mother pregnant and at the mercy of her mother.'

She had filled in the gaps in his story.

He let out a long sigh. Would she ever let him forget?

'You know that's what happened, Pippa. I tried to keep in touch with her. I wrote for eighteen months but my letters were intercepted.'

It was all ancient history now.

But the three young people were transfixed. They all knew versions of the story but to hear it from his own lips was completely unexpected. Louis turned to Pippa as if he wanted her to know their mothers had both shared the same experience.

'It seems our father has a history of seducing women and getting them pregnant,' Louis said, with a half laugh.

He turned then to look at Sebastian.

'I've heard your mother and my father were very close friends after she first came to work for him. Maybe she was lucky not to be left pregnant and without a husband too. Or is that why she snapped up your father so quickly after my parents married?'

No one could misunderstand his meaning.

In that moment—in that awful moment when Philippe knew he must lie and lie convincingly for Sebastian's sake—it was Jessica who came to his rescue.

'You are so ridiculous, Louis. You just want to create trouble where none exists.'

Louis laughed.

'I didn't expect anyone to take me seriously, Jess,' he said, gesturing apologetically for his poor attempt at humour.

But the words, once spoken, had taken on a life of their own. Sebastian looked from one to the other and then to Pippa, who averted her gaze, not knowing what to say.

Philippe, above all others, saw the danger of how a few careless words had the potential to tear the family apart. He knew what would happen if the truth emerged. Walter and Arabella's marriage would crumble. Sebastian would be left in a world of uncertainty. And Karen might well file for divorce. And where would that leave him? The family split beyond repair. And he would be left a lonely old man paying a price for his past sins.

'Don't take any notice of Louis,' he said firmly. 'Jessica's right. He's just being ridiculous.'

'Thanks, Uncle, I always thought the gossip I heard about the two of you was ridiculous,' he said, 'but I'm pleased to hear you say it's ridiculous.'

Philippe frowned. Why would anyone still be gossiping about them, so long after Sebastian's birth? It worried him yet he knew he could not probe further. To ask more questions would simply raise new suspicions. And yet he knew the conversation would continue to trouble him.

'I must go and get ready,' he said, rising from his chair with an agility that surprised them all.

As if on cue, Karen appeared in the doorway and clapped her hands, which startled them all.

'Time to get ready,' she said, conspicuously consulting her watch.

One by one they drifted from the room while she waited for Philippe.

'I'm a bit slower these days, my darling,' he said with a grimace. Arthritis was making its presence felt, despite his attempts to remain active and keep it at bay.

She smiled. In a few days' time, they would celebrate twenty-five years of marriage. Her life with him had been everything she had hoped for. And then she saw the photograph on the coffee table. Curious, she picked it up.

'A memory from your deep past, by the look of it,' she said. 'She was a beautiful young girl. No wonder you fell for her.'

'It was another life,' he said, looking fondly at the picture. 'Another life altogether.'

'Jessica is very much like her, isn't she?'

He nodded.

'She is. Remarkably so. She gets on very well with Julia.'

'And Pippa? Does she get on with her mother?'

'She does. Of course she does. But part of her could never quite forgive Julia for giving her up for adoption.'

'Or quite forgive you for giving up her mother,' Karen said.

He sighed deeply.

'We can't always please our children, can we?'

'No, we can't. I didn't tell you I've had to quietly overturn some decisions Louis has made about the car dealerships. He'll find out when he gets back to Sydney.'

'Expect fireworks,' Philippe said with a smile. 'He has a lot of your father in him.'

'I know he does. A lot. But then so do I,' she said. 'So do I.'

He laughed quietly to himself. He had every confidence Karen would be a match for their headstrong son. Together, they headed along the corridor to the master bedroom suite where she had already laid out his suit.

'You look after me very well,' he said.

She kissed him on the cheek.

'It's a pleasure,' she said. 'It's a pleasure because I love you.'

'I love you too,' he said, realising he had not said those words so much lately.

As he dressed, his mind drifted back to Sebastian's comment. Was it recent gossip, he wondered? Or was it something he'd heard as a child? Would Arabella know?

But he was in two minds about asking her. Did he really need to revisit this issue now? Wouldn't it be better to let it go and hope it was never raised again?

But something told him he had not heard the last of it. And then he decided. If someone is still spreading gossip, money might well be the answer. And if money was the answer, he was prepared to pay whatever it would take to ensure the truth never emerged. To ensure the truth lay buried forever.

That evening, all of Philippe's anxieties were forgotten as he sat at the head of the glittering dining table surrounded by family members. He wondered how it was that a barefoot boy who could number his family members on one hand now found himself at a table surrounded by fourteen members of his family. Life had delivered him a strange and unpredictable journey. Had he really controlled his own life, he wondered, or had events directed it in ways he could never have predicted nor controlled.

He thought back to the day he learned he was the principal heir to the Cox wealth. Would his life have been better if that decision had never been made? Would he have lived a more contented life as a doctor? He was no longer sure. With wealth had come new challenges. And new horizons. And temptations to which he had succumbed. And he had paid the price. But if asked he would have described himself as a contented man mostly.

Amid the chatter and laughter, Walter caught his eye.

'A more contented family than the one you came into, Philippe,' he observed, indicating the group at the table with a sweep of his hand. 'You should be proud of that. This is more than my grandfather achieved. And my father certainly wouldn't have achieved it.'

It seemed Walter too was remembering.

'I'm pleased you think that, Walter,' he said. 'What little I knew of my father was enough to convince me I didn't want to be like him in my old age. He was very embittered towards the end.'

Walter nodded.

'He was, sadly. It rather overshadowed what he'd achieved.'

And what of the next generation, Philippe wondered? He looked along the table to where Louis sat alongside Sebastian and Allana, across the table from Virginia's two daughters Mia and Sylvie and, further along, Pippa's daughter Jessica. He envied them their youth. At twenty-five, he remembered embarking on his medical career with such high hopes yet by the end of the following year, he was in the army. It all seemed so long ago now.

At the far end, Karen was keeping an eagle eye on proceedings. She too was remembering. Remembering the first meal she had hosted at that very table, nearly twenty-five years earlier. And after that, the family lunch had become a Sunday ritual each time she was with Philippe at Eastbury Hall. Her efforts had made the difference. And she had insisted the young children be included as soon as they were old enough to sit on a chair.

She turned towards Pippa, their old enmities forgotten, if not entirely forgiven.

'I'm so pleased you got here in time. Your father would have been very disappointed if you hadn't made it.'

'We all would have been disappointed, Karen,' she said, 'especially Jessica. And carrying her secret commission too.'

'You mean the photograph of your mother? I saw it on the coffee table. I thought perhaps you'd brought it with you.'

Pippa shook her head and smiled.

'No, it was something my mother and Jessica cooked up between them.'

'I take it Jessica sees a lot of your mother?'

'She does. She's spending more and more time with my mother at Prior Park.'

'Is that where her life is headed?' She was curious. She and Philippe rarely discussed Pippa's family. It was as if he preferred to keep that part of his life separate from her and Louis, as if his divorce from Pippa's mother still haunted him.

'Possibly. She likes the country life. Joel is a little disappointed she didn't follow him into medicine, but I reminded him it's something you really need to have a passion for. My father had it. Joel has it. But I could never find it. Not to the same degree.'

Across the table, Arabella sat quietly, but she too was wondering what would happen with the next generation. Before long, there'll be marriages, she mused, and then children and she and Walter would be grandparents. She wondered how Walter would cope, taking on the management of the Cox wealth but he had reassured her he was well prepared. He already had joint control over many aspects of the investments. And then she looked at Philippe and realised, since his marriage, they had never spoken of their previous relationship. It had been a forbidden topic. And now it no longer matters, she thought. She had made the right choice in marrying Walter. But on her right wrist, she wore the diamond and gold bracelet, Philippe's final gift to her. He had spotted it and smiled but said nothing as she greeted him that evening.

Of all his family seated at the table, it was only Joel who noticed Philippe lurch forward and clutch his chest briefly as if in pain before he settled back in his chair as if nothing had happened. He made a mental note to check up on Philippe at the end of the dinner.

Working swiftly and silently around the table, Edmund Bailey Temple carefully refilled wine and champagne glasses almost before anyone had noticed their glass was nearly empty. Tall, dark haired and quiet, he had spent more than a decade at Eastbury Hall, firstly as deputy to Clarence, and then as his replacement. To Philippe's relief the transition had been an easy one. He ran the house with the same quiet efficiency that had been Clarence's trademark.

As the main course was being removed, to Philippe's surprise, it was Louis who rose from his seat to propose a toast for his birthday. He had supposed it might be Walter or Karen who would undertake the task.

All eyes were on Louis as he stood facing towards his father, his wine glass held aloft

'Husband, father, grandfather, uncle, friend - my father is all these things. Everyone knows his modest beginnings. Everyone knows the story of how he came to inherit the Cox family fortune. These are all now part of family folklore,' Louis said.

'And before I was born, he was, of course, a very fine surgeon. And before that, an army medic.

'When we are eighty, will we all have similar extraordinary achievements to look back on?

'Somehow, I doubt it because he has made life easy for all of us. I want you all to join me in drinking to the health of an extraordinary man who is dear to us all.

'Happy eightieth birthday, old man. May there be many more.'

Beneath the glittering chandelier, crystal glasses were raised in his honour. He marvelled at his son's unexpected eloquence, but he struggled to know how he should respond. Simply with thanks? Or was this the moment, with everyone gathered, to make an important point about the future?

He rose to his feet, the chatter quietened by the scrape of his chair.

'I'm really delighted to see everyone here, enjoying themselves. I feel as though this is the crowning achievement of my life, bringing the Cox family together.'

He nodded in Barbara Cox's direction. She looked away, not willing to meet his eye.

'The early days when I took over were not easy because I was an outsider, but I was determined to treat everyone fairly. And I believe I have achieved that aim. So this is what I pass on to you all now.

Apart from Walter, Virginia and Pippa, we have a younger generation of Cox family heirs. Louis, Sebastian and Allana, Mia and Sylvie, and Jessica. When I'm no longer here, Walter will take over, as you all know.

But after that, who knows? But I want you all to be clear. My father, whom I hardly knew, elevated me above his other potential heir. After Walter, I want everyone to be clear it is my wish that the next generation understands something important: you are all equal in your entitlement to the Cox legacy. I have made certain the situation that occurred where I inherited the bulk of the estate will never occur again. Legally, I have made sure of that. But it will be equally important that one person, or perhaps two, manage the family investments for the benefit of all. That should come down to ability. And not necessarily seniority. It should all be managed in a spirit of cooperation.'

He could see he had their undivided attention now. It was as if this was the first time most of them had seriously considered the inheritance that awaited them.

Walter too was listening intently, now understanding some of the legal steps Philippe had taken to ensure no one, in future, would be disadvantaged. He was pleased Philippe had taken the opportunity to explain it. He had not been relishing the task himself.

But it was Louis who seemed the most intent on listening to Philippe as if everything his father said was directed at him.

Is he warning me, Louis wondered? He smiled to himself at his father's earnestness. Does he not realise I'm the only one with the business experience to step into Walter's shoes? He wanted to say it out loud but he did not. He did not want to spoil the mood. Nor did he want to spoil the dinner over which his mother had taken so much time and effort.

As if a distant voice was echoing in his head, he heard his father thank everyone for coming and thank his wife for having organised the dinner but his thoughts remained on what his father had said.

Louis had grudgingly accepted Walter as the next head of the family but he saw no reason why the tradition of appointing a single person to the primary role should end. He was the next principal heir. It had to be that way, he thought. It must be that way.

But he feared that his father, knowing how much he desired it, had taken steps to ensure it would never be. Had he wanted to avoid me clashing with Sebastian, he wondered? He glanced at Sebastian and for the first time he began to wonder if the gossip was true. Was Sebastian's father really Walter? Or had his father engaged in one last fling before his remarriage? But he knew he could not pursue it, not for his father's sake, or Sebastian's sake, but for his mother's sake. He would not be the one to puncture the fairytale of their marriage.

As he left the dining room with Sebastian, he did not notice how his father clung to his chair for support for just a moment. But Joel was looking out for further signs. Without any fuss, he moved to Philippe's side. He put his hand on his arm.

'Do you need help, Philippe?' he asked quietly.

Philippe shook his head.

'Just a bit of a chest pain, Joel. Nothing serious.'

But Joel ignored him.

'So you're a cardiac specialist now, are you?'

Philippe managed a weak smile.

'I've got some medication, Joel, if that's what you're worried about.'

'But are you taking it?'

He nodded.

'I am,' he said, determined to cut the conversation short as he started to walk away.

'And what have you told Karen? Or Pippa? Or Walter?'

'Nothing,' he said. 'Nothing at all. I don't want them to worry. And I don't want you to say anything either.'

He put his hand on Joel's arm.

'I don't want people fussing about me, Joel,' he insisted. 'Do you understand?'

'Of course I do but I think you need to have another full check up.'

'I will,' he promised. 'I will.'

'Before you get on the plane back to Sydney?'

'Yes, before I get on the plane back to Sydney.

And with that, Joel had to be content.

CHAPTER 24

America—January 1995

'YOU MUST BE PLEASED,' Arabella said, as, days later, she surveyed the crowded reception rooms at Eastbury Hall. She had insisted that Philippe's milestone birthday should be celebrated with a reception hosted by the Ella Duval Foundation.

More than twenty-five years after it had been set up, the Foundation was now well established and respected for the integrity of its research grant program. Yet Philippe was inclined to dismiss his own role in the success of the Foundation.

'Any success the Foundation has had is down to you, Arabella,' he said. 'It's your achievement, not mine.'

She shook her head, determined to acknowledge the important role he had played.

'Without your backing, none of this would have happened,' she said.

He shrugged. It had been a worthwhile project, something that had gone some way to replacing the medical career that had once consumed most of his attention.

She turned to face him.

'Is there something troubling you?' she asked quietly. 'I've had the sense you've wanted to say something to me ever since your birthday dinner.'

'Yes, there's something we need to talk about privately,' he replied, 'but not here. Not with Walter around.'

Across the room, they could see Walter in an animated discussion with a small group of guests. He had always been an enthusiastic supporter of the Foundation and of Arabella's work in particular.

For a few moments, they stood together in silence, each consumed by their own thoughts.

For Arabella, there was a rising tide of anxiety at his unexpected request. Did he know about Sebastian? Had he figured it out? Was this the problem that was troubling him now? And if it was, what was he planning to do about it?

In their twenty-five years working together, he had never asked the question she most feared. In fact, there were times she wondered if he even knew what she had hidden so successfully from him. And from Walter. But he must know, she had reasoned with herself. He must know. And now she was certain. He did know. And something in that knowledge now troubled him.

'There's a board meeting tomorrow,' she said quietly. 'Why don't you attend? Walter doesn't attend. It would be an opportunity.'

He nodded. It would be the perfect opportunity.

'I will,' he said. 'I'll do that.'

He turned away then to greet one of the Foundation's most generous benefactors.

The following day Philippe's presence was warmly welcomed by the Foundation's board members. His presence was unusual but not unwelcome. He sat back while Arabella took charge of the meeting, just as she had for years. In just over an hour, all the business had been discussed and agreed.

The room emptied quickly, much to Philippe's relief. He sat back down at the table, the agenda still in front of him. He waited while Arabella farewelled the directors until, finally, she came back into the room, closing the door behind her.

'I'd forgotten what a good meeting you run,' he said. 'Everything is kept on track. No pointless discussions.'

She smiled at the compliment.

'I learnt very quickly how to keep the discussions moving along,' she said, as she sat down alongside him. 'Besides, everyone's busy these days. They don't have time to sit around.'

'Will you bring Sebastian in on this work?' he asked.

She was surprised at the suggestion.

'Do you think it would suit him? I'm in two minds. Anyway, I think Walter has plans for him now he's finished college. Is that what you wanted to talk to me about? What happens in the future with the Foundation? Or was there …' Her voice trailed off.

He shook his head.

'No, it wasn't but now you mention it, we should think about it. I thought you might like to give it up at some stage?'

'Well, I have a very able deputy. She takes a lot of the workload now. Another year or two and I'll ease up.'

Philippe had left the appointment of a deputy entirely in Arabella's hands.

'You chose well. Marie Grenville is very competent from what I've seen.'

'I'm pleased you approve,' she said with a smile, 'but that's not what you really want to talk about, is it?'

She paused, watching him closely. She could see he was struggling with how to begin.

'Is it something to do with Sebastian?'

He nodded slightly.

'It is. I had a conversation with him on the day of my birthday.'

'And that conversation was about?'

She wasn't going to jump to conclusions.

'He'd overheard some gossip apparently. Gossip about us.'

'Really? After such a long time? Are you sure?'

She leant forward, fully alert now, listening carefully to what Philippe was saying.

'I thought it was odd too. After all this time. Why would anyone still be gossiping about us?'

Arabella sat back in her chair. She did not respond immediately. For the first time, Philippe noticed she was looking tired. Her honey blonde hair was streaked with grey. But, still, the years had not dimmed her lively nature.

'I wonder …'

She paused. Should she tell him what she was thinking?

'Wonder about what?' he asked.

'My secretary of many years retired last year. You must remember her. Margaret Kelly. She became great friends with Mrs Anderson, your housekeeper at the time. They attended the same church, I believe. There were times when I had the feeling she disapproved of me.'

'But not recently, surely?' he asked.

'No, but as she got older, she seemed to become more …'

She was struggling to find the right words.

'More judgemental perhaps?' he volunteered.

'I guess that's what I'm trying to say. And envious too, I think. Envious because she believed that somehow luck had smiled on me where it hadn't smiled on her.'

'And now you think because she's no longer working for you, she finally feels free to gossip about us. But why would anyone still be interested?'

And then he thought for a moment.

'Seeing Sebastian about the place, I suppose, now that he's finished college. I'm told he often works in the gardens. He seems to like the work.'

She laughed quietly.

'Yes, Walter told him to make himself useful until such time as he had worked out what he wanted to focus on. And he'd much rather do outdoor work than indoor work.'

'Just the way Walter was by the sound of it,' he said.

'While we're talking about the next generation, your birthday speech was quite eye opening,' she said. 'Walter thinks Louis won't take easily to the idea he won't be first among equals if you know what I mean.'

'I know what you mean,' Philippe said, 'but that won't make me change anything. Anyway, Sebastian might have felt it was his right to succeed his father in the role as primary heir and take charge of everything.'

Arabella shook her head. It would be out of character for her son, she was sure. And she knew Louis had the capacity to intimidate him, if he felt like it.

'Sebastian isn't like that. I don't think he would want confrontation. I think he'd probably just let Louis have his way. Anyway, in the end, they'll just have to sort it out themselves.'

'Is Walter OK with what I've decided?'

'I think so,' she said. 'Besides, he's very pragmatic. He pointed out he wouldn't be around to find out whether it was a good idea or not.'

He smiled. It was exactly what Walter had said to him. Let the future take care of itself.

'And the current problem?' she asked.

He brought his mind back to the present.

'If you challenge your former secretary, she'll deny it of course. Are you in touch with her?'

'I sent her a small gift at Christmas. She replied with thanks and a card, but I haven't spoken to her recently.'

'How is she placed financially?' he asked.

'I'm not sure,' she admitted. 'I don't like to ask such questions.'

'Of course not,' he said, 'but it might be wise to visit her on some pretext. You could always give her some honorary job that's not honorary, if you get my meaning. Nothing so obvious it looks like you're trying to buy her favour but generous enough that she feels obligation.'

'Such as?'

He shrugged.

'Perhaps doing garden tours or house tours when the reception rooms are open for inspection.'

She smiled at his practical solution.

'I'll give that a try,' she said. 'I certainly don't want Sebastian to feel there's something I'm hiding from him. It's too late for revelations.'

'I agree,' he said. 'There is nothing to be gained from raking over the past. Nothing at all.'

With that he got up and then he turned back towards her. Had they avoided a potential problem? He hoped so. But he felt he had to say something more. To acknowledge what she had done. To acknowledge she had been right to do it.

'I'll always be grateful for what you did,' he said gently. 'Always.'

It was the first time he had ever thanked her. The first time they had ever even spoken together about what she had done.

'When did you know …?'

'That I was pregnant?'

He nodded.

'Not long after you left for Sydney.'

He looked around nervously to make sure they wouldn't be overheard.

'I'm sorry I left you with that problem,' he said. He reached out and touched her cheek. 'But I don't regret being with you. You made those lonely months bearable. For me it was like a golden summer. Carefree. Indulgent. But always knowing it would end.'

'For me too,' she said. 'It was delightful for me too. And you were always honest with me. I was grateful for that but you still broke my heart.'

'I'm sorry,' he said. 'You know I didn't mean to. But I was promised elsewhere.'

And even as he heard himself saying the words he was remembering how, so many years before, he had said the same thing to Karen. *I'm promised elsewhere.*

He looked at her closely. A single tear ran down her cheek unchecked as if it had been waiting a very long time to be shed.

'We should not have waited so long to have this conversation,' he said, embracing her. 'The heartbreak wasn't all on one side. And then I was pleased to know you were marrying Walter. Jealous but pleased.'

'It seemed an obvious solution,' she said quietly. 'I didn't want to be the one to break up your relationship with Karen. Louis needed a father.'

He inclined his head slightly. It was as if she was saying Karen and Louis had a stronger claim to him.

'Thank you for doing that,' he said gently. 'I've always been pleased that your marriage worked out so well.'

She smiled slightly.

'When did you realise Sebastian was your … ?

He paused, thinking back to his shock at finding out Arabella had consulted his first wife, Jennifer. He had understood immediately why Arabella had turned to Jennifer.

'I had my suspicions when you consulted Jennifer.

'I thought she would help me. I was determined my baby wouldn't pay the price for …' Her voice trailed away.

He nodded, knowing what she had been about to say.

'For those months of madness.'

She smiled. It seemed so far in the past, yet she could still recall the passion they had once felt for one another. It had been real.

'It's in the past,' she said finally. 'It must stay in the past, for everyone's sake.'

He kissed her on the cheek.

'It must indeed,' he said. 'I just hope, in the years to come, it won't be a bitter rivalry between the two boys that undermines everything we've worked for.'

Against all odds, he now presided over a settled family that had grown close. He did not want the family to return to its old acrimonious ways.

'You've done what you can, Philippe.' She felt he needed reassurance. 'The family is changing but in a good way. But it's good to see the settled marriages: Walter and me; Virginia and Matthew; Pippa and Joel. And look at how well Virginia and Karen get along. It's fashion and more fashion with them.'

He laughed.

'It's not a friendship I could have predicted but they love going to the fashion shows together.'

'And don't forget Allana, Mia and Sylvie now tag along too.'

'You're not inclined to go along with them?'

She shook her head.

'Actually, no. Allana thinks I'm dull because I'd rather go to a literary event or to a gallery opening.'

'Not boating?'

'No, I leave that to the boys. They all seem to like it.'

Philippe smiled wistfully.

'They're lucky. I never had the leisure or the money to pursue hobbies like that when I was young.'

'But you've covered a lot of ground in your life. You've done many good things in your life.'

It was as much a statement of fact as a question.

'I have,' he agreed, 'but I've made some mistakes too.'

'But the memories are mostly good, aren't they?'

'Yes, they're mostly good,' he said. He paused then. 'Except I have a son I can't acknowledge.'

'Nothing can change that now, Philippe. That decision was made years ago.'

He paused. She was right. The decision has been made years ago.

'Yes, it was. And you were right to make it. At least I found and acknowledged my daughter. That might easily never have happened.'

'She's special to you, isn't she? She and Jessica.'

'She is, but sadly I broke her heart too in a different way, leaving her mother as I did.'

'Did you regret that?'

He sighed. It was time for honesty.

'Yes, I did regret that. It was the price I had to pay.'

'Because of Karen and Louis.'

He nodded.

'Because of Karen and Louis.'

They had not spoken together like this in years but Arabella marvelled at how quickly their previous intimacy resurfaced. They had once spoken about so much. And now, it seemed easier. Much easier, as if the years that had passed had given them breathing space.

'And if she had not been pregnant? If she had not borne you a child?'

'I've never been able to answer that question,' he said quietly. 'I've never been able to answer it.'

He looked at her then.

'For a brief moment, I thought there might be another option.'

'Another option?'

But he would not elaborate. He had said enough. He had gone further and said more than he had ever intended.

Anyway, it was too late for revelations. Too late for speculating on what might have been. He turned and headed out of the room leaving Arabella to finish tidying away the board papers.

CHAPTER 25

PHILIPPE'S BODY LAY at the foot of the staircase for only minutes. But it was too late when Arabella discovered him. Too late when Joel was summoned to his side. Too late when the ambulance arrived at the front door of Eastbury Hall. And too late when Karen returned home to be greeted by her son, tears streaming down his face.

Death, when it came, had come swiftly. Silently. Without fuss. But the suddenness of it shocked everyone. How was this possible, they all asked? He had been a doctor. If he had heart problems, he would have known.

In the days that followed, Eastbury Hall—and the people who loved him—slowly came to terms with the death of the man who had defied the odds of his birth to become head of the wealthy Cox family from which he had once been excluded.

But there was nothing that offered any consolation to the woman who had loved him for so long. She wept until she could weep no more. From the moment she had met Philippe, she had loved him.

But in loving him and finally winning him, she knew she had broken another woman's heart. And now, with his death, she too felt the deep visceral pain of loss.

Pippa wept too. Tears streamed unchecked down her cheeks as she mourned the father who had moved his life across the world for her. There were times he had tested her love. But deep in her soul, she had loved him without reserve. And now he was gone. And with him, part of her history was gone. But she was left with the most precious memory. The memory of the day he had knocked on her Aunt Edith's door. She had been a young teenager, almost alone in the world. Bereft. Without a future. Without a family who cared for her. And then he had rescued her. And married her mother.

For nearly ten glorious years, her world had been perfect. He had given her that. And now he had left a void in her life that no one else could fill. Not her mother. Not her husband. Not her daughter. Her father had been special. No one could replace him. Ever. And she cried long into the night. Inconsolable.

For Arabella, grief came in quiet waves of sadness that threatened at times to overwhelm her. She had loved him too.

Her son, quietly observing this, guessed that the gossips might have been right. His mother had been in love with Philippe. But still the question he could not ask haunted him. And it would go on haunting him. As he mourned Philippe's death, the unanswerable question remained: am I mourning the man I can never claim as my father?

Ten thousand miles away, across a vast expanse of ocean, another woman wept for him. She wept for what might have been. What should have been.

For Julia, Philippe's death would end a long, bittersweet chapter in her life. He had been her first love. And deep within her soul she had never stopped loving him. For a long time, he had been the centre-piece of her life. And now that part of her story was finished.

But she could remember it all as if it was yesterday. The passion and excitement of their wartime romance. The anguish of Pippa's birth. The fleeting glimpse of her baby daughter as she was whisked away. The acceptance of a life without her daughter. And without Philippe.

Then the joy of their unexpected meeting more than a decade later. Their marriage. Pippa's teenage years. Their happy family years. All shattered by the lure of a woman he could not resist. And the child he would not turn his back on.

As she remembered, she would close her eyes. She could still feel the pain. The pain of having loved him. And now it was over. But in her heart, she held on to the final words he had written to her.

I'm sorry for having hurt you the way I did. You were the love of my life. I realised that too late. I discovered too late there was a price to pay for my foolishness.

Please don't hate me. You should know that I have always loved you. And that I will always love you. I once said we should have grown old together. It was my fault we did not.

But I will always cherish the time we spent together. More than you will ever know.

She remembered smiling at the words *a price to pay*. Hadn't they both paid a price?

Epilogue

ON A COLD JANUARY day on the other side of the world, Julia would cling to her daughter Pippa and to her granddaughter Jessica.

She would not speak to Karen. Or to Karen's son. She did not trust herself to speak. She did not trust herself to speak the platitudes expected of her.

Through a haze of grief, she remembered her daughter guiding her away from the graveside, but then she had stopped to look back at the grave. It was a mound of flowers. And at the very top, she saw Karen's extravagant bouquet of red roses proclaiming her love.

'He didn't love her like he loved me,' she remembered saying.

And she remembered her daughter's words exactly.

'I know,' Pippa had replied. 'I know. He told me. He talked about *paying a price.*'

And she had simply nodded.

'He paid a price. We all paid a price. There is always a price to pay,' she had said, as they walked away together, arm in arm.

❄❄❄